"Perhaps the love affairs of Kings are to be ignored by all, including their wives."

"But he was not unfaithful, Your Grace."

"No, the lady's brother and her husband intervened in time. It is naught to do with the King's virtue. I think that is why he is so angry with me, Maria . . . because he failed."

"He is young, Your Grace."

"Five years younger than I. He reminded me of it."

"It will pass, dearest lady."

"Oh, Maria, I am so tired. I feel bruised and wounded. I have not felt so sad . . . so lost . . . since the old days in Durham House when I thought everyone had deserted me."

Maria took the Queen's hand and kissed it. "All did not desert Your Grace."

"No. You were always there, Maria. Oh, it is good to have staunch friends."

"Let me cover you. When you are rested you will feel stronger."

Katharine smiled and closed her eyes. . . .

By Jean Plaidy
Published by Fawcett Books:

LILITH
MELISANDE
THE SCARLET CLOAK
KATHARINE, THE VIRGIN WIDOW
THE SHADOW OF THE POMEGRANATE

The Queens Of England Series:
MYSELF, MY ENEMY
QUEEN OF THIS REALM
VICTORIA VICTORIOUS
THE LADY IN THE TOWER
THE QUEEN'S SECRET
THE RELUCTANT QUEEN
THE PLEASURES OF LOVE
WILLIAM'S WIFE

The Georgian Saga:
THE PRINCESS OF CELLE
QUEEN IN WAITING
CAROLINE, THE QUEEN
THE PRINCE AND THE QUAKERESS
THE THIRD GEORGE
SWEET LASS OF RICHMOND HILL
INDISCRETIONS OF THE QUEEN
THE REGENT'S DAUGHTER
GODDESS OF THE GREEN ROOM
VICTORIA IN THE WINGS

Books published by The Ballantine Publishing Group
are available at quantity discounts on bulk purchases for
premium, educational, fund-raising, and special sales
use. For details, please call 1-800-733-3000.

THE SHADOW
OF THE
POMEGRANATE

Jean Plaidy

FAWCETT CREST • NEW YORK

A Fawcett Crest Book
Published by Ballantine Books
Copyright © 1962 by Jean Plaidy

http://www.randomhouse.com

Library of Congress Catalog Card Number: 96-97116

ISBN 0-449-22346-9

This edition published by arrangement with G. P. Putnam's Sons.

Manufactured in the United States of America

First Ballantine Books Edition: January 1997

10 9 8 7 6 5 4 3 2 1

Contents

I	"Sir Loyal Heart"	1
II	The King's Indiscretion	23
III	The Secret Life of Thomas Wolsey	54
IV	Spanish Intrigue	71
V	Murder in Pamplona	86
VI	The French Disaster	100
VII	The Perfidy of Ferdinand	108
VIII	Henry at War	136
IX	The Flowers of the Forest	145
X	Bessie Blount	152
XI	The French Marriage	179
XII	The Open Rift	198
XIII	A Venetian Embassy and a Cardinal's Hat	204
XIV	The Death of Ferdinand	223
XV	The Princess Mary	228
XVI	" 'Prentices and Clubs"	233
XVII	The King Triumphant	237
	Bibliography	248

CHAPTER I

"Sir Loyal Heart"

In the royal bedchamber at the Palace of Richmond the Queen of England lay alone. "She should rest now," the doctors said. "Leave her to sleep."

Yet, tired as she was, Queen Katharine, who was known to the people as Katharine of Aragon although it was ten years since she had left her native land to come to England, had no desire to sleep. It was long since she had known such happiness. She had come through humiliation to enjoy the greatest esteem; she who had once been neglected was now courted and treated with great respect. There was no woman in England who was accorded more homage than the Queen. During the month just past she had celebrated her twenty-fifth birthday; she was reckoned to be handsome and, when she was dressed in her jewelled garments and her lovely hair with its tints of reddish gold fell loose about her shoulders, the looks of admiration which were bestowed upon her were those given to a beautiful woman, whether she were Queen or beggarmaid.

Her husband was devoted to her. She must share in all his pastimes; she must be present to watch his prowess at the joust; she must applaud his success at tennis; and it was to her he presented the spoils of the hunt. She was the luckiest of women because her husband was the King—five years her junior, it was true, but an open-hearted boy, generous, passionate, loving, who, having escaped from the tiresome restrictions of a miserly parent, was determined to please his people and asked only adoration and admiration from those surrounding him.

Katharine smiled thinking of this big handsome boy whom she had married, and she was glad that she was older than he

1

was; she was even glad that she had suffered such poverty and humiliation when she had lived in England as the widow of Henry's brother Arthur and had been used by her father-in-law, Henry VII, and her father, Ferdinand of Aragon, as a counter in their game of politics.

All that was over. Henry, headstrong, determined to make his own decisions, had chosen her as his bride; and as a result he, like some sixteenth-century Perseus, had rescued her, had cut her free from the chains of poverty and degradation and had declared his intention of marrying her—for she pleased him better than any other woman—and setting her beside him on the throne of England.

How could she ever show enough gratitude? She smiled. *He* was never tired of her gratitude; his small blue eyes, which seemed to grow more blue with emotion, would glisten like aquamarines when he looked back into the not very distant past and compared her state then with what it was now.

He would place a heavy arm about her shoulders and give her one of those hugs which took her breath away; she was not sure whether he was unaware of his strength or liked to pretend he was, and so make others the more aware of it.

"Ah, Kate," he would cry; Kate was his name for her; he liked to be thought bluff and blunt, a King who could talk on equal terms with his humblest subject. Kate was a good old English name. " 'Tis not so long, eh, since you were languishing in Durham House, patching your gowns. A different story now, eh, Kate!" And he would burst into that loud laughter which brought tears to those blue eyes and made them brighter than ever. Legs apart he would survey her, head on one side. "I brought you up, Kate. Never forget that. I . . . the King . . . who would let no other choose my woman for me. 'You shall not marry Katharine,' they said. They made me protest against the betrothal. That was when I was but a child and powerless. But those days are past. Now it is my turn to decide, and none shall say me nay!"

How he revelled in his power . . . like a boy with new toys! He was twenty, strong and healthy; he was well nigh perfect in the eyes of his subjects, and quite perfect in his own.

And Katharine, his wife, loved him; for who could help loving this golden boy?

"How happy you make me," she had told him once.

"Ay," he had answered proudly. "I have, have I not, Kate? And you shall make me happy too. You shall give me sons."

The blue eyes looked complacently into the future. He was seeing them all—boys, big boys, with red in their hair and their cheeks; with eyes as blue as aquamarines, boys strong and healthy, all made in the image of their glorious sire.

She had determined that he should not be denied his desires. He should have sons; and within a few weeks of their marriage she had become pregnant. She had been very unhappy when her still-born daughter had been born. She, who had suffered in dry-eyed silence for so many years, wept at the sight of Henry's disappointment. But he could not long believe in failure. The gods were smiling on him even as his Court and subjects did. All Henry desired must be his.

But she had quickly become pregnant again, and this time she had given him all that he needed to make his contentment complete.

In the cradle lay their son. What a happy omen that he should have been born on New Year's Day!

Henry had stood by her bed, his eyes ablaze with triumph.

"Here lies Your Grace's son and heir," she had said. "My New Year's gift to you."

Then Henry had fallen on his knees beside her bed and kissed her hand. She had thought that he was but a boy himself, for all his joy, all his pleasure in her and his son, was in his face for everyone to see.

"I would ask a boon of you," Katharine had whispered.

"Name it, Kate," he had cried. "You have but to name it . . . and it is yours."

He was ready to give her anything she asked because he wanted her to know how he felt; he wanted the whole Court, the whole world, to know of his gratitude to the Queen who had given him his son.

"It is that this Prince shall be called Henry after his most noble, his most beloved Sire."

Henry's eyes had been moist for a moment; then he had leaped to his feet.

"Your wish is granted!" he cried. "Why, Kate, as if I could deny you aught!"

She smiled, remembering. Almost at once he had been impatient to leave her, because he was planning the christening ceremony which he had decided must be more magnificent than any such ceremony had ever been before.

This was his first-born son, the heir to the throne, who was to be called Henry. He was the happiest of Kings; so she, in whom love for him had grown out of her great gratitude, was the happiest of Queens.

It was small wonder that she had no wish to slip into the world of sleep, when waking she could savour such happiness.

The King smiled with affection at his opponent in the game of tennis which they had just finished. It had been a close game, but there had never been any doubt in the mind of the King that he would be the victor. There had been no doubt in the mind of Charles Brandon either. He was not such a fool as to think of beating the King, although, he was ready to admit, it was questionable whether he would have been able to. Henry excelled at the sport.

Now Henry slipped his arm through that of his friend with the familiarity which was so endearing. They were almost the same height, but not quite; Charles Brandon was tall but Henry was taller. Charles was handsome but he lacked the pink and golden perfection of his King; he was wily and therefore he always saw to it that, although he jousted as a champion and excelled at all sports, he just failed to reach the perfection of his master.

"It was a good game," murmured Henry. "And I thought at one time you would beat me."

"Nay, I am no match for Your Grace."

"I am not sure, Charles," answered the King, but his expression showed clearly that there could be no doubt whatsoever.

Brandon shook his head with feigned sorrow. "Your Grace is . . . unrivalled."

The King waved a hand. "I would talk of other matters. I wish to plan a masque for the Queen as soon as she is able to rise from her bed, and to show in this my pleasure in her."

"Oh fortunate Katharine to be Queen to such a King!"

Henry smiled. Flattery delighted him and the more blatant it was the better he liked it.

"I fancy the Queen is not displeased with her state. Now, Charles, devise some pageant which will please me. Let us have a tournament in which we shall appear disguised so that the Queen will have no notion who we are. We will surprise the company with our daring and then, when we are acknowledged the champions, let us throw off our disguise."

"That would give Her Grace much pleasure, I am sure."

"You remember how I surprised her at the Christmas festivities in the guise of a strange knight, and how I astonished all with my skill. And how surprised she was when I unmasked and she found in the strange knight her own husband?"

"Her Grace was delighted. She had been wondering how it was possible for any to rival her husband and when she had seen one who showed the same skill it was only to discover that it was the King in disguise!"

Henry burst into loud laughter at the memory. "I remember a time when I, with my cousin Essex, forced my way into her apartments dressed as Robin Hood and his men," he mused. "And there was that occasion when, with Essex and Edward Howard and Thomas Parr . . . there were others also . . . we appeared dressed as Turks and we blacked the faces of our attendants so that they looked like blackamoors."

"I remember the occasion well. Your Grace's sister, the Princess Mary, danced disguised as an Ethiopian Queen."

"She did well," said the King fondly.

"It was a goodly sight though her pretty face was veiled."

" 'Twas well that it should be." Henry's mouth was a little prim. "My sister grows too fond of her pretty face."

"Is that so?" murmured Brandon.

"She is a witch who can twist me about her finger," murmured the King fondly. "But what would you? She is my only sister now that Margaret is away. It may be that I am over-indulgent."

"It is difficult not to indulge one so charming," agreed Brandon.

Henry was faintly impatient. "But the masque, man. I would have you devise some pageant which will amuse the Queen."

"I will give the matter my earnest attention."

"And remember that there must be little delay. The Queen cannot lie abed much longer."

It was on the tip of Brandon's tongue to remind the King that the Queen had, in less than two years of marriage, twice been brought to bed for the purpose of bearing a child. But one only reminded the King of that which he wished to remember. He himself enjoyed perfect health; those who did not he considered to be rather tiresome.

"I'll swear Her Grace is all impatience to join the revels," said Brandon.

"It is so. So let us give her a worthy spectacle, Charles."

"Your Grace commands, and it is my pleasure to obey. There shall be a spectacle such as none of your courtiers have ever seen before."

"Then I shall go to the Queen and bid her hasten her convalescence."

As they approached the Palace they were joined by many of the courtiers who hastened to pay compliments to the King.

"Listen," commanded Henry, "I would have the Queen know our pleasure. There is to be a pageant. . . ."

They listened, all eager to join in the fun. The new King was a complete contrast to his father, and in this new reign to be young, gay, witty, to excel at the jousts, could lead the way to fortune. There was not a courtier, as there was not a man or woman in the street, who did not rejoice in the accession of Henry VIII.

They were joined by the King's sister, the young Princess Mary, said by many to be the loveliest girl at Court. Henry's eyes glistened with affection as they rested on her. She was now fifteen, full of life as became a Tudor, inclined to take liberties with her brother which no one else would dare; and he seemed to like it.

"Well, sister," he said, "are you ready to join in our fun?"

Mary swept a deep curtesy and smiled at her brother. "Always ready to be at Your Grace's side."

"Come here to me," said Henry.

She came and he slipped his arm through hers. She was a beauty, this little sister. Tudor, all Tudor. By God what a handsome race we are! thought Henry; then he remembered his father's somewhat sere, sour face, and laughed.

"It will be necessary for you to show a little decorum, my child," said Henry.

"Yes, Your Grace. I live but to please Your Grace."

She was laughing at him, imitating his sycophantish courtiers, but he did not object. He took her cheek between his fingers and pinched it.

Mary cried out. "Too much pressure of the royal fingers," she explained, taking those fingers and kissing them.

"I shall miss you, sister, when you leave us."

Mary frowned. "It will be years yet."

Henry looked at her; he could see the shape of her breasts beneath her bodice. Fifteen! She was a woman. It could not be long before she left England for Flanders to marry Charles, grandson of Maximilian and Ferdinand of Aragon, and heir to great dominions. He did not want to lose Mary, but, as he told himself sadly, a King must not think of his own feelings.

She guessed his thoughts and pouted. She was going to raise difficulties when the time came for her to go.

"It may be," she said suddenly, and her lovely face was radiant, "that Your Grace will discover he cannot bear to part with his little sister—and Charles will then not get his bride."

There was an appeal in the lovely eyes; they had strayed to Brandon's face and rested there. Fifteen! thought Henry. She has the provocation of a girl some years older. He must warn her not to look at men like Brandon in that way. Charles Brandon had not lived the life of a monk. That was something Mary was as yet too young to understand; he should warn her, for he was not only her King but, since she had neither father nor mother, he must be her guardian too.

"Enough, enough," he said. "Come turn your wits to the pageants. I expect you to give the Queen a goodly spectacle."

The King's thoughts had gone to the Queen and his son and purposefully he made his way through the Palace to her apartments.

In her bedchamber the Queen was awakened by the fanfares which announced the King's coming. Her doctors had said that she must rest, but the King did not know this, or had forgotten.

She spread her hair about her pillows, for he liked it in that way and her hair was her one real beauty.

He burst into the apartment, and she saw him standing on the threshold with Mary on one side of him and Brandon on the other. Behind him were other friends and courtiers.

"Why, Kate," he cried advancing, "we come to see how you are. Are you not weary of bed? We plan a great entertainment for you. So get well quickly."

"Your Grace is kind to me," answered the Queen.

"Your King takes pleasure in pleasing you," replied Henry.

The courtiers were surrounding her bed, and she felt very tired but she smiled, because one must always smile for the King, that golden boy whose strict upbringing under his father's rule had been perhaps a little too severe for his exuberant nature.

He was a little irritated by the sight of her. She must lie a-bed, and he was impatient with all inactivity. He was urging her to shorten the period of rest, but she dared not. She had to preserve her strength; she had to remember that this was one of many births which must follow over the coming years.

The baby in his cradle cried suddenly as though he came to his mother's aid.

The King immediately swung round and the procession, with him at its head, went towards the cradle.

Henry took the child in his arms, and he looked at it with wonder.

"Do you realize," he said, to those who crowded about him, "that this infant could one day be your King?"

"We trust not until he is an old graybeard, Your Grace."

It was the right answer. The King laughed. Then he began to walk up and down the Queen's bedchamber, the child in his arms.

The Queen watched smiling.

He is but a boy himself, she thought.

As soon as Katharine left her bed she prepared to leave Richmond for Westminster. The King had gone on before her; impatient and restless, he had already journeyed to Walsingham, there to give thanks for his son at the Shrine of the Virgin.

But he had now returned to Westminster and was there waiting to receive the Queen.

Katharine, who still felt weak, would have enjoyed some respite, perhaps a few weeks of quiet at Richmond; but she knew that was too much to hope for because Henry begrudged every day he spent hidden from the public gaze. So did the people. Wherever he went they crowded about him to bless his lovely face and express their pleasure in him.

The people would not be excluded from the festivities at Westminster. One of the reasons why they loved their new King was because he showed them with every action, every gesture, that he was determined to be a very different King from his father. One of his first acts had been the public beheading of his father's ministers, Dudley and Empson, those men whom the people had regarded as the great extortioners of the previous reign. Nothing could have been more significant. "These men imposed great taxes on my beloved people; they have brought poverty and misery to thousands. Therefore they shall die." That was what the young King was telling his people. "England shall now be merry as she was intended to be." So they cheered themselves hoarse whenever they saw him.

It seemed fitting to them that their handsome young King should be covered in glittering jewels, that his satin and velvet garments should be more magnificent than anyone had ever worn before. And because he was always conscious of the presence of the people, always determined to extract every ounce of their affection, he constantly won their approval.

They were now looking forward to the festivities at Westminster almost as eagerly as Henry was himself. Therefore there could be no delay merely because the Queen would have liked a little longer to recover from giving the King and country an heir.

All along the route the people cheered her. She was Spanish and alien to their English ways, but their beloved King had chosen her for his wife and she had produced a son; that was enough to make the people shout: "Long live the Queen!"

Beside Katharine rode her beautiful and favourite lady-in-waiting, Maria de Salinas, who had been with her ever since she had left Spain. It was significant that even when they were alone together she and Maria spoke English nowadays.

"Your Grace is a little weary?" asked Maria, anxiously.

"Weary!" cried Katharine, faintly alarmed. Did she look weary? The King would be hurt if she did. She must never show him that she preferred to rest rather than to frolic. "Oh no . . . no, Maria. I was a little thoughtful, that was all. I was thinking how my life has changed in the last few years. Do you remember how we suffered, how we patched our gowns and often had to eat fish which smelt none too good because it was the cheapest that could be bought in the market, how we wondered whether my father would send for us to return ignobly to Spain, or whether the King of England would ever pay me an allowance?"

"After such humiliation Your Grace can now enjoy all the fine gowns that you wish for, all the good food that you care to order for your table."

"I should be ungrateful indeed, Maria, if I allowed myself to be tired when so much is being arranged for my pleasure."

"Yet weariness is something over which we have no control," began Maria.

But Katharine laughed: "We must always have control over our feelings, Maria. My mother taught me that, and I shall never forget it."

She smiled, inclining her head as the people called her

name. Maria had guessed that she was weary; no one else must.

The Queen was seated in the tiltyard, for the tournament would soon begin. All about her were signs of the King's devotion. His enthusiasm was such that when he was gratified the whole world must know it. This woman whom his father had tried to withhold from him, but whom he had insisted on marrying, had proved his wisdom in marrying her, for she had quickly given him a son. He wanted everyone to know in what esteem he held her, and everywhere Katharine looked she could see those entwined initials H and K. They were on the very seat on which she sat—gold letters on purple velvet.

If my mother could see me now, she would be happy, thought Katharine. It was nearly seven years since her mother had died and ten since she had seen her, yet she still thought of her often and when something happened which was particularly pleasing, it was almost as though she shared her pleasure with her mother. Isabella of Castile had been the greatest force in her daughter's life and when she had died it seemed to Katharine that something very beautiful and vital had gone from her life. She believed that perhaps in the love she would bear towards her own children she would find some consolation for this aching loss; but that was in the future.

The ordinary people were crowding into the arena. They seemed always to be present. Henry would be pleased; he would triumph of course at the tournament and he liked his people to see him victorious. He would seem like a god to them in his glittering armour, with his looks which were indeed unrivalled, and his great height—no one at Court was taller than Henry. Katharine wondered what chance of favour a man would have who happened to be an inch taller than the King.

She suppressed such thoughts. They came to her now and then but she constantly refused to entertain them. Her Henry was a boy and he had the faults of a boy. He was young for his years, but she must always remember that he had been repressed during his boyhood by a father who had always feared he might be spoiled by others, and who was eager that the eighth Henry should rule in a manner similar to that of the seventh.

All about her was the glittering Court. Henry was not present so she knew that he would appear later in the guise of some wandering king, perhaps a beggar, or a robber, some role which would make the people gasp with surprise. He would either tilt in his new role and as the conqueror disclose who he really was, or show himself before the joust and then proceed to conquer. It was the old familiar pattern, and every time Katharine must behave as though this were the first time it had happened. Always her surprise that the champion was in truth the King must appear to be spontaneous and natural.

What is happening to me? she asked herself. There had been a time when she was happy enough to enter into his frolics. Was that because in the first year of their marriage she had felt as though she were living in a dream? The period of humiliation had been so close in those days; now that it was receding, was she less grateful?

A hermit was riding into the arena and there was a hush in the crowd. He wore a grey gown and tattered weeds.

No, thought Katharine, he is not quite tall enough. This is not the great masquerade.

The hermit was approaching her throne and, when he was before her, he bowed low and cried aloud: "I crave the Queen's Grace to permit me to tilt before her."

Katharine said as was expected: "But you are no knight."

"Yet would I ask your royal permission to test my skill, and it shall all be for Your Grace's honour."

"A hermit . . . to tilt in my honour!"

The crowd began to jeer, but Katharine held up her hand.

"It is strange indeed to find a hermit in the tiltyard, and that he should wish to tilt stranger still. But our great King has such love for all his subjects that he would please them each and every one. The lowliest hermit shall tilt before us if it is his wish. But I warn you, hermit, it may cost you your life."

"That I would willing give for my Queen and my King."

"Then let it be," cried Katharine.

The hermit stepped back, drew himself to his full height,

threw off his grey tattered robe, and there was a Knight in shining armour—none other than Charles Brandon himself.

The Princess Mary, who was seated near the Queen, began to clap her hands, and all cheered.

Brandon now asked the Queen's permission to present to her a knight of great valour who was desirous, like himself, of tilting in her honour.

"I pray you tell me the name of this knight," said Katharine.

"Your Grace, his name is Sir Loyal Heart."

"I like well his name," said Katharine. "I pray you bring him to me."

Brandon bowed and there was a fanfare of trumpets as Sir Loyal Heart rode into the arena.

There was no mistaking that tall figure, that gold hair, that fresh fair skin which glowed with health and youth.

"Sir Loyal Heart!" shouted the ushers. "Who comes to tilt in honour of the Queen's Grace."

Before the Queen's throne Henry drew up, while the people roared their approval.

Katharine felt that her emotions might prevent her in that important moment making the right gesture. Sir Loyal Heart! How like him to choose such a name. So naïve, so boyish, so endearing.

Surely I am the most fortunate of women, she thought; Mother, if you could but see me now, it would make up for all you have suffered, for my brother Juan's death, for my sister Isabella's death in childbirth, for Juana's madness. At least two of your daughters inherited what you desired for them. Maria is the happy Queen of Portugal, and I am happier still, as Queen of England, wife of this exuberant boy, who shows his devotion to me by entwining my initials with his, by riding into the arena as Sir Loyal Heart.

"How happy I am," she said in a voice which was not without a tremor of emotion, "that Sir Loyal Heart comes hither to tilt in my honour."

There was nothing she could have said which would have pleased Henry more.

"The happiness of Sir Loyal Heart equals that of Your Grace," cried Henry.

He had turned—ready for the joust.

The tournament was opened.

Darkness came early in February, and the Court had left the tiltyard for the whitehall of Westminster. This did not mean that the festivities were over. They would go on far into the night, for the King never tired and, until he declared the ball closed, it must go on.

He had scored great success in the tiltyard to the delight of the people. But none was more delighted than Henry. Yet now that the party had entered the Palace he had disappeared from Katharine's side.

This could only mean one thing. Some pageant or masque was being planned in which he would play a major part. Several of his friends had crept away with him, and Katharine, talking to those who remained about her, tried to compose her features, tried to display great expectation while she hoped that she would be able to register that blank surprise when she was confronted with some denouement which she had guessed even before the play had begun.

One must remember, she reminded herself, that he has been brought up in a most parsimonious fashion. She knew that his father had ordered that his doublets must be worn as long as they held together and then turned if possible; he and the members of his household had been fed on the simplest foods and had even had to save candle ends. All this had been intended to teach him the ways of thrift. The result? He had rebelled against thrift. He was ready to dip into his father's coffers to escape from the parsimony, which had been anathema to him, in order to satisfy his extravagance. His nature was such that he must passionately long for all that was denied him—so for him the scarlet and gold, the velvet and brocade; for him the rich banquets, the pomp and the glory. It was fortunate that the thrift of Henry VII had made it possible for Henry VIII to indulge his pleasure without resorting to the unpopular methods which his father had used to amass his wealth.

Katharine looked about the hall, which had been so lavishly decorated, and tried to calculate the cost to the exchequer. The English love of pageantry was unquestionable. What great pains had been taken to turn this hall into a forest. There were artificial hawthorns, maples and hazels, all so finely wrought that they looked real enough. There were the animals, a lion, an antelope, and an elephant all cleverly made. She did not know the price of the commodities necessary to make these things but she guessed it was high, for clearly no expense had been spared. There were beautiful ladies to roam the mock forest and they, with the wood-woos, who were wild men of the forest, had to be specially apparelled. The maids of the forest wore yellow damask, and the wood-woos russet sarcenet; she knew the high cost of these materials.

Should she remonstrate with the King? Should she point out that such pageants were well enough when there was some great event to celebrate—as there was at this time the birth of their son—but this was one among many. Since Henry had come to the throne feasting had followed feasting, and pageant, pageant.

She imagined herself saying: "Henry, I am older than you . . . and I had the advantage of spending my early years with my mother who was one of the wisest women in the world. Should you not curb these extravagances?"

What would be his response? She pictured the brows being drawn together over those brilliant blue eyes, the pout of a spoiled boy.

Yet was it not her duty?

One of the courtiers was at her elbow. "Your Grace?"

"You would speak with me?"

"Your Grace, I know of an arbour of gold, and in this arbour are ladies who would show you their pastime in the hope that they might please your Grace. Would you wish to see this arbour?"

"I greatly desire to see it."

The courtier bowed, and then, drawing himself to his full height, he declaimed: "Her Grace Queen Katharine wishes to see the arbour of gold."

A curtain which had been drawn across one end of the hall was then pulled back to disclose a pavilion in the form of an arbour. This was composed of pillars about which artificial flowers made of silk and satin climbed naturalistically. There were roses, hawthorn and eglantine, and the pillars had been decorated with ornaments of pure gold.

This arbour was carried by stout bearers and placed close to the Queen's throne. She saw that in it were six of the most lovely girls, and that their dresses were of white and green satin which appeared to be covered with gold embroidery; but as they came closer she realized that what she had thought was embroidery were two letters entwined—the familiar H and K. She stared in admiration, for it was indeed a pretty sight, and as she did so six men dressed in purple satin which, like the gowns of the girls, was adorned with the entwined letters, sprang forth to stand three on either side of the arbour.

Each of these knights had his name on his doublet in letters of real gold; and there was one among them who stood out distinguished by his height and golden beauty; and across his doublet were written the words Sir Loyal Heart.

The ordinary people who revelled in these antics of the Court had pressed into the hall and now cheered loudly, calling "God bless his Grace! God bless the Queen!"

Henry stood before her, his face expressing his complete joy.

Katharine applauded with her ladies, and the King clapped his hands—a signal for the ladies to step from the arbour.

Each of the six ladies was taken as a partner by one of the six men.

"Make a space for us to dance!" commanded Sir Loyal Heart. And the bearers wheeled the arbour back through the forest to the end of the hall where the people who had crowded into the Palace from the streets stood agog watching all this splendour.

"Come," cried the King to the musicians, and the music began.

Henry danced as he loved to dance. He must leap higher than any; he must cavort with greater verve. Katharine watching him thought: He seems even younger now than he did the day we married.

"Faster! Faster!" he commanded. "Who tires? What you, Knevet?" The glance he threw at Sir Thomas Knevet was scornful. "Again, again," he commanded the musicians, and the dance continued.

So intent were all on the dancing of the gay young King that they did not notice what was happening at the other end of the hall.

One man, a shipmaster whose trade had brought him to the port of London, murmured: "But look at the trimmings on this arbour. These ornaments are real gold!"

He put up his hand to touch one, but another hand had reached it before him. A gold ornament was taken from the arbour, and several crowded round to look at it.

In a few moments many of the spectators had plucked a gold ornament from the arbour; and those at the back, who saw what was happening, determined not to be left out, pressed forward and in the space of a few minutes that arbour was denuded of all the gold ornaments which had made it such a thing of beauty.

Meanwhile the King danced on, smiling at the ladies, now and then glancing in the Queen's direction. Was she watching? Was she marvelling?

Katarine was ready every time his eyes met hers; and she had managed to infuse that look of wonder into her expression which he constantly demanded.

At last the music stopped, and Henry stood smiling benignly at the company.

"You see," he announced, "that the dresses of the performers are covered in gold letters. These form my own initial and that of the one who is most dear to me. I now invite the ladies to come and help themselves to these entwined letters and I trust they will treasure them and when their time comes to marry they will endeavour to live in perfect harmony and follow the example set by their Queen and ... Sir Loyal Heart."

The ladies rushed forward. There were many, Katharine

noticed, to gaze coquettishly at the King, and then she was grateful to him for his loyalty and ashamed of her criticisms. He is but a boy, she told herself; a boy who wishes to be good.

There was a sudden shout from the back of the hall, where the once golden arbour had been transformed into a few sticks of wood. The populace who, as custom demanded, were permitted to see their King at his meals, at his dancing and games, rushed forward.

The ladies had been invited to strip the King of his ornaments; well, so they should; and the men would help them in the game.

There was a startled cry of surprise from the dancers as they found themselves surrounded. The King himself was in the hands of half a dozen laughing men and women, but in their eyes there was something more than laughter. They had looked on at the luxury of Westminster and had compared it with their own homes; they had seen men and women whose garments were covered in glittering jewels and gold ornaments, one of which would keep them in luxury for a very long time.

This was their King and their beloved King, but the mob stood together against its rulers and when the call came it was invariably ready. But this was merely a masque; and the people had caught the spirit of the masque. They would not have harmed their handsome King; but they wanted his jewels.

Listening to the cries of protest of his friends, being aware of the people—who smelt none too fresh—pressing close to him, Henry ceased to be a pleasure-loving boy. He was a man at once—shrewd and cunning. He knew no fear; he had always felt himself to be capable of dealing with any situation and, because it had been his pleasure to go among his people as often as possible, he was able to understand them; and of all the noblemen and women in that hall there was none more calm, more wise than the King.

There was no sign of anger in those blue eyes which could so easily grow stormy at a courtier's careless word. They were purposely full of laughter. He had played his own game; now he must play the people's game; but he did not forget that he was still the central player.

He smiled into the eyes of a pretty young seamstress who had snatched a gold button from his doublet.

"May it continue to make your pretty eyes shine," he said.

She was startled, flushed scarlet, then she turned and ran.

They had stripped him of all his jewels; they had torn his cloak from his shoulders so that he was wearing nothing but his doublet and his drawers. He laughed aloud being aware that his courtiers were being more roughly handled than he was himself while they were being stripped of their valuables. Moreover he saw too that the guards had rushed into the hall, halberds raised, and were doing their duty. They had taken several of the people and were hustling them into a corner of the hall, from where they were loudly abusing the guards.

Henry glancing quickly round the company saw that the dishevelled ladies looked bewildered and that Sir Thomas Knevet who had climbed up one of the pillars was clinging there stark naked. Sir Thomas had protested so vigorously that the mob had denuded him not only of his jewels but of all his clothes.

Looking at Knevet clinging to the pillar Henry burst into sudden loud laughter; it was the signal. Clearly the King intended to treat the affair as part of the masque and everyone was expected to do the same. Those of the people who had been muttering now joined in the laughter. "God Save the King!" they cried, and they meant it. He had not disappointed them. He was a true sportsman and they had nothing to fear from such a king.

He was shouting to his courtiers: "Why do you look so glum? My people have helped themselves to largesse. Let us leave the matter at that, for I confess to a hunger which must be appeased, and I am thirsty too."

The people were not loth to be hustled from the hall grasping the spoils they had snatched. The sound of their laughter came floating back to the hall. They were delighted. They loved their King. Now when he rode through the streets they would cheer him more loudly than ever.

Katharine, who had watched the incident with rising horror, had been much astonished by the attitude of the King. She had expected him to roar his anger, to summon the guard, to have the people punished; yet she, whose eyes had not left him, had seen no sign of anger in the bright flushed face.

He was not merely a boy, she realized now. He was a King. And his crown was more dear to him than all the jewels in the world; he was more than a feckless boy, because he knew that he kept that crown by the will of the people. He would rage against his courtiers; he would without hesitation send them to the block; but when he came face to face with the mob he would have nothing for them but smiling tolerance.

Then she did not know this man she had married as she had believed she did, and the knowledge that this was so filled her with faint misgivings.

He was at her side, mischievous in his doublet and drawers.

"Come, Kate," he said. "I starve. Let us lead the way to the banquet that awaits us."

He took her hand and led her into his own chamber where the feast awaited them; and seated at the place of honour at that table with Katharine on his right hand, he was very merry as he surveyed his courtiers in their tattered garments; nor would he allow any to leave the banquet except Sir Thomas Knevet who, he said, for dear decency's sake must find himself some garments.

"My friends," said Henry, "your losses are largesse to the commonalty. That is an end of the matter. Now to work!"

And laughing he tackled the good red meat which he loved.

The Countess of Devonshire came unceremoniously to the Queen's apartment. Katharine received her husband's favourite aunt graciously but she was quick to see that the Countess was alarmed.

"It is the Prince, Your Grace," she burst out. "He has had an uneasy night and seems to find breathing difficult."

Katharine was filled with apprehension.

"I must go to him at once," she said.

The Countess looked relieved. "I have called the physicians to look at him. They think his Royal Highness has caught a chill, and may be better in a few days."

"Then I will not tell the King . . . as yet."

The Countess hesitated; then she said: "It might be well that the King is told, Your Grace. He will wish to see his son."

Katharine felt sick with fear. So the child was worse than they pretended. They were trying to spare her, to break bad news gently.

"I will tell the King," she said quietly, "and I am sure he will wish to make all speed with me to Richmond."

It could not be true, Henry would not believe it. This could not happen to him. The son, of whom he had been so proud, little Henry his namesake, his heir—dead! The child had lived exactly fifty-two days.

He stood, his face puckered, his legs apart, looking at the Queen. The courtiers had left them together, believing that one could comfort the other and thus make their grief more bearable.

Katharine said nothing; she sat in the window seat looking out over the river, her body drooping, her face drawn. She looked like an old woman. Her eyes were red, her face blotched, for she had shed many bitter tears.

"We should have taken greater care of him," she whispered.

"He had every care," growled Henry.

"He caught a chill at the christening. He was robust until then."

Henry did not answer. It had been a splendid christening, with the Archbishop of Canterbury officiating and the Earl of Surrey and the Countess of Devonshire standing as sponsors; he had enjoyed every minute of it. He remembered thinking, as he watched the baby being carried to the font, that this was one of the happiest moments of his life. He had thanked God for His grace.

And now . . . the baby was dead.

He felt the anger bubbling within him. That this should happen to him! What he wanted more than anything in the world, he told himself, was a son—strong and healthy like himself—a boy whom he could watch grow up and teach to be a King.

He felt bewildered because Fate had dared take from him his greatest prize.

"It was well that he was christened, since he is now dead," he said sullenly.

She could not be comforted. She longed for children; she needed them even as he did.

He thought how old she looked, and he felt angry with her because he wanted to feel angry with someone. He had been so grateful to her because she had given him a son; and now he was no longer grateful.

Katharine glancing up suddenly saw his eyes upon her—small, narrowed, cruel.

She thought: Dear God. Holy Mother, does he then blame me?

And her sorrow was tinged with an apprehension so faint that it was gone before she realized fully what it meant.

Even as he gazed at her his expression softened. He said: "This is a bitter blow, Kate. But I am no greybeard and you are young yet. We'll have more children, you see. We'll have a son this time next year. That's the way to chase away our sorrow, eh?"

"Oh Henry," she cried and held out her hand.

He took it.

"You are so good to me," she told him. "I only live to please you."

He kissed her hand. He was too young, too sure of himself, to believe that ill luck awaited him. This was an unfortunate accident. They would have more sons; so many that the loss of this one would cease to matter.

CHAPTER II

The King's Indiscretion

The King sat in the window seat strumming his lute and trying out a song of his own composition; there was a dreamy expression in his eyes and he did not see the courtyard below; he was picturing himself in the great hall, calling for his lute and surprising all present with the excellence of his song.

They would say: "But who is the composer? We must bring him to Court. There are few who can give us such music."

He would put his head on one side. "I do not think it would be an *impossible* task to bring this fellow to Court. In fact I have a certain suspicion that he is with us now."

They would look at each other in surprise. "But, Sire, if such genius were among us surely we could not be so blind as to be unaware of it. We pray Your Grace, summon him to your presence and command him to continue to delight us."

"I doubt he would obey my command. He is a rash fellow."

"Not obey the command of the King!"

Then he would laugh and say: "Now I will play you one of my own songs. . . ." And he would play and sing the very same song.

They would look at each other in amazement—but not too much surprise. They must not run the risk of implying that they did not believe him capable of writing such music. They would quickly allow their bewilderment to fade and then it would be: "But how foolish of us. We should have known that none but Your Grace could give us such a song."

In a little while the song would be sung throughout the Court. The women would sing it, wistfully, and with yearning in their eyes and voices. There were many women who looked

23

at him with longing now. He knew he had but to beckon and they would be ready for anything he should suggest whether it was a quick tumble in a secluded garden or the honour of being the recognized mistress of a King.

His mouth was prim. He intended to be virtuous.

He sang quietly under his breath:

> "The best I sue,
> The worst eschew:
> My mind shall be
> Virtue to use;
> Vice to refuse
> I shall use me."

He would sing that song, and as he did so he would look at those wantons who tried to lure him into sin.

Of course, he told himself often, I am a King, and the rules which are made for other men are not for Kings. But I love my wife and she is devoted to me. She will bear me children in time, and to them and to my people will I set an example. None shall say of me: There was a lecher. It shall be said: There goes the King who is strong, not only in battle, not only in state councils, but in virtue.

So his little mouth was prim as he sat playing his lute and practising the song with which, later that day, he would surprise the Court.

And watching at the window he saw her. She was neither tall nor short, and she was very beautiful. She looked up and saw him, and she dropped a curtsey. There was invitation in the way she lifted her skirts and lowered her eyes. He knew her. Her name was Anne and she was Buckingham's younger sister who had recently married her second husband. Images of Anne Stafford with her two husbands came into his mind. The primness left his mouth which had slackened a little.

He bowed his head in acknowledgment of her curtsey and his fingers idly strummed the lute, for he had momentarily forgotten the song.

Anne Stafford went on her way, but before she had taken more than a few steps she turned to look again at the window.

This time she smiled. Henry's lips seemed to be frozen; he did not acknowledge the smile but after she had disappeared he went on thinking of her.

He found that one of the grooms of the bedchamber was standing beside him. He started and wondered how long the man had been there.

"So 'tis you, Compton," he said.

"'Tis I, Your Grace," answered Sir William Compton. "Come to see if you have work for me to do."

Henry strummed on the lute. "What work should I have for which I should not call you?"

"I but seek excuses to speak awhile with Your Grace."

Henry smiled. There were times when he liked to live informally among his friends; and Sir William Compton, a handsome man some ten years older than himself, amused him. He had been Henry's page when he was Prince of Wales and they had shared many confidences. When he had become King, Henry had given Compton rapid promotion. He was now chief gentleman of the bedchamber, as well as Groom of the Stole and Constable of Sudeley and Gloucester castles.

"Well, speak on," said Henry.

"I was watching Lady Huntingdon pass below. She's a forward wench."

"And why did you think that?"

"By the glance she threw at Your Grace. If ever I saw invitation it was there."

"My dear William," said Henry, "do you not know that I receive such invitations whenever I am in the company of women?"

"I know it, Sire. But those are invitations discreetly given."

"And she was not . . . discreet?"

"If she seemed so to Your Grace I will say that she was."

Henry laughed. "Ah, if I were not a virtuous married man. . . ." He sighed.

"Your Grace would seem to regret that you *are* a virtuous married man."

"How could I regret my virtue?" said Henry, his mouth falling into the familiar lines of primness.

"Nay, Sire. You, being such a wise King, would not; it is only the ladies who are deprived of Your Grace's company who must regret."

"I'll not say," said the King, "that I would ask for too much virtue in a man. He must do his duty, true, duty to state, duty to family; but when that is done. . . ."

Compton nodded. "A little dalliance is good for all."

Henry licked his lips. He was thinking of Anne Stafford; the very way she dipped a curtsey was a challenge to a man's virility.

"I have heard it said that a little dalliance away from the marriage bed will often result in a return to that bed with renewed vigour," murmured Henry.

"All are aware of Your Grace's vigour," said Compton slyly, "and that it is in no need of renewal."

"Two of my children have died," said the King mournfully.

Compton smiled. He could see how the King's mind was working. He wanted to be virtuous; he wanted his dalliance, and yet to be able to say it was virtuous dalliance: I dallied with Anne Stafford because I felt that if I strayed awhile I could come back to Katharine with renewed vigour—so powerful that it must result in the begetting of a fine, strong son.

Compton, who had lived many years close to Henry, knew something of his character. Henry liked to think of himself as a deeply religious man, a man devoted to duty; but at heart he had one god and that was himself; and his love for pleasure far exceeded his desire to do his duty. Moreover, the King was not a man to deny himself the smallest pleasure; he was a sensualist; he was strong, healthy, lusty like many of his friends; but, whereas some of them thoughtlessly took their pleasures where they found them, Henry could not do this before he had first assured himself that what he did was the right thing to do. He was troubled by the voice of his conscience which must first be appeased; it was as though there were two men in that fine athletic body: the pleasure-seeking King and the other, who was completely devoted to his duty. The former would always be forced to make his excuses to the latter, but Compton had no doubt of the persuasive powers of one and the blind eye of the other.

"There are some ladies," mused Compton, "who are willing enough to give a smile of promise but never ready to fulfil those promises."

"That is so," agreed Henry.

"There are some who would cling to their virtue even though it be the King himself who would assail it."

"A little wooing might be necessary," said Henry, implying his confidence that if he were the wooer he could not fail to be successful.

"Should the King woo?" asked Compton. "Should a King be a suppliant for a woman's favours? It seems to me, Your Grace, that a King should beckon and the lady come running."

Henry nodded thoughtfully.

"I could sound the lady, I could woo her in your name. She has a husband and if her virtue should prove overstrong it might be well that this was a matter entirely between Your Grace, myself and the lady."

"We speak of suppositions," said Henry, laying a hand on Compton's shoulder. He picked up his lute. "I will play and sing to you. It is a new song I have here and you shall tell me your opinion of it, good Compton."

Compton smiled and settled himself to listen. He would sound the lady. Kings were always grateful to those who arranged their pleasures. Moreover Anne Stafford was the sister of Edward Stafford, Duke of Buckingham, an arrogant man whom Compton would delight in humiliating; for such was the pride of the Staffords that they would consider it humiliation for a member of their family to become any man's mistress—even the King's.

So, while Henry played his lute and sang his song, Sir William Compton was thinking of how he could arrange a love affair between the sister of the Duke of Buckingham and the King.

* * *

Anne Stafford was bored. She was of the Court, but it was her sister Elizabeth who had found favour with the Queen; and this was because Elizabeth was of a serious nature which appealed to Katharine.

The Queen, thought Anne, was far too serious; and if she did not take care the King would look elsewhere for his pleasure.

Anne laughed to herself; she had very good reason to believe that he was already looking.

Anne had had two husbands and neither of them had satisfied her. In a family such as theirs there had been little freedom. They would never forget, any of them, their closeness to the throne, and they were more conscious of their connection with royalty than the King himself. Through her father Anne was descended from Thomas of Woodstock, a son of Edward III; and her mother was Catharine Woodville, sister of Elizabeth Woodville who had been Edward IV's Queen.

Anne's father had been an ardent supporter of the House of Lancaster, and Richard III had declared him a traitor and the "most untrue creature living." He was beheaded in the marketplace at Salisbury, thus dying for the Tudor cause, a fact which had endeared his family to Henry VII; and Henry VIII carried on his father's friendship for the Staffords.

And what was the result? Anne had been married twice without being consulted and given a place at Court; but there she was merely a spectator of the advancement of her elder sister.

Being a Stafford, Anne was not without ambition, so she thought how amusing it would be to show her family that the way to a King's favour could be as effectively reached in the bedchamber as on the battlefield. How amusing to confront that arrogant brother of hers, that pious sister, with her success! Once she and Henry were lovers, neither brother nor sister would be able to prevent the liaison's continuance, and then they would have to pay a little attention to their younger sister.

One of her maids came to tell her that Sir William Compton was without and would have speech with her.

Sir William Compton! The King's crony! This was interesting; perhaps the King had sent for her.

"I will see Sir William," she told the maid, "but you should remain in the room. It is not seemly that I should be alone with him."

The maid brought in Sir William and then retired to a corner of the room, where she occupied herself by tidying the contents of a sewing box.

"Welcome, Sir William," said Anne. "I pray you be seated. Then you can comfortably tell me your business."

Compton sat down and surveyed the woman. Voluptuous, provocative, she certainly was. A ripe plum, he thought, ready enough to drop into greedy royal hands.

"Madam," said Compton, "you are charming."

She dimpled coquettishly. "Is that your own opinion, or do you repeat someone else's?"

"It is my own—and also another's."

"And who is this other?"

"One whose name I could not bring myself to mention."

She nodded.

"You have been watched, Madam, and found delectable."

"You make me sound like a peach growing on a garden wall."

"Your skin reminds me—and another—of that fruit, Madam. The peaches on the walls are good this year—warm, luscious, ripe for the plucking."

"Ah yes," she answered. "Do you come to me with a message?"

Compton put his head on one side. "That will come later. I would wish to know whether you would be prepared to receive such a message."

"I have an open mind, Sir William. I do not turn away messengers. I peruse their messages; but I do not always agree to proposals."

"You are wise, Madam. Proposals should always be rejected unless they are quite irresistible."

"And perhaps even then," she added.

"Some proposals would be irresistible to any lady; then it would be wise to accept them."

She laughed. "You keep company with the King," she said. "What is this new song he has written?"

"I will teach it to you."

"That pleases me." She called to her maid and the girl put down the box and hurried forward. "My lute," said Anne. And the girl brought it.

"Now," went on Anne.

Compton came close to her and they sang together.

When they stopped he said: "I shall tell the King that you sang and liked his song. It may be that His Grace would wish you to sing for him. Would that delight you?"

She lowered her eyelids. "I should need some time to practise. I would not wish to sing before His Grace until I had made sure that my performance could give the utmost satisfaction to him . . . and to myself."

Compton laughed.

"I understand," he murmured. "I am sure your performance will give the utmost pleasure."

Anne was passing through an ante-room on her way from an interview with her sister. She was feeling annoyed. Elizabeth had been very severe. She had heard that Sir William Compton had visited Anne on several occasions and such conduct, she would have Anne know, was unseemly in a Stafford.

"I was never alone with him," Anne protested.

"I should hope not!" retorted Elizabeth. "Do behave with more decorum. You must keep away from him in future. The Queen would be displeased if she knew; and what of your husband? Have you forgotten that you are a married woman?"

"I have been twice married to please my family, so I am scarcely likely to forget."

"I am glad," replied Elizabeth primly.

Anne was thinking of this as she hurried through the rooms. The Queen would be displeased! She laughed. Indeed the Queen would be displeased if she knew the true purpose of Sir William's visits. Perhaps soon she would be ready for that encounter with the King, and once that had taken place she was sure that Queen Katharine's influence at Court would be a little diminished. There would be a new star, for Anne Stafford, Countess of Huntingdon, would be of greater importance even than her brother, the Duke of Buckingham.

As she came into an ante-room a woman rose from a stool and came hurriedly towards her.

"My lady Huntingdon," the voice was low and supplicating, and vaguely familiar. The accent was foreign and easily recognizable as Spanish since there had been so many Spaniards at Court. This was a very beautiful woman. "You do not know me," she said.

"I know your face. Were you a lady-in-waiting to the Queen?"

"I was, before she was Queen. My name is Francesca de Carceres and I am now the wife of the Genoese banker, Francesco Grimaldi."

"I do remember," said Anne. "You ran away from Court a few months before the Queen's marriage."

"Yes,'" said Francesca and her lovely face hardened. She had schemed for power; she had imagined that one day she would be the chief confidante of the Queen; but the Queen had been surrounded by those whom Francesca looked upon as her enemies, and in despair Francesca had run away from Court to become the wife of the rich and elderly banker.

Her banker was ready to lavish his fortune upon her, but it was not jewels and fine garments which Francesca wanted; it was power. She realized that fully, now that she had lost her place at Court; and she cursed herself for a fool because she had run away two months before Henry had announced his intention to marry Katharine. Had she waited two months longer, as one of Katharine's ladies-in-waiting, as a member of one of the noble families of Spain, she would have been given a husband worthy of her background; she would have remained in the intimate circle of the Queen.

Having lost these things Francesca now realized how much they meant to her, and she presented herself at Court in the hope of getting an audience with Katharine, but Katharine had so far declined to see her. Francesca had been a troublemaker; she had quarreled with Katharine's confessor, Fray Diego

Fernandez; she had intrigued with Gutierre Gomez de Fuensalida who had been the Spanish ambassador at the time and
whose arrogance and incompetence had aroused Katharine's
indignation and had resulted in his being sent back to Spain.

Moreover in Katharine's eyes Francesca had committed the
unforgivable sin of marrying a commoner, and she wished her
former maid of honour to know that there was no longer a
place at Court for her.

But Francesca was not one to give way lightly; and she was
constantly to be seen in ante-rooms, hoping for a glimpse of the
Queen that she might put her case to her and plead eloquently
for that for which she so much longed.

Francesca now said eagerly: "I wonder if you could say a
word in my favour to Her Grace the Queen."

"You mistake me for my sister," Anne answered. "It is she
who is in the service of Her Grace."

"And you . . . are in the service of . . . ?"

Anne smiled so roguishly that Francesca was immediately
alert.

"I am the younger sister," said Anne. "My brother and sister
think me of little account."

"I'll warrant they're wrong."

Anne shrugged her shoulders. "That may well be," she
agreed.

"The Queen has changed since her marriage," went on
Francesca. "She has grown hard. There was a time, when she
lived most humbly in Durham House and I waited on her. Then
she would not have refused an audience to an old friend."

"She disapproved strongly of your marriage; she is very
pious and surrounds herself with those of the same mind."

Francesca nodded.

"My sister is one of them. I have just received a letter on the
lightness of my ways, when all I did was to receive a gentleman—one of the *King's* gentlemen—in the presence of my
maid."

"It is natural," said Francesca slyly, "that the Queen's
friends should be disturbed when a gentleman of the King's

household visits a lady as beautiful as yourself . . . on the King's orders."

"But I did not say . . ." began Anne, and then she burst into laughter. She went on incautiously: "She is indeed so much older than he is, so much more serious. Is it to be wondered at?"

"I do not marvel," replied Francesca. "And, Lady Huntingdon, if ever you should find yourself in a position to ask favours, would you remember that I have a desire to return to Court?"

Anne's eyes gleamed. It was a glorious thing to be asked such favours; the power of the King's mistress would be infinite.

She bowed her head graciously.

"I would be your friend for evermore," murmured Francesca.

Anne laughed lightly and said: "I shall not forget you."

She walked on as though she were a Queen instead of a potential King's mistress.

Little fool! thought Francesca. If she ever does reach the King's bed she will not stay there long.

There was a constricted feeling in Francesca's throat which was the result of bitterness. She was the most unfortunate of women. She had endured all the years of hardship as Katharine's friend; and then two months before the coming of power and glory she had run away to Grimaldi—she, who longed to live her life in an atmosphere of Court intrigue, whose great delight was to find her way through the maze of political strategy.

She went back to the luxurious house where she lived with her rich husband.

He watched her with a certain sadness in his eyes. To him she was like some gorgeous bird which had fluttered into the cage he had prepared for her and was now longing to escape.

She was so young and so beautiful, but lately the lines of discontent had begun to appear on her brow.

"What luck?" he asked.

"None. When do I ever have luck? She will not receive me. She will never forgive me for marrying you. I have heard that she thinks I did it to cover up a love affair with Fuensalida. Our Queen cannot understand a noblewoman's marrying a commoner except to avoid a great scandal. Fuensalida was of a family worthy to match my own."

"And I am a vulgar commoner," sighed Grimaldi.

Francesca looked at him, her head on one side. Then she smiled and going to him she took his head in her hands and laid her lips lightly on the sparse hair. She loved power and he gave her power over him. He would do anything to please her.

"I married you," she answered.

He could not see her mouth, which had twisted into a bitter line. I married him! she thought. And in doing so I brought about my exile from the Court. It was so easy to offend. She thought of the frivolous Anne Stafford who was hoping—so desperately hoping—to begin a love affair with the King.

Then she smiled slowly. Such a woman would never keep her place for more than a night or two. Francesca could not place herself on the side of such a woman; and if it was going to be a matter of taking sides there would be another on which she could range herself.

If Katharine were grateful to her, might she not be ready to forgive that unfortunate marriage?

Katharine was on her knees praying with her confessor, Fray Diego Fernandez, and the burden of her prayer was: Let me bear a son.

Fray Diego prayed with her and he comforted her. He was a young man of strong views and there had been certain rumours, mainly circulated by his enemies, the chief of whom was the ambassador Fuensalida with whom he had clashed on more than one occasion; and another was Francesca de Carceres who had been convinced, first that he was preventing her returning to Spain and, now that she was married and exiled from Court, that he was preventing her being received again.

The pugnacious little priest was the kind to provoke enemies; but Katharine trusted him; indeed in those days, immediately before her marriage, when she had begun to despair of ever escaping from the drab monotony of Durham House, and had discovered the duplicity of her duenna, Doña Elvira and the stupidity of her father's ambassador, Fuensalida, she had felt Fray Diego to be her only friend.

Katharine was not likely to forget those days; her memory was long and her judgment inflexible. If she could not forgive her enemies, she found it equally difficult to forget her friends.

Fuensalida had been sent back to Spain; Francesca had proved her treachery by deserting her mistress and escaping to marriage with the banker; but Fray Diego remained.

She rose from her knees and said: "Fray Diego, there are times when I think that you and Maria de Salinas are the only part of Spain that is left to me. I can scarcely remember what my father looks like; and I have almost as little esteem for our present ambassador as I had for his predecessor."

"Oh, I do not trust Don Luis Caroz either, Your Grace," said the priest.

"I cannot think why my father sends such men to represent him at the English Court."

"It is because he knows his true ambassador is the Queen herself. There is none who can do his cause more good than his own daughter; and none more wise or understanding of the English."

Katharine smiled tenderly. "I have been blessed in that I may study them at the closest quarters . . . singularly blessed."

"The King is full of affection towards Your Grace, and that is a matter for great rejoicing."

"I would I could please him, Fray Diego. I would I could give him that which he most desires."

"And is there any sign, Your Grace?"

"Fray Diego, I will tell you a secret, and secret it must be, for it is as yet too soon to say. I believe I may be pregnant."

"Glory be to the saints!"

She put her fingers to her lips. "Not a word, Fray Diego. I could not endure the King's disappointment should it not be so. You see, if I told him he would want to set the bells ringing; he would tell the entire Court . . . and then . . . if it were not so . . . how disappointed he would be!"

Fray Diego nodded. "We do not wish Caroz to prattle of the matter."

"Indeed no. Sometimes I wonder what he writes to my father."

"He writes of his own shrewdness. He believes himself to be the greatest ambassador in the world. He does not understand that Your Grace prepared the way for him. He does not know how you continually plead your father's cause with the King."

"I do not see it as my father's cause, Fray Diego. I see it as friendship between our two countries. I would have perfect harmony between them, and I believe we are working towards it."

"If Caroz does not ruin everything, it may well be. He is such an arrogant man that he does not know that Your Grace's father sent him to England because he had sufficient wealth to pay his own way."

"Ah, my father was always careful with the gold. He had to be. There were so many calls upon it."

"He and the late King of England were a pair. The King, your husband, is of a different calibre."

Katharine did not say that her husband's extravagance sometimes gave her anxiety; she scarcely admitted it to herself. Henry VII had amassed a great fortune, and once his successor had had a surfeit of pleasure he would shoulder his responsibilities and turn his back on it. Katharine often remembered his behaviour when the people had robbed him of his jewellery so unexpectedly; and she believed that when he was in danger he would always know how to act. He was a boy as yet—a boy who had escaped from a parsimonious upbringing. He would soon grow tired of the glitter and the gold.

Fray Diego went on: "Your Grace, Francesca de Carceres was at the Palace today, hoping for an audience."

"Did she ask it?"

"She did and I told her that Your Grace had expressed no desire to see her. She abused me, telling me that it was due to me that you had refused, that I had carried evil tales about her. She is a dangerous woman."

"I fear so. She is one who will always scheme. I do not wish to see her. Tell her I regret her marriage as much as she evidently does; but since she made it of her own free will I should admire her more if she were content with the station in life which she herself chose."

"That I will do, Your Grace."

"And now, Fray Diego, I will join my ladies. And remember I have not even told Doña Maria de Salinas or Lady Elizabeth Fitzwalter of my hopes."

"I shall treat it as a secret of the confessional, Your Grace; and I shall pray that ere long the whole Court will be praying with me that this time there may be an heir who lives."

Francesca de Carceres was furiously angry as she left the Palace. She had always hated Fray Diego Fernandez but never quite so much as she did at this time. She had persuaded herself that it was due to his influence that Katharine would not receive her; and she decided to seek the help of the Spanish ambassador, Don Luis Caroz.

This was not difficult to arrange, because her husband transacted business for Caroz as he had done for Fuensalida, and the ambassador was a frequent visitor to the Grimaldi household.

So on his very next visit Francesca detained him and told him that she had news of an intrigue which was taking place at Court and of which she felt he should not be kept in ignorance.

She then told him that she believed that the King was either conducting, or preparing to conduct, a love affair with Lady Huntingdon.

The ambassador was horrified. It was essential to Spanish interests that Katharine should keep her influence with the King, and a mistress could mean considerable harm to those interests.

"The affair must be stopped," he said.

"I doubt whether it has begun," answered Francesca. 'The King has been a faithful husband so far, in spite of temptations; but I think he is eager to subdue his conscience and take a mistress. I believe therefore that we should take some action . . . quickly. The Queen will not see me. Could you approach her, tell her that *I* have discovered this and am sending the news to her through you? You might hint that if she would see me I could tell her more."

The ambassador shook his head. "It would be dangerous to approach the Queen. We cannot be sure what action she would take. She might reproach the King, which could have disastrous results. Nay, this woman has a sister who is in the service of the Queen. We will approach the sister, Lady Fitzwalter. She will almost certainly call in the help of her brother the Duke and I am sure that the proud Staffords would not wish their sister to become the mistress even of the King. They will doubtless realize that the relationship with this rather foolish woman would be of short duration."

Francesca was silent. She did not see how this was going to help her win the Queen's favour, which was her sole object; but she had grown wise since making her fatal mistake. Her most powerful friend was the ambassador, and if she wished to keep his friendship she must fall in with his wishes.

"You are right," she said at length. "The important thing is to prevent the Queen from losing her influence over the King."

Caroz smiled slowly. "I think you might ask for an audience with Lady Fitzwalter. Tell her what you know. We will then watch how the Staffords receive the news. If things do not work out as we wish, we might take other action."

"I shall do exactly as you say," Francesca assured him.

He answered: "You are a good friend to Spain, Doña Francesca."

She felt more hopeful than she had for a long time. Perhaps previously she had been wrong to count so much on getting an audience with the Queen. She must work her way back through more devious paths. The Spanish ambassador might even report to Ferdinand her usefulness. It was possible that Katharine's father would command his daughter to take such a useful servant of Spain back into her service.

Edward Stafford, third Duke of Buckingham, looked at his elder sister in dismay which was quickly turning to anger.

Buckingham's dignity was great. Secretly he believed that

he was more royal than the King himself, for the Tudor ancestry could not bear too close a scrutiny; but the Staffords had royal blood in their veins and the present Duke could never forget that he was directly descended from Edward III.

Buckingham was a member of the King's most intimate circle, but Henry had the Tudor's suspicion of any who had too close a connection with the throne, and would never have the same affection for the Duke as he had for men like Sir William Compton.

In spite of his ambition Buckingham could not overcome his pride. Because he himself could never forget his royal descent he could not help making others aware of it on every conceivable occasion. Often his friends had warned him to beware; but Buckingham, although being fully conscious of possible danger, could not curb his arrogance.

As yet the danger was not acute. Henry was young with a boy's delight in sport and pageantry. He enjoyed perfect health and his bursts of ill temper, although liable to occur suddenly, were quickly over and forgotten. So far he was sure of his popularity with his people and therefore inclined to be a little careless of the ambitions of others. But there were times when those suspicions, which had been so much a part of his father's character, made themselves apparent.

Buckingham's reactions to the news his sister was telling him were so fierce that he forgot that the King was involved in this matter.

He burst out: "Has the woman no family pride! Does she forget she is a Stafford?"

"It would seem so," answered Elizabeth Fitzwalter. "I am informed that it can only be a matter of days before she surrenders."

"She is such a fool that she would not hold the King's attention more than a night or so," growled Buckingham. "Moreover, the King is still too enamoured of the Queen for a mistress to have any chance of making her position really secure."

Elizabeth bowed her head. She was deeply shocked that a sister of hers should be ready to indulge in such immorality, but she was after all an ambitious Stafford and did know that the families of King's mistresses rarely suffered from their connection with royalty. But she, like her brother, realized that Anne's triumph would be short-lived; therefore it was advisable to stop the affair before it went too far.

"I suppose the whole Court is gossiping of this matter!" said Buckingham.

"I do not think it is widely known as yet; but of course as soon as she has shared the King's bed for one night it will be known throughout the Court. So far Compton is acting as go-between, and the final arrangements have not yet been made. Our sister is behaving like a simpering village girl—clinging to her chastity with reluctant fingers."

"And likely to let go at any moment. Well, she shall not do so. I trust that we may rely on our informants."

"I am sure of it. You remember Francesca de Carceres? She is a clever woman and very eager to return to Court. She is anxious to show the Queen that she is still her humble servant. Anne—the little fool—allowed this woman to wheedle her secret from her; and I believe that Carceres feels that if she can prevent our sister's becoming the King's mistress she will have earned the Queen's gratitude. She makes a good spy, that woman."

The Duke nodded. "There is one thing to be done. I will send immediately for Huntingdon. He shall take his wife away to the country with all speed."

"I was sure you would know what should best be done, Edward." She looked anxious. "And the King? I am a little worried concerning his feelings when he knows that she has been whisked away from him."

"He will have to understand," said Buckingham haughtily, "that if he wants to take a mistress he must not look for her among the Staffords, whose blood is as royal as his own."

"Edward, do not let anyone hear you say that."

Buckingham shrugged his shoulders. "It does not need to be said. It is known for the truth by any who care to look into the matter."

"Still, have a care, Edward. I shall be so pleased when her husband has taken her out of danger."

Anne's maid came to tell her that Sir William Compton was begging an audience.

"Then bring him to me," said Anne, "and do not forget to remain in the room."

He came in and once again the maid set about tidying the sewing box.

"I declare you grow more beautiful every time I have the pleasure of seeing you."

"You are gracious, sir."

"I come to tell you that impatience is growing strong in a certain breast."

"And what should *I* do about that?"

"It is only yourself who can appease it. I come to ask you if you will allow me to arrange a meeting between you and this impatient one."

"It would depend. . . ."

"On what, Madam?"

"On when and where this meeting should take place?"

Compton came closer and whispered: "In one of the royal apartments. None would see you come to it. It should be a matter between you and him who bids me tell you of his impatience."

"Then it seems this would be a command rather than a request."

"It could seem so," agreed Compton.

She smiled, her eyes gleaming. "Then I have no alternative but to say, Tell me when . . . tell me where. . . ."

The door opened suddenly. The Countess of Huntingdon gave a little cry of alarm, and the maid dropped her sewing box as the Duke of Buckingham strode into the room.

"Why, brother, is it indeed you?" stammered Anne.

"Whom else did you expect? Your lover! Or is this one he? By the saints, Madam, you forget who you are! This is conduct worthy of a serving wench."

"My lord Buckingham," began Compton sternly, "I come on the King's business."

"Neither the King nor anyone else has business in the private apartment of a married woman of my family."

"The King, I had always believed, might have business with any subject, an he wished it."

"No, sir, you are mistaken. This is my sister, and if she has forgotten the dignity due to her name, then she must be reminded of it." He turned to Anne. "Get your cloak at once."

"But why?"

"You will understand later, though it is not necessary for one so foolish to understand, but only to obey."

Anne stamped her foot. "Edward, leave me alone."

Buckingham strode forward and seized her by the arm. "You little fool! How long do you think it would last for you? Tonight? Tomorrow night? Disgrace to your name. *That* you are ready to bear. But, by God and all the saints, I'll not suffer disgrace to mine. Come, you would-be harlot, your cloak." He turned to the maid. "Get it," he shouted, and the girl hurried to obey.

Compton stood looking at the Duke. He wondered how long such arrogance could survive at Court. But Buckingham was no youngster; he was well past his thirtieth birthday; he should be able to look after himself, and if he valued his family pride more than his life, that was his affair.

Compton shrugged. He was faintly amused. It would be interesting to see how the spoiled golden boy responded to this.

Buckingham snatched the cloak from the maid's trembling hands and roughly threw it about his sister's shoulders.

"Where are you taking me?" she asked.

"To your husband who, if he takes my advice, will place you this night in a convent. A pallet in a cell for you, sister; that is what your lust shall bring you."

Compton plucked the sleeve of the Duke's doublet.

"Do you realize that His Grace will not be pleased with you?"

"I," retorted Buckingham haughtily, "am far from pleased with His Grace's attempt to seduce my sister. Nor do I care for pimps—even though they be the King's own—to lay hands on me."

"Buckingham," murmured Compton, "you fool, Buckingham."

But Buckingham was not listening; he had taken his sister by the shoulders and pushed her before him from the room.

"And so, Your Grace," said Compton, "the Duke burst into his sister's apartment, bade her maid bring her cloak, and thereupon hustled her from the apartment with threats that he was taking her to her husband, and that the pair of them would see that this night she would lie in a convent."

The King's eyes were narrow and through the slits shone like pieces of blue glass; his fresh colour was heightened.

"By God and our Holy Mother!" he cried.

"Yes, Sire," went on Compton. "I warned the Duke. I told him of Your Grace's pleasure."

"And what said he?"

"He cared only for his sister's honour."

"I planned to honour the woman."

"'Tis so, Sire. The Duke has another meaning for the word."

"By God and his Holy Mother!" repeated the King.

Anything can happen now, thought Compton. The frisky cub is a young lion uncertain of his strength. He will not be uncertain long. Soon he will know its extent, and then it will go ill for any who oppose him.

Compton tried to read the thoughts behind those pieces of blue flint.

Frustrated desire! Now the lady seemed infinitely desirable. Out of reach in a convent! Could he demand her release? Could he have her brought to his apartments, laid on his bed? But what of the people, the people who adored him, who shouted their approval of their golden boy? They had seen him embrace his wife whom he had married because he said he loved her more than any woman. The people wanted their handsome King to be a virtuous husband. What would they say if they heard the story of the King and Buckingham's sister?

They would laugh; they would snigger. They might say: Well, he is a King, but he is a man as well. They would forgive him his frailty; but he wished to have no frailty in their eyes. He wished to be perfect.

His eyes widened and Compton saw that they were the eyes of a bewildered boy. The cub was not yet certain of his strength; he had not yet grown into the young lion.

Now there was anger on the flushed face . . . vindictive anger. He would not send for the woman and there would be no scandal. Yet he would not lightly forgive those who had frustrated him.

He turned on Compton. "How did Buckingham discover this?"

"It was through his sister—Your Grace may recollect that the Duke has two sisters—Anne, your Grace's . . . friend, and Elizabeth, Lady Fitzwalter."

"I know her," growled Henry. "She is with the Queen."

"A lady of high virtue, Your Grace. And much pride, like her brother."

"A prim piece," said Henry, and his eyes were cruel. Then he shouted: "Send for Buckingham."

Compton left him, but Buckingham was not at Court. He, with Anne and Lord Huntingdon, were on their way to the convent which Buckingham had ordered should be made ready to receive his erring sister.

The King's anger had had time to cool by the time Buckingham stood before him; but Henry was not going to allow anyone to interfere in his affairs.

He scowled at the Duke.

"You give yourself airs, sir Duke," he said.

"If Your Grace will tell me in what matter I have displeased you I will do my best to rectify my error . . . if it be in my power."

"I hear you have sent your sister into a convent."

"I thought she needed a little correction, Your Grace."

"You did not ask our permission to send her there."

"I did not think Your Grace would wish to be bothered with a family matter."

The King flushed hotly; he was holding fast to his rising temper. The situation was delicate. He was wondering how much of this had reached the Queen's ears and hoping that he could give vent to his anger in such a manner that Katharine would never hear of it.

"I am always interested in the welfare of my subjects," he grumbled.

"Her husband thought she was in need of what the convent could give her."

"I could order her to be brought back to Court, you know."

"Your Grace is, by God's mercy, King of this realm. But Your Grace is a wise man, and knows the scandal which would be bruited about the Court and the country itself, if a woman who had been sent by her husband into a convent should be ordered out by her King."

Henry wanted to stamp his feet in rage. Buckingham was older than he was and he knew how to trap him. How dared he stand there, insolent and arrogant! Did he forget he was talking to his King?

For a few moments Henry told himself that he would send for Anne; he would blatantly make her his mistress and the whole Court—ay, and all his subjects too—must understand that he was the King, and when he ordered a man or woman to some duty they must obey him.

But such conduct would not fit the man his subjects believed him to be. He was uncertain. Always he thought of the cheering crowds who had come to life when he appeared; he remembered the sullen looks which had been thrown his father's way. He remembered too the stories he had heard of his father's struggle to take the throne. If he displeased the people they might remember that the Tudor ancestry was not as clean as it might be—and that there were other men who might be considered worthy to be Kings.

No. He would remain the public idol—perfect King and husband; but at the same time he would not allow any subject of his to dictate to him what should be done.

"My lord Buckingham," he said, "you will leave Court. And you will not present yourself to me until I give you leave to do so."

Buckingham bowed.

"You may go," went on the King. "There is nothing more I have to say to you. I should advise you to be gone in an hour, for if I find you lingering after that I might not be so lenient."

Buckingham retired, and the King paced up and down like a lion in a cage.

He summoned one of his pages to him and said: "Send for Lady Fitzwalter, I would have immediate speech with her."

The page rushed to do his bidding and soon returned with Elizabeth Fitzwalter.

She looked disturbed, Henry was pleased to notice. A prim woman, he thought, with none of her sister's voluptuousness. The sight of her reminded him of Anne, and he was furious once more to contemplate what he had lost.

"Lady Fitzwalter," he said, "you are, I believe, one of the Queen's women."

She was bewildered. Surely he knew. He had seen her so often when he was in the Queen's company.

"Did I say you *are* one of Her Grace's women? It was a mistake, Lady Fitzwalter. I should have said you *were*."

"Your Grace, have I offended . . . ?"

"We do not discuss why we banish from our Court those who do not please us, Lady Fitzwalter. We merely banish."

"Your Grace, I beg to . . ."

"You waste your time. You would beg in vain. Go back to your apartment and make all haste to leave Court. It is our wish that you are gone within the hour."

The startled Lady Fitzwalter curtseyed and retired.

Henry stared at the door for a few minutes. He thought of voluptuous Anne and realized suddenly how urgently he desired a change, a new woman who was as different from his wife as could be.

Then he began to pace up and down again . . . a lion, not sure of his strength, but aware of the cage which enclosed him. The bars were strong, but his strength was growing. One day, he knew, he would break out of the cage. Then there would be nothing—no person on Earth to restrain him.

Elizabeth Fitzwalter came unceremoniously into the apartment where the Queen sat sewing with Maria de Salinas.

Katharine looked with surprise at her lady-in-waiting, and when she saw how distraught Elizabeth was she rose quickly and went to her side.

"What has happened to disturb you so?" she asked.

"Your Grace, I am dismissed from the Court."

"You, dismissed! But this is impossible! None has the authority to dismiss you but myself. Why. . . ." Katharine paused and a look of horror spread across her face. There was one other who had the power, of course.

Elizabeth met Katharine's gaze, and Katharine read the truth there.

"But why?" demanded the Queen. "On what grounds? Why should the King dismiss you?"

"I find it hard to say, Your Grace. I am to leave at once. I have been told to make ready and go within the hour. I pray you give me leave to make ready."

"But surely the King gave you a reason. What of your brother?"

"He has already gone, Your Grace; and my sister also."

"So the King is displeased with all your family. I will go to see him. I will ask him what this means. He will keep nothing from me."

Maria de Salinas, who loved Katharine sincerely and with a disinterested devotion, laid her hand on the Queen's arm.

"Well, Maria?"

Maria looked helplessly at Elizabeth as though asking for permission to speak.

"What is it?" asked Katharine. "If it is something I should know, it is your duty to tell me."

Neither of the women spoke, and it was as though each was waiting for the other to do so.

"I will go to the King," said Katharine. "I will ask him what this means, for I see that you both know something which you believe you should keep from me."

Maria said: "I must tell Her Grace. I think she should know."

Katharine interrupted sternly: "Come Maria, enough of this. Tell me at once."

"The Countess of Huntingdon has been taken away from Court by her husband and brother because they . . . they feared the King's friendship."

Katharine had grown pale. She was almost certain now that she was with child and had been wondering whether she could tell the King. She had looked forward to his pleasure and had told herself how thankful she should be to have such a faithful husband.

She looked from Maria to Elizabeth and her gaze was bewildered. The King's friendship for a woman could surely mean only one thing.

But they must be mistaken. They had been listening to gossip. It was not true. He had always been faithful to her. He had firm notions on the sanctity of marriage: he had often told her so.

She said quietly: "Pray go on."

"Sir William Compton acted as His Grace's emissary in the matter," said Elizabeth. "Francesca Carceres discovered what was happening and warned me. I told my brother and, as a result, my sister has been sent to a convent. But the King was displeased with my brother and myself."

"I cannot believe this to be true."

"Your Grace, pray sit down," whispered Maria. "This has been a shock."

"Yes," said the Queen, "it has been a shock, a shock that such rumours can exist. I believe it all to be lies . . . lies. . . ."

Maria looked frightened. Elizabeth whispered: "Your Grace, give me leave to retire. I have to prepare with all speed to leave Court."

"You shall not go, Elizabeth," said Katharine. "I will speak to the King myself. There has been some terrible mistake. What you believe has happened is . . . an impossibility. I will go to him now. You will see, he will give me the explanation. I will tell him that I wish you to remain. That will suffice."

Katharine walked from the apartment, while Maria looked after her sadly; and Elizabeth, sighing, went to make ready to leave.

It seemed to Henry that he saw his wife clearly for the first time.

How sallow her skin is! he thought comparing her with Anne Stafford. How serious she was! And she looked old. She was old of course, compared with him, for five years was no small matter.

She seemed distasteful to him in that moment, because he felt guilty, and he hated to feel so.

"Henry," she said, "I have heard some disturbing news. Elizabeth Fitzwalter comes to me in great distress and says that you have commanded her to leave Court."

"It is true," he said. "She should be gone within an hour of our giving her the order to leave."

"But she is one of my women, and I do not wish her to go. She is a good woman and has given me no offence."

The colour flamed into his face. "We will not have her at Court," he shouted. "Mayhap it escapes your notice, but our wishes here are of some account."

Katharine was afraid, yet she remembered that she was the daughter of Isabella of Castile, and it ill became any—even the King of England—to speak to her in such a manner.

"I should have thought I might have been consulted in this matter."

"No, Madam," retorted Henry. "We saw no reason to consult you."

Katharine said impetuously: "So you had the grace to try to keep it from my notice."

"We understand you not."

She realized then that he was using the formal "we", and she guessed he was attempting to remind her that he was the King and master of all in his dominions, even his Queen. She saw the danger signals in his eyes, for his face always betrayed his feelings, but she was too hurt and unhappy to heed the warning.

"It is true then," she burst out, "that the woman was your mistress. . . ."

"It is not true."

"Then she was not, because Buckingham intervened in time."

"Madam, if the King wishes to add to his friends it is no concern of any but himself."

"If he has sworn to love and cherish a wife, is it not his wife's concern if he takes a mistress?"

"If she is wise and her husband is a King, she is grateful that he is ready to give her children . . . if she is able to bear them!"

Katharine caught her breath in horror. It is true then, she thought. He blames me for the loss of our two children.

She tried to speak but the words would not pass the lump of misery in her throat.

"We see no reason to prolong this interview," said Henry.

Her anger blazed suddenly. "Do you not? Then I do! I am your wife, Henry. You have told me that you believe that husband and wives should be faithful to each other; and as soon as a wanton woman gives you a glance of promise you forget your vows, you forget your ideals. The people look upon you as a god—so young, so handsome, so model a king and a husband. I see now that your vows mean nothing to you. You think of little but seeking pleasure. First it is your pageants, your masques . . . now it is your mistresses!"

He was scarcely handsome in that moment. His eyes seemed to sink into his plump red face. He hated criticism and, because he was so deeply conscious of his guilt, he hated her.

"Madam," he said, "you should do your duty. It is what is expected of you."

"My duty?" she asked.

"Which is to give me sons. You have made two attempts and have not been successful. Is it for you to criticize me when you have failed . . . so lamentably?"

"I . . . failed? You would blame *me*, then. Do you not know that I long for sons as much as you do? Where have I failed?

How could I have saved the lives of our children? If there is a way, in the name of the saints tell it to me."

Henry would not look at her. "We lost them both," he mumbled.

She turned to him. She was about to tell him that she had hopes of bearing another child; but he looked so cruel that she said nothing. She was bewildered, wondering if this man who was her husband was, after all, a stranger to her.

Henry felt uneasy. He hated to know that Katharine had become aware of his flirtation with Anne Stafford. Looking back it was such a mean little affair—it had not even approached its climax. He felt small, having sent Compton to do his wooing for him, and taking such a long time to make up his mind whether he should or shouldn't, and so giving Buckingham time to whisk his sister away.

He was angry with everyone concerned in the affair and, as Katharine was the only one present, he gave vent to his venom and let it fall upon her.

"It may be," he said coldly, "that the difference in our ages is the cause. You are five years older than I. I had not realized until today how old you are!"

"But," she stammered, "you always knew. I am twenty-five, Henry. That is not too old to bear healthy children."

Henry looked past her, and when he spoke—although he did so more to himself than to her—she felt a cold terror strike at her.

"And you were my brother's wife," was what he said.

She could bear no more. She turned and hurried from his presence.

Before Lady Fitzwalter had left Court the news was circulating. "The King and Queen have quarrelled bitterly. This is the first quarrel. Perhaps there will be fewer of those entwined initials. Perhaps this is the end of the honeymoon."

Maria de Salinas helped the Queen to her bed. Never had Maria seen Katharine so distraught; for even in the days of humiliating poverty she had never given way to her grief but had stoically borne all her trials.

"You see, Maria," said Katharine, "I feel I did not know him. He is not the same. I have glimpsed the man behind my smiling happy boy."

"He was angry," said Maria. "Perhaps Your Grace should not have spoken to him on the matter yet."

"Perhaps I should never have spoken to him on the matter. Perhaps the love affairs of Kings are to be ignored by all, including their wives. My father was not entirely faithful to my mother. I wonder if she ever complained. No, she would be too wise."

"You are wise too. Perhaps your mother had to learn also to curb her jealousy."

Katharine shivered. "You speak as though this is but a beginning, the first of many infidelities."

"But he was not unfaithful, Your Grace."

"No, the lady's brother and husband intervened in time. It is naught to do with the King's virtue. I think that is why he is so angry with me, Maria . . . because he failed."

"He is young, Your Grace."

"Five years younger than I. He reminded me of it."

"It will pass, dearest lady."

"Oh, Maria, I am so tired. I feel bruised and wounded. I have not felt so sad . . . so lost . . . since the old days in Durham House when I thought everyone had deserted me."

Maria took the Queen's hand and kissed it. "All did not desert Your Grace."

"No. You were always there, Maria. Oh, it is good to have staunch friends."

"Let me cover you. Then you should try to sleep. When you are rested you will feel stronger."

Katharine smiled and closed her eyes.

It was later that night when she was awakened by pains which gripped her body and brought a sweat upon her skin.

She stumbled from her bed, calling to her ladies as she did so; but before they could reach her she fell groaning to the floor.

They put her to bed; they called her physicians; but there was nothing they could do.

On that September night Katharine's third pregnancy ended. It had been brief, but the result was no less distressing.

Once more she had failed to give the King the son for which he longed.

She was ill for several days, and during that time she was tormented with nightmares. The King figured largely in these—an enormous menacing figure with greedy, demanding hands which caressed others, but when he turned to her, held out those hands, crying: "Give me sons."

CHAPTER III

The Secret Life of Thomas Wolsey

As the days passed they took some of Katharine's sorrow with them, and she began to look at her life in a more philosophical way. Through the ages Kings had taken mistresses who bore them children, but it was the children who were born in wedlock who were heirs to their father's crown. She must be realistic; she must not hope for impossible virtue from her lusty young husband.

More than ever she thought of her mother, who had borne the same tribulations before her; she must endeavour as never before to emulate Isabella and keep the memory of her as a bright example of how a Queen should live.

As for Henry, he was ready enough to meet her half way. Reproaches would only result in sullen looks; and the pout of the little mouth, the glare of the little eyes in that large face implied that he was the King and he would do as he wished. But any signs of a desire on her part to return to the old relationship brought immediate response; dazzling smiles would light up his face; he would be boisterously affectionate, sentimental, calling her his Kate—the only woman who was of any real importance to him.

So Katharine set aside her illusions and accepted reality; which was, she assured herself, pleasant enough. If she could have a child—ah, if she could have a child—that little creature would make up to her for all else. That child would be the centre of her existence; and her husband's philandering would be of small importance compared with the delight that child would bring her.

In the meantime she would concern herself with another

important matter. Since she had become Queen of England she had been in close contact with her father. She waited for his letters with the utmost eagerness, forgetting that, when she had been living in neglected seclusion at Durham House, he had not written to her for years.

"What a joy it is to me," Ferdinand assured her, "that you, my daughter, are the Queen of England, a country which I have always believed should be my closest ally. I am beginning to understand that a father can have no better ambassador than his own daughter."

Ferdinand in his letters to her artfully mingled his schemes with his news of family affairs. His daughter was the beloved wife of young Henry, and if the King of England was occasionally unfaithful to his marriage bed, what did that matter as long as he continued to regard his wife with affection and respect!

"If your dear mother could know what a comfort to me you have become, what a clever ambassadress for her beloved country, how happy she would be."

Such words could not fail to move Katharine, for the very mention of her mother always touched all that was sentimental in her nature.

After receiving her father's letters she would put forward his ideas to Henry, but never in such a manner that it would appear she was receiving instructions from Spain.

"The King of France," Ferdinand wrote, "is an enemy to both our countries. Singly we might find it difficult to subdue him. But together. . . ."

Henry liked to walk with her in the gardens surrounding his palaces. When he felt particularly affectionate towards her he would take her arm and they would go on ahead of the little band of courtiers, and occasional he would bend his head and whisper to her in the manner of a lover.

On such an occasion she said to him: "Henry, there are certain provinces in France which are by right English. Now that there is a young King on the throne, do you think the people would wish to see those provinces restored to the crown?"

Henry's eyes glistened. He had always longed for the conquest of France. He was beginning to think he had had enough of empty triumphs at the jousts and masques. He wished to show his people that he was a man of war no less than a sportsman. Nothing could have given him greater pleasure at that time than the thought of military conquest.

"I'll tell you this, Kate," he said. "It has always been a dream of mine to restore our dominions in France to the English crown."

"And what better opportunity could we have than an alliance with my father who also regards the King of France as his enemy?"

"A family affair. I like that. Your father and I standing together against the French."

"I believe my father would be ready enough to make a treaty in which you and he would agree to attack the French."

"Is it so, Kate? Then write to him and tell him that, having such regard for his daughter, I would have him for my friend."

"You have made me happy, Henry . . . so happy."

He smiled at her complacently. "We'll make each other happy, eh Kate?" His eyes were searching her face. There was a question in them which he did not need to put into words. It was the perpetual question: Any sign, Kate? Any sign yet that we may expect a child?

She shook her head sadly. He did not share her sadness today. The thought of war and conquest had made him forget temporarily even the great need for a son.

He patted her arm affectionately.

"Have no fear, Kate. We'll not suffer ill luck for ever. I have a notion, Kate, that England and Spain together are . . . invincible! No matter what they undertake."

She felt her spirits rising. It was a great pleasure to see that his thoughts were turned for a while from the matter of childbearing; and it was equally gratifying that he was so willing to fall in with her father's desires. Thus she could please them both at the same time. And surely her next pregnancy must result in a healthy child!

* * *

Richard Fox, Bishop of Winchester and Lord Privy Seal, was deeply disturbed, and he had asked Thomas Howard, Earl of Surrey, and William Warham, Archbishop of Canterbury, to call upon him.

Fox, some sixty-four years of age, was as much a politician as a man of the church. He had stood staunchly by Henry VII and had worked in co-operation with the King since the victory at Bosworth, receiving from that monarch the offices of Principal Secretary of State and Lord Privy Seal. When he had died Henry VII had recommended his son to place himself under the guidance of Richard Fox, and this young Henry had been prepared to do, particularly when Warham had declared himself against the marriage with Katharine.

Fox, the politician, had supported the marriage because he believed that an alliance with Spain was advantageous. Warham, as a man of the Church, had felt that a more suitable wife than the widow of his brother might have been found for the King. The fact that Fox had supported the marriage had placed him higher in the King's favour than the Archbishop of Canterbury; but Fox was now becoming disturbed to see that the country's wealth, which he so carefully had helped Henry VII to amass, was being extravagantly squandered by the young King.

But that was not the matter he intended to discuss with his two colleagues at this time—something of even greater importance had arisen.

William Warham, who was perhaps a year or two younger than Fox, had also served the Tudors well. Henry VII had made him Lord Chancellor and he had held the Great Seal for some nine years. Although he disagreed with Fox on certain matters they both felt deeply the responsibility of guiding a young king who lacked his father's caution and thrift.

The third member of the party was the choleric Thomas Howard, Earl of Surrey, who was the eldest of the three by some five years.

His record was not one of loyalty to the Tudors for he and his father had both fought as Bosworth on the side of Richard III. At this battle Surrey had been taken prisoner and his father killed. There had followed imprisonment in the Tower and forfeiture of his estates; but Henry VII had never been a man to allow desire for revenge to colour his judgment; he realized the worth of Surrey who believed in upholding the crown and the nobility, no matter who wore the first and whatever the actions of the latter, and it seemed to the crafty King that such a man could be of more use to him free than a prisoner. It cost little to restore his titles—but Henry kept the greater part of his property, and sent him up to Yorkshire to subdue a rebellion against high taxation.

The King proved his wisdom when Surrey turned out to be a first-class general and as ready to work for the Tudor as he had for Richard III. For his services he was made a member of the Privy Council and Lord Treasurer.

When Henry VII had died, Surrey, on account of his age and experience, had become the chief of the new King's advisers; and recently, to show his appreciation, young Henry had bestowed upon his faithful servant the title of Earl Marshal.

As soon as these three men were together Fox told them of his concern.

"The King contemplates war with France. I confess that the prospect does not please me."

"The expense would be great," agreed Warham, "and what hope would there be of recovering that which we laid out?"

They were looking at Surrey, the soldier, who was thoughtful. The prospect of war always thrilled him; but he was becoming too old to take an active part in wars and therefore could consider them, not in terms of adventure and valour, but of profit and loss.

"It would depend on our friends," he said.

"We should stand with Spain."

Surrey nodded. "Spain could attack from the South; we from the North. It does not sound a pleasant prospect for the French."

"The late King," said Fox, "was against wars. He always said that it was a sure way of losing English blood and gold."

"Yet, there could be riches from conquest," mused Surrey.

"Victory," put in Warham, "is more easily dreamed of than won."

"The King is enamoured of the prospect," Fox declared.

"Doubtless because the Queen has made it sound so attractive to him," added Warham. "Can it be that Ferdinand has placed an ambassador nearer to the King than any of his own advisers could hope to be?"

He was looking ironically at Fox, reminding him that he had been in favour of the marriage while he, Warham, had seen many disadvantages—of which this could be one.

"The King is pleased with his Queen as a wife," put in Fox. "Yet I believe him to be wise enough to look to his ministers for advice as to how matters of state should be conducted."

"Yet," Surrey said, "he would seem eager for war."

"How can we know," went on Warham, "what has been written in Ferdinand's secret despatches to his daughter? How can we know what the Queen whispers to the King in moments of intimacy?"

"It always seemed to me that the young King must tire of his sports and pageants in time," said Fox. "Now the time has come and he wishes to turn his energies to war. This was bound to happen, and the conquest of France is a natural desire."

"What course do you suggest we should take in this matter?" Warham asked.

"Why," Fox told him, "I believe that if we advised His Grace to send a few archers to help his father-in-law in his battles, that would suffice for the time."

"And you think the King will be satisfied with that?" demanded Surrey. "Young Henry is yearning to place himself at the head of his fighting men. He wishes to earn glory for his country . . . and himself."

"His father had turned a bankrupt state into one of some consequence," Warham reminded them. "He did it through peace, not through war."

"And," put in Surrey, remembering the confiscation of his own estates, "by taxes and extortions."

"I was not speaking of the method," Fox told him coldly,

"but of the result." He went on: "I have asked the King's almoner to join us here, for there are certain matters which I feel we should lay before him; and he is such an able fellow that he may help us in our counsels."

Surrey's face grew purple. "What!" he cried. "That fellow, Wolsey! I will not have the low-born creature sharing in my counsels."

Fox looked at the Earl coldly. "He has the King's confidence, my lord," he said. "It would be well if you gave him yours."

"That I never shall," declared Surrey. "Let the fellow go back to his father's butcher's shop."

"Ah," said Warham, "he has come a long way from that."

"I'll admit he has sharp wits," conceded Surrey. "And a quick tongue."

"He also has the King's ear, which is something we should not forget," Fox told him. "Come, my lord, do not allow your prejudices to affect your judgment of one of the ablest men in this country. We have need of men such as Thomas Wolsey."

Surrey's lips were tightly pressed together and the veins in his temples stood out. He wanted them to know that he was a member of the aristocracy and that he supported his own class. If there were honours to be earned they should be earned by noblemen; to his bigoted mind it was inconceivable that a man of humble origin should share the secrets of the King's ministers.

Fox watched him ironically. "Then, my lord," he said, "if you object to the company of Thomas Wolsey, I can only ask you to leave us, for Wolsey will be with us in a very short time."

Surrey stood undecided. To go would mean cutting himself off from affairs; he was growing old; he believed that Fox and this upstart of his would be delighted to see him pass into obscurity. He could not allow that.

"I'll stay," he said. "But, by God, I'll stand no insolence from a butcher's cur."

* * *

Thomas Wolsey had taken time from his duties to visit his family. This was one of the pleasures of his life; not only did he enjoy being a husband and father but the fact that he must do so with secrecy gave his pleasure an added fillip.

He was a priest but that had not prevented his being uncanonically married; and when he had fallen in love with his little "lark", and she with him, it became clear that their relationship was no light matter of a few weeks' duration and must therefore be set on as respectable a basis as was possible in the circumstances.

So he had gone through a form of marriage with Mr. Lark's daughter; he had made a home for her which he visited from time to time, leaving his clerical garments behind, and dressed so that he could pass through the streets as an ordinary gentleman returning to his home.

It was a rather splendid little home, for he enjoyed ostentation and could not resist the pleasure of making his family aware that he was rising in the world.

As he entered the house he called: "Who is at home today? Who is ready to receive a visitor?"

A serving maid appeared and gave a little cry of wonder. She was followed by a boy and a girl who, having heard his voice, rushed out to greet him.

Thomas Wolsey laid his hand on the boy's shoulder and put an arm about the girl. The smile on his face made him look younger than his thirty-seven years. The alertness in the eyes almost disappeared; Thomas Wolsey briefly looked like a man who is contented.

"Why, my son, my little daughter, so you are pleased to see your father, eh?"

"We are always pleased to see our father," said the boy.

"That is as it should be," answered Thomas Wolsey. "Now Tom, my boy, where is your mother?"

There was no need to ask. She had started to come down the stairs, and as Thomas looked up she paused and for a few seconds they gazed at each other. The woman, thought Thomas, for whom I was ready to risk a great deal. Not everything, and perhaps what he had risked was not very much—for

why should not a priest have a wife as long as he did not prate
of it—but the fact that he was ready to risk anything, that he
was ready to pause in his journey up the steep and difficult
slopes of ambition to spend a little time with this woman and
their children, was an indication of the extent of his feelings
for her.

"Thomas, had I known . . ." she began; and she came down
the stairs slowly, almost reverently, as though she marvelled
yet again that this great man should have time to spare for her.

He took her hand and kissed it.

"Well met, Mistress Wynter," he said.

"Well met, Master Wynter."

It was the name behind which they sheltered from the world.
She longed to boast that she was the wife of the great Thomas
Wolsey, but she knew well the folly of that. He had given so
much; he could not be expected to give more. She was happy
enough to be plain Mistress Wynter, with a husband whose
business frequently called him away from home but who was
now and then able to visit his family.

The future of her children was secure. Thomas was rising
rapidly in the service of the King; he was proud of the children;
he would not forget them, and their way would be easier than
his had been. Honours, riches would come to them—that
would be when they were of an age to receive them—and by
that time Thomas would be the most important man in the
realm. Mistress Wynter believed that, for Thomas had determined it should be so; and Thomas always achieved his ends.

The children stood aside while their parents embraced.

"How long will you stay, Thomas?" she asked.

"Naught but a few hours, my lark." Even as he uttered the
endearment he wondered what certain members of the King's
entourage would say if they could see and hear him now. Fox?
Warham? Surrey? Lovell? Poynings? They would snigger
doubtless; and the wise among them would not be displeased.
They would tell themselves that he had his weaknesses like all
other men, and such weaknesses were not to be deplored but
encouraged, for they were as a great burden hung upon the
back to impede the climb to the heights of success.

There are some who are afraid of Thomas Wolsey, thought Thomas, and the thought pleased him; for when men began to fear another, it meant that that one was high upon the ladder since others could see him mounting.

But I must take care, he thought as he stroked his wife's hair; no one however dear must prevent my taking every opportunity; the road to disaster and failure is one of lost opportunities.

But for a few hours he was safely hidden from the Court, so for that time he would be happy.

"Why, Mistress Wynter," he said, "you were not warned of my coming, but I smell goodly smells from your kitchen."

The children began to tell their father what was for dinner. There was a goose, capon and chicken; there was a pastie which their good cook had made in the shape of a fortress; there was pheasant and partridge.

Thomas was pleased. His family lived as he would have them live. It made him happy to think that he could pay for their comforts; and the sight of the rosy cheeks and plump limbs of his children was an immense satisfaction to him.

Mistress Wynter in a flurry of excitement went off to the kitchen to warn the servants that the master was in the house; and there the cook harried the lower servants to do their best and prove that, although the master of the house was often absent on his important business, the house was so well managed that he need have no fears.

So Thomas sat at the table and watched the food brought in, while his wife sat facing him and on either side of the table was a child.

It was very humble compared with the King's table, but here was contentment; and in such moments he deeply wished that he was not a priest and that he might take this charming family with him to Court and boast of the health of the boy and the good looks of the girl.

He now wished to know how young Tom was getting on with his studies, and he put on a sternly paternal expression when he discovered that the boy was not quite so fond of his studies as his tutor would wish.

"That must be remedied," said Thomas, shaking his head.

"Doubtless you think that you are young yet and that there is always time. Time is short. It is hard for you to realize it at your age, but soon you must understand that it is so, for when you do you will have learned one of the first lessons of life. It is those who dally by the wayside, my son, who never reach the end of the road."

There was quiet at the table, as there always was when he spoke; he had a melodious voice and a way of driving home his points which demanded attention.

And as they sat eating their way through meat and pies to the marchpane and sugar-bread he told his family how he himself had once defeated time in such a way that he had convinced the King that he had a little more than ordinary men to offer in his service.

"It was when I was in the service of the old King . . ." He did not tell them that he had been the King's chaplain; children often talked freely in the hearing of servants, and he must keep secret his connection with the Church. "This was not the King you have seen riding through the streets. This was the old King, his father, a King with a very serious mind and one who had learned the value of time.

"He called me to him and he said: 'I wish you to go on a journey to Flanders as a special envoy to the Emperor Maximilian. Prepare to leave as soon as possible.' So I took the message which I was to deliver and I set out for my lodgings. My servant said: 'You will leave tomorrow, my lord?' And I answered: 'Tomorrow! Nay, I shall leave today . . . at this very hour.' He was astonished. He had thought I should need time to prepare for such a journey; but I was conscious of time and I knew that the message I carried was of great importance. It might be that if it arrived a day later than I intended to deliver it, the answer to that letter would not be the same favourable one that I was determined to get. Circumstances change . . . and it is time which changes them.

"The message I carried was the King's request for the hand of Maximilian's daughter in marriage. If I could bring a favourable reply from Maximilian, the King would be happy, and that would make him pleased with me; and if that reply came quickly, the better pleased he would be.

"I crossed the water. I rode hot foot to Flanders; I saw the Emperor, delivered the King's message and received his reply; then back to the coast and home. It had been three days since I left England. I presented myself to the King, who frowned in anger when he saw me. He said: 'I had thought you received orders to take a message to Flanders. I expected you would have left by now. I like not dilatory service.' Then my heart leaped in exultation and I waited a few seconds for the King's anger to grow, for the greater it grew the more surprised he must be when he heard the truth. 'Your Grace,' I told him, 'I left for Flanders within an hour of receiving your instructions to do so. I have now returned and bring you the Emperor's reply.' The King was astonished. Never had he been served with such speed. He grasped my hand and said: 'You are a good servant.' "

"And that was all, Father?" demanded young Thomas. "It seems a small reward to shake your hand and tell you you were a good servant."

"He did not forget me," said Thomas.

No, indeed he had not. Thomas Wolsey had become Dean of Lincoln and, had Henry VII lived longer, doubtless more honours would have come his way. But the old King had died; yet that was not a matter for mourning, because the new King was as interested in his servant Wolsey as the old one had been.

From this young King Thomas Wolsey hoped for much. He understood the eighth Henry. Here was a young man, lusty, sensual, far less interested in matters of state than in pleasure. He was the sort of King who is always beloved of ambitious ministers. Henry VII had conducted all state business himself; he had indeed been head of the state. But the joust, tennis, dancing, possible fornication and adultery gave no pleasure to his rheumaticky body. How different was his young and lusty son! This King would wish to place at the helm of the ship of state a man with capable hands; there was every opportunity for ambitious ministers to rule England under such a King.

The King's almoner saw great possibilities ahead.

He smiled at the eager faces about the table—flushed with good food and drink. This was his oasis of pleasure, of humanity; here it was possible to stray from the road of heated ambition to dally in a cool green meadow.

He saw Mistress Wynter through a veil of gratitude and desire, and she seemed fairer to him than any Court lady.

He said to the children: "You will leave your mother with me for a while. We have matters to speak of. I shall see you again before I leave."

The children left their parents together, and Thomas took Mistress Wynter in his arms and caressed her body.

They went through to her sleeping chamber and there made love.

As she lay in his arms she thought: It is like a pattern, always the same. Will it remain so? What when he is the first minister at the King's Court? This he would be, for in a moment of confidence he had told her so.

If it were not so, she thought, if he lost his place at Court, he might come home to us.

It was a wicked thought. He must not lose his place. It meant more to him than anything . . . more than this, his home, more than her and their children.

When he had dressed in that precise manner of his, he said: "I will see the children before I go."

He noticed that she looked a little sad but he did not mention this. He knew that she was wishing they lived a normal married life, that they did not have to go to bed in the middle of the day because it was the only time they had. She was picturing him, being there every day—a merchant, a lawyer, a goldsmith . . . a man of some profession such as those of her neighbours. She thought of cosy conversations over the table, of discussions as to what should be planted in the garden, about the education of the children; she pictured them retiring to bed each night by the light of candles, the embrace that had become almost a habit, the slipping into sleep afterwards. It was normality she craved.

Poor little Mistress Wynter, he thought, she can only share one very small portion of my life and she wants to share the whole.

It was unfortunate for her that she loved not a man of ordinary ability, but one who had risen from a humble Ipswich butcher's shop to his present position and was determined to go to the very heights of ambition.

He said: "Let us go to the children. I have little time left to me."

He kissed her once more, but this time he did not see the sadness in her eyes. He saw only Wolsey, going higher and higher. He saw the Cardinal's hat, but that of course was not the end. There was still the Papal Crown; and since even he must realize that he could never be the King of England, his ultimate ambition was that he should be head of the Church.

He went to his children, smiling happily, for his ambition did not seem an impossible one to achieve. Thomas Wolsey, who had learned so many lessons from life, believed that all that which he desired would eventually be his.

As soon as he returned to Court a messenger informed him that the Archbishop of Canterbury and the Bishop of Winchester with the Earl of Surrey requested his presence.

He donned his clerical garments and washed his hands before making his way to their presence, for this was one of those occasions when time should be used to create an impression of his own power and importance.

They were waiting rather impatiently when he arrived.

"My lords," he said, "you requested my presence."

Surrey looked with distaste at Thomas Wolsey. He reeks of vulgarity, thought Surrey. That coarse skin, that over-red complexion—they proclaim him the vulgarian he is.

Surrey was scarcely pale himself, nor was his skin extra fine, but he was determined to find fault with Wolsey and looked for opportunities to remind him that he was not of noble blood and was only admitted to their counsels as a special privilege for which he should be perpetually grateful.

Fox welcomed him with a smile of pleasure. Fox had believed in his exceptional powers from the first and was determined to be proved right.

"We have been discussing the possibility of war with France," Warham told him.

Wolsey nodded gravely.

"You, Mr. Almoner, should know how much we could put into the field," Surrey pointed out, implying by his tone that it was as a lower servant of the King's that Wolsey had been invited and that his opinion must be confined only to questions of goods and gold.

"Ah," said Wolsey ignoring Surrey and turning to Fox and Warham, "it would depend on what scale the war was to be carried on. If the King should put himself at the head of his men that could be costly. If we sent a small force under the command of some noble gentlemen . . ." Wolsey glanced at Surrey. . . . "that would be well within our means."

"I see you are of our opinion," Fox put in. "At the moment any action should be kept on a small scale."

"And," continued Wolsey, "I dare swear we would not move until we had an assurance from the King of Spain that he also would take action."

"Any alliance with the King of Spain," Surrey interrupted hotly, "should surely be no concern of Mr. Almoner."

"My lord is mistaken," Wolsey said coolly. "That the alliance should be made and adhered to is of the utmost importance to every subject in this land, including the King's Almoner."

The veins seemed to knot in Surrey's temples. "I cannot see that matters of state policy are the concern of every *Tom*, Dick or Harry."

"Might it be that there is much that the noble lord fails to see?" retorted Wolsey. "But since he is now aware of his blindness he may seek a cure for it."

Surrey lifted his fist and brought it down on the table.

"This is insolence!" he shouted. He glared at Fox and Warham. "Did I not tell you that I had no wish to consort with . . . tradesmen!"

Wolsey looked round the apartment in astonishment.

"Tradesmen?" he said, but the hot resentment was rising within him. "I see no tradesmen present." He was fighting his anger because his very love of ostentation grew out of his desire to live as the nobility lived—and a little more richly—that he might leave behind him the memory of the butcher's shop.

"No," sneered Surrey, "how could you? There is no mirror in this room."

"My lord," said Wolsey almost gently, "I am not a tradesman. I graduated at Oxford and was elected Fellow of Magdalen College. Teaching was my profession before I took Holy Orders."

"I pray you spare us an account of your achievements," sneered Surrey, "which I admit are remarkable for one who began in a butcher's shop."

"How fortunate," retorted Thomas, "that you, my lord, did not begin in such an establishment. I fear that if you had you would still be there."

Warham lifted a hand. "I pray you, gentlemen, let us return to the point of discussion."

"I prefer not to continue with it," Surrey shouted. "There is scarce room for myself and Master Wolsey in this council."

He waited for Warham and Fox to request Wolsey to retire. Wolsey stood still, pale, but smiling; and both Fox and Warham looked beyond the now purple-faced Earl. Surrey! Fox was thinking. With his inflated ideas of his own nobility he was scarcely likely to continue in favour with the King. Wolsey, with his quick and clever mind, his ability to smooth out difficulties, and make easy the King's way to pleasure, was by far the better ally. Moreover, Fox had always looked upon the almoner as one of his protégés. Let Surrey stomp out of the apartment. They could well do without him.

As for Warham, he also recognized the almoner's brilliance; he had no love for Surrey either. Surrey belonged to the old school; the days of his youth had been lived in that period when valour in battle brought glory; but Henry VII had taught his people that the way to make a country great was by crafty statesmanship rather than through battles, even if they should be victorious.

With an exclamation of disgust, Surrey flung out of the room.

Wolsey smiled in triumph. "The atmosphere, gentlemen, is now more conducive to thoughtful reasoning," he said.

Fox returned his smile in a manner implying that they were well rid of Surrey.

"And your opinion?"

Wolsey was ready. He was not going to say that he was against sending an army to France, because it might well be that the King wished to send one; it was almost certain that the Queen did, because that was the desire of her father, and the Queen was naturally working for her father's interests. If a decision was made which was contrary to the King's wishes, let Fox and Warham make it.

"As my lord of Surrey pointed out," he said almost demurely, "matters of state are scarcely the concern of the King's Almoner. Should His Grace decide to go into battle I will see that all available armaments are made ready for him; but it is only reasonable to suppose that the mustering of arms to equip a small force, say under some nobleman, would be a simpler matter and one which would give us practice in this field before embarking on the great campaign."

"I see," said Fox, "that you are of our opinion."

They discussed the matter in detail, and, although he seemed outwardly calm, inwardly Thomas Wolsey felt his pride to be deeply bruised. He could not forget the scorn in Surrey's eyes when he had referred to the butcher's shop. Would he ever escape such slights?

They could not be forgotten; therefore they could not be forgiven. Surrey's name was on that list he kept in his mind of those who must one day pay for the indignity they had made Thomas Wolsey suffer.

CHAPTER IV

Spanish Intrigue

Katharine rejoiced to see the change in her husband. She was sure that the irresponsible boy had been left behind and the King was growing to maturity.

He had forgotten their differences and talked with her of his ambitions; this made her very happy; he had even ceased to ask questions as to whether or not she had conceived again.

She had said to him: "It may be that the fact that we concern ourselves so constantly with my pregnancies is the reason that I am not with child. I have heard that constant anxiety can make one sterile."

He may have taken this to heart, but on the other hand the prospect of war may have been entirely responsible for turning his interest into other channels.

One day he swept into her apartments, and she was aware that instead of glancing appreciatively at the prettiest of her women with that glazed look in his eyes which she had noticed with some alarm on previous occasions, he waved his hands for their dismissal.

"Ah, Kate," he cried when they were alone, "I chafe at this delay. I would I could set out this day for France. These ministers of mine think the time is not meet for me to leave the country."

"I have heard from my father," she told him. "He writes that he knows that you would be welcomed in Guienne. The people there have never taken kindly to French rule, he says, and have always considered the English their true rulers. He says that once they see Your Grace they would rally to your banner."

Henry smiled complacently. He could well believe that. He

was certain that the wars with France should never have been allowed to die out while the position was so unsatisfactory for England. England had been torn by her own Wars of the Roses—which was a matter he could not regret as out of that had come the victorious conclusion which had set the Tudors on the throne; but now that there was peace within England and there was a King on the throne who was as strong and eager for conquest as Henry V had been, why should not the struggle be continued?

But Guienne! His ministers were a little anxious. It would have been so much simpler to have attacked nearer home. Calais was the natural starting point.

He would of course be near his ally if he attacked in the south; delay galled him. He could not imagine defeat, so he longed to set forth, to show the people his conquests.

"It would please me, Kate," said Henry, "to lead my army and join up with that of your father. Together we should be invincible."

"I am sure that you would. My father is considered one of the greatest soldiers in Europe."

Henry frowned. "You would imply, Kate, that I should find it necessary to learn from him?"

"He is a man of great experience, Henry."

Henry turned from her. "There are some who are born to be conquerors. They are endowed with the gift. They do not need lessons in bravery."

She went on as though she had not heard him. "He and my mother had to fight for their kingdoms. She often said that without him she would have been lost."

"I like to hear of a wife who appreciates her husband."

"She appreciated him . . . although he was often unfaithful to her."

"Ha!" cried Henry. "You have no such complaint."

She turned to him smiling. "Henry, never give me cause for such complaint. I swear to love and serve you with all my might. I picture us growing old together with our children about us."

His eyes were misted with sentiment. The thought of children could always produce this result. Then his face puckered suddenly.

"Kate, I do not understand. We have been unfortunate, have we not?"

"Many are unfortunate, Henry. So many children die in infancy."

"But three times. . . ."

"There will be many times, Henry."

"But I cannot understand. Look at me. See my strength. My good health is something all marvel at. And yet . . ." He was looking at her almost critically.

She said quickly: "I too enjoy good health."

"Then why . . . I could almost believe that some spell has been cast upon us . . . that we have offended God in some way."

"We cannot have done that. We are devout worshippers, both of us. No, Henry, it is natural to lose children. They are dying every day."

"Yes," he agreed. "One, two, three or four in every family. But some live."

"Some of ours will live."

He stroked her hair, which was her claim to beauty, and as he watched the sun bring out the red in it he felt a sudden rush of desire for her.

He laughed and taking her hand he began to dance, twirling her round, releasing her to caper high in the air. She watched him, clapping her hands, happy to see him so gay.

He grew excited by the dancing and he seized her and hugged her so tightly that she could not breathe.

"A thought comes to me, Kate," he said. "If I go to France with my armies, you must stay behind. We shall be apart."

"Oh Henry, that will make me very sad. I shall miss you so sorely."

"Time will pass," he assured her "and while we are separated how can I get you with child?" Then he began to laugh afresh. "And we squander our time in dancing!"

Then with a swift gesture—eager even in this moment of excitement that she should marvel at his strength—he swung her into his arms and carried her across the apartment to the bedchamber.

Ferdinand, King of Aragon and Regent of Castile until his grandson Charles should come of age, was eagerly awaiting despatches from England.

His great desire at the moment was for the conquest of Navarre. He had made Naples safe and this left him free to make new conquests. It had always been one of his ambitions that Navarre should be under Spanish dominion; his great concern now was to persuade the Archbishop of Toledo and Primate of Spain, Francesco Ximenes de Cisneros, of the justice of this.

He had summoned Ximenes to his presence with the sole purpose of winning his approval of the project. Ximenes came, but from the moment he entered the King's apartments in the Alhambra he showed his reluctance to be torn from his beloved University of Alcalá, which he himself had built and where he was now finishing that great work, his polyglot bible.

Ferdinand felt a surge of resentment as Ximenes entered the apartment. Whenever he saw the man he remembered how his first wife, Isabella, had bestowed the Archbishopric of Toledo on this recluse when he, Ferdinand, had so deeply desired it for his illegitimate son. He had to admit that Isabella's trust in Ximenes had not been ill-founded; the man was a brilliant statesman as well as a monk; yet the resentment lingered.

Even now, thought Ferdinand, I must make excuses for my conduct to this man. I must *win* him to myself, because he wields as much power as I do, since while I am Regent for my grandson, he is Primate in his own right.

"Your Highness wished to see me," Ximenes reminded Ferdinand.

"I am concerned about the French, and the dilatory ways of the English."

"Your Highness is eager to make war on the French for, I believe, the purpose of annexing Navarre."

Ferdinand felt the warm blood rushing to his face.

"Your Eminence has forgotten that I have a claim to Navarre, through my father's first wife."

"Who was not Your Highness' mother."

"But I claim through my father."

"Through his marriage into the royal house of Navarre," Ximenes reminded Ferdinand, "it would seem that Jean d'Albret is the rightful King of Navarre."

Ferdinand said impatiently: "Navarre is in a strategic position. It is necessary to Spain."

"That is scarcely a reason for making war on a peaceful state."

You old fool! thought Ferdinand. Go back to your university and your polyglot bible. Leave me to fight for my rights.

But he said craftily: "How can we be sure that their intentions are peaceful?"

"We have no evidence to the contrary, and it is scarcely likely that such a small kingdom would seek to make war on Spain."

Ferdinand changed the subject.

"The English are eager to take Guienne."

"A foolish project," said Ximenes, "and one doomed to failure."

Ferdinand smiled slyly. "That is a matter for them to decide."

"Your Highness has doubtless roused these ambitions in the mind of the young King of England."

Ferdinand lifted his shoulders. "Should it be my concern if the King of England becomes ambitious to regain territories in France?"

"It could well be," retorted Ximenes, "since the English could harry the French, leaving you free to walk into Navarre."

The sly old fox! thought Ferdinand. There was little he did not know of European affairs. There he sat in his gloomy cell in his grim old university, scratching away with his scholars at their polyglot bible. Then he took one look at affairs and saw the position as clearly as those did who studied it hourly.

The man had genius. Trust Isabella to discover it and use it.

If I could but lure him to my side, the conquest of Navarre would be as good as achieved.

But the Primate was not with him; it was against his principles to make war on a peaceful state. Ximenes did not wish for war. He wanted peace, that he might make a great Christian country, a country which was the strongest in the world, and in which no man could live and prosper unless he was a Christian. The Inquisition was dear to his heart; he was eager that every Spaniard should be as devout as himself and he was ready to torture them to make them so—for he was a man who did not hesitate to torture himself. Ferdinand knew that, beneath the grand robes of his office—which he wore only because he had been ordered to do so by the Pope—was the hair shirt and the rough serge of the Franciscan habit.

We shall always pull one against the other, thought Ferdinand. It was inevitable that he, the ambitious, the sensuous, the avaricious, should be in continual conflict with the austere monk.

Yet, he thought, he shall not hold me back. I must lure the English to France, and this I shall do for I have the best ambassador a man could have at the Court of England. My daughter is the Queen, and the King cherishes her, and as the King is young, inexperienced and inordinately vain, it should not be difficult.

He began to talk of other matters because he saw it was useless to try to convince Ximenes of the need to take Navarre. But all the time he was thinking of the instructions he would give to Katharine and Luis Caroz in London. With the English as his ally he would do without the approval of Ximenes.

He hid his resentment and feigned such friendship for his Primate that he accompanied him to his apartments. A faint sneer touched his lips as he saw the elaborate bed—worthy of the Cardinal, Inquisitor General and Primate of Spain—because he knew that Ximenes used it only for ceremonial occasions and spent his nights on a rough pallet with a log of wood for a pillow. It was incongruous that such a man should hold such a position in a great country.

Ferdinand, however, lost no time in returning to his own apartments and writing to his ambassador in London.

The King of England must be persuaded to join Spain in the war against France without delay. The Queen of England must influence her husband. It would not be good policy of course to let her know how, in inducing England to make war, she was serving Spain rather than England; but she must be made to use all her power to persuade the King. It was clear that certain of the King's ministers were restraining him. Those ministers should be promised bribes . . . anything they wished for . . . if they would cease to dissuade the King of England from war. But the most important influence at the Court of England was the Queen; and if Caroz could not persuade her to do what her father wished, he should consult her confessor and let the priest make Katharine see where her duty lay.

Ferdinand sealed the despatches, called for his messengers and, when they had gone, sat impatiently tapping his foot. He felt exhausted, and this irked him for it was yet another indication that he was growing old. He thought with regret of those days of glowing health and vitality; he was a man of action and he dreaded the thought of encroaching old age.

If he could not be a soldier leading men into battle, a statesman artfully seeking to get the better of his opponents, a lusty lover of women, a begetter of children, what was left to him? He was not one who could enjoy the quiet pleasures of old age. He had always been a man of action, first and foremost.

And now there was grey in his beard, pouches beneath his eyes and a stiffness in his limbs. He had a young and beautiful wife, yet his pleasure in her was spoilt by the contrast in their ages; he could not forget his age when he was with her, but rather was more conscious of the years.

He longed for sons, because he was feeling a growing animosity towards his young grandson Charles, a boy who was being brought up in Flanders and who could inherit not only the dominions of his grandfather, the Emperor Maximilian, but those of Isabella and Ferdinand and all the Spanish dependencies . . . unless Ferdinand's wife Germaine gave him a son to whom he could leave Aragon.

So much! thought Ferdinand. For one young boy who has done nothing to win it for himself!

He thought of the early struggles he and Isabella had endured in order to win Castile, and he longed afresh for his youth. With mingled feelings he remembered Isabella—a great Queen but at times an uncomfortable wife. His Germaine was more pliable; there was no question of her attempting to use her authority in defiance of his—she had none in any case. And yet . . . those days of struggle and triumph with Isabella had been great days.

But she was gone these many years, and her daughter Juana, Queen of Spain in name only, passed her tragic days in seclusion at the Castle of Tordesillas, roaming from room to room, her mentality so clouded that she talked to those who had died years before, or fell into silences which lasted for weeks; ate her meals from the floor like an animal, never cleaned herself, and constantly mourned the dead husband who had been noted for his infidelity and his beauty.

Tragic for her of course, but not so for Ferdinand, since it was due to Juana's insanity that he ruled Castile. But for that he would be merely a petty ruler of Aragon realizing how much he owed to his marriage with Isabella.

But the past was done with, and the once active, lusty man was feeling his age.

Unless he got Germaine with child, young Charles could inherit everything his maternal and paternal grandparents had to leave. But his younger brother, Ferdinand, should not be forgotten. His grandfather and namesake would see to that. All the same he longed for a son of his own.

He had thought at one time that his wish was to be fulfilled. Germaine had two or three years before given birth to a son; but the little boy had died only a few hours after birth.

Ferdinand sat musing on the past and the future, and after a while he rose and went through the main apartments to a small chamber in which he kept certain important documents.

He opened a cabinet in this room and took out a small bottle which contained certain pills, which he slipped into his pocket.

Unobtrusively he would take one half an hour before retiring. He had proved the efficacy of these pills and would reward his physician if the desired result were achieved.

Germaine would be surprised at his powers.

He smiled; yet at the same time he felt a little sad that a man who had once been noted for his virility should be forced to resort to aphrodisiacs.

Don Luis Caroz, waiting in an ante-chamber of the Queen's apartments at Westminster, chafed against this mission which he felt to be an indignity to a man of his position. Don Luis flicked at the elaborate sleeve of his doublet; it was an unnecessary gesture; there was no dust on his sleeve; but it conveyed his fastidiousness and his contempt for the streets through which he had passed.

His garments were more magnificent than those of most ambassadors at the King's Court; indeed he vied with the King and he assured himself that it was merely because Henry favoured the brightest colours that he appeared to be more dazzling. It was a matter of English vulgarity against Spanish good taste. Don Luis had a very high opinion of himself; it seemed to him that his diplomacy succeeded brilliantly; he lost sight of the fact—if it ever had occurred to him—that it was the Queen who made it easy for him, not only to gain an audience with the King whenever he wished to do so, but, receiving hints of her father's desires, by preparing the King's mind favourably towards them before Caroz appeared.

Vain, immensely rich—which was the reason why Ferdinand had chosen him to be his ambassador in England since he could pay his own expenses and thus save Ferdinand's doing so—Don Luis was determined that his suite should be more grand than that of any other ambassador, and that the Court should not forget that his position was a specially favourable one on account of the Queen's being the daughter of his master.

It was therefore galling for such a grand gentleman to be

kept waiting—and by a humble priest at that. At least he should have been humble; but Caroz had reason to know that there was nothing humble about Fray Diego Fernandez.

Katharine, who was almost as pious as her mother had been, naturally placed great confidence in her confessor, and the friar who held such a position was certain to wield an influence over her.

Don Luis paced up and down the ante-room. How dare the priest keep the ambassador waiting! The vulgar fellow. It was the ambassador's belief that the little priest was itching to get a finger into the political pie. Let him keep to his post and the ambassador would keep to his.

But Fray Diego's task was to be the Queen's confessor— and a woman such as Katharine would consider her actions always a matter of conscience.

Don Luis made a gesture of impatience. "The saints preserve us from saintly women," he murmured.

At length the priest appeared. Don Luis looked at him— uncouth, he thought, in his priestly robes, a smug satisfaction on his young but clever face.

"Your Excellency wished to see me?"

"I have been waiting this last half hour to do so."

"I trust you have not found the waiting tedious."

"I always find waiting tedious."

"It is because you are a man of such affairs. I pray you therefore let me know your business."

Don Luis went swiftly to the door; he opened it, looked out, then shut it and stood leaning against it. "What I have to say is for you alone . . . for Spanish ears, you understand me?"

The priest bowed his head in assent.

"Our master is eager that the King of England should declare war on France without delay."

The priest lifted his hands. "Wars, Excellency, are beyond my sphere."

"Nothing is beyond the sphere of a good servant of Spain. That is what our master thinks. And he has work for you."

"I pray you proceed."

"King Ferdinand believes that the Queen could help us. She

has much influence with King Henry. Indeed her influence must surely be of greater account than that of his ministers."

"I doubt that, Excellency."

"Then it must become so. If it is not, mayhap it is because the Queen has not worked hard enough to obey her father's wishes."

"Her Grace wishes to please her father and her husband. Her father is far away and did little to succour her when she needed his help. Her husband is here at hand; and I doubt he could be led too far from his own desires."

"What do you know of these matters? He is young and ardent. If the Queen used skill, the utmost tact . . . she could win his promise immediately."

"It is my opinion that this would not be so."

"Your opinion was not asked. And how can you, a celibate, understand that intimacy which exists between a man and woman in the privacy of the bedchamber? My dear Fray Diego, there are moments, I assure you, which if chosen with skill can be used to great advantage. But you do not know of these matters—or do you?"

There was a sneer behind the words, a suggestion that the rumours of a secret life, attributed to Fray Diego, might be true. If such rumours were proved to be true they could cost him his position, Fray Diego knew; for Katharine herself would be so shocked that, much as she relied on him, she would let him go if she discovered his secret.

The priest knew that the ambassador was not his friend; but he had triumphed over enemies before. He remembered with relish his battle with Francesca de Carceres; she had hated him and had schemed for his recall to Spain. But look what had happened to her! Now married to the banker Grimaldi she was desperately trying to regain her position at Court, whereas he was higher in the Queen's favour than he had ever been, and so important that the ambassador was forced, though much against his will, to seek an interview with him.

Fray Diego was young; he was somewhat arrogant. He really did not see why he should take orders from Caroz. It was Ferdinand's wish that he should do so, but he no longer regarded Ferdinand as his master. His influence seemed slight from such a great distance. Ferdinand had neglected his daughter during the years of her widowhood; it was only now that he wrote to her so frequently and so affectionately. Katharine remembered this; and in Fray Diego's opinion she was more Queen of England than Infanta of Spain.

He was determined therefore that he was not going to allow his fear of Ferdinand to rob him of the ascendancy he felt he possessed over Ferdinand's ambassador, towards whom the Queen did not feel as affectionate as she did towards her friend and confessor.

"It is true," he said, "that I have not your experience, Don Luis, of these matters. But what you ask is for the Queen's conscience, and for Her Grace to decide."

"Nonsense!" retorted Caroz. "It is a confessor's duty to guide those who are in his spiritual care. A few careful words, spoken at the appropriate moment, and the Queen will realize her duty."

"You mean her duty to her father, I am sure. But there is the possibility that Her Grace might also realize the duty to her husband."

"Do you mean that you refuse to obey our master's commands?"

"I mean," said Fray Diego with dignity, "that I will give the matter my consideration and if, after meditation and prayer, I can convince myself that what you ask is good for the soul of Her Grace, I shall do as you say."

"And if not . . . ?" burst out Caroz, fuming with indignation.

"This is a matter for my conscience as well as the Queen's. That is all I can say."

Caroz curtly took his leave and went away fuming. The arrogance of that upstart! he was thinking. A vulgar fellow. It was a great mistake that any but the highest nobility should be entrusted with state matters—and the Queen's confessor should have been a man of highest integrity and that noble birth which would have kept him loyal to his own kind.

Caroz soothed his anger by thinking of the account he would send to Ferdinand of this interview.

You will not long remain in England, my little priest, he prophesied.

His next call was on Richard Fox, Bishop of Winchester—a man who, he knew, had great influence among the King's ministers.

Promise them anything, Ferdinand had said, but get in exchange for your promise theirs to work for the English invasion of France.

Here was a man, thought Luis, who could surely be bribed because as an ambitious man he must be eager for the prizes of power and fame.

Caroz was proud of his ingenuity, for he had made up his mind what he was going to promise Richard Fox.

Fox received him with seeming pleasure, but beneath that calm expression of hospitality there was an alertness.

"I pray you be seated," said Fox. "This is indeed both an honour and a pleasure."

"You are kind, my lord Bishop, and I thank you. I have come here today because I believe it is in my power to do you some service."

The Bishop smiled rather ambiguously. He knew that it was a bargain the ambassador would offer rather than a gift.

"Your kindness warms my heart, Excellency," he said.

"It would not be an easy matter to achieve," admitted Caroz, "but I would ask my master to work for this with all his considerable power—and he has great power."

The Bishop was waiting, now almost unable to curb his eagerness.

"His Holiness plans to create more Cardinals. There are two French Cardinals and it has been suggested that he will present the hat to more Italians and Spaniards. My master is of the opinion that there should be some English holders of the office. I think he would be prepared to consider those for whom he felt some . . . gratitude."

The Bishop, who had been sceptical until this moment, could scarcely hide the great excitement which possessed him. The Cardinal's hat! The major step towards the highest goal of all churchmen—the Papal Crown.

Fox had assured himself that he was a man of integrity; he would work for the good of England—but what an honour for England if one of her bishops became a Cardinal; what great glory if one day there should be an English Pope!

Caroz, exulting inwardly, knew of the conflict which was going on behind the immobile features of the Bishop. What a stroke of genius on his part to think of hinting at a Cardinal's hat! It was the irresistible bribe. No matter if there was no possibility of the offer's ever being made; promises such as this were all part of statecraft. How delighted Ferdinand would be with his ambassador when he heard of his ingenuity. It was worthy of Ferdinand himself.

"I agree with His Highness, King Ferdinand, that there should be a few English Cardinals," said Fox. "It will be interesting to see if the Pope shares that opinion."

"There are few whom I would consider for the office," said Caroz. "But there are some . . . there is one. . . ."

The Bishop said fervently: "That man would never cease to be grateful to those who helped him to attain such office, I can assure you."

"I will pass on your words to my master. As you know, since the alliance of his daughter and the King he has had a great affection for your countrymen. It is something which he does not bear towards the French. Nothing would please him more than to see our two countries set out side by side to conquer our mutual enemy."

The Bishop was silent. The terms had been stated. Withdraw your opposition to the project of war, and Ferdinand will use all his considerable influence with the Pope to win you a Cardinal's hat.

Was it such a great price? Fox asked himself. Who could say? It might well be that those territories which had once been in English hands would be restored. Surely a matter for rejoicing. And his help might mean that an English Cardinal would be created, and English influence would be felt in Rome.

Caroz wanted to laugh aloud. It has succeeded, he thought.

And why not? What bishop could turn aside from the glory of receiving his Cardinal's hat?

He took his leave of the Bishop and went to his own apartments, there to write to his master.

He wrote that he believed he had found a means of breaking down the opposition to the beginning of military operations. He added a footnote: "It would seem to me that the Queen's confessor, Fray Diego Fernandez, works more for England than for Spain, and I would recommend his recall to Spain."

CHAPTER V

Murder in Pamplona

Jean d'Albret, that rich nobleman who owned much of the land in the neighbourhood of the Pyrenees, had become King of Navarre through his marriage to Catharine, the Queen of that state.

It was an ambitious marriage and one which had pleased him at the time he had made it, and still did in some respects. But to possess a crown through a wife was not the most happy way of doing so, and Jean d'Albret, a man who was more attracted by pleasure than ambition, by a love of literature than of conquest, was far from satisfied.

The times were dangerous and he saw himself caught between two great and militarily minded powers. His was a small state but it was in a strategic position and could be of importance to both France and Spain. Jean knew that Ferdinand had long cast acquisitive eyes on his and Catharine's crown; and that Louis was determined to keep Navarre as a vassal state.

It was tiresome. There were so very many interesting matters to occupy a man. War seemed to Jean senseless; and he knew that, if there should be war over Navarre, the Spanish and French sovereigns would see that it took place on Navarrese soil.

Jean began to think that had he made a less ambitious marriage, say with the daughter of a nobleman as rich as himself, their possessions could have been joined together and they would have remained happily French; and moreover lived the rest of their days in comfort without this perpetual fear of invasion of their territory.

His wife Catharine came to him, and he saw by the anxious expression on her face that she was even more worried than he was. She was pleased for once to find him alone; usually the fact that he preferred to live as an ordinary nobleman with as little royal style as possible, irritated her; but today she had something of importance to say to him.

"My agents have brought news of negotiations which are going on between Ferdinand and Henry of England. It is almost certain that the English will invade France."

Jean shrugged his shoulders. "Louis will laugh at their puny efforts."

"You have missed the point as usual," she told him tartly. "Ferdinand's plan is not to invade France but to take Navarre. As soon as the English engage the French he will march on us."

Jean was silent. He was watching the sun play on a fountain and thinking of a poem he had read a short while ago.

"You are not listening!" she accused. Her eyes flashed. "Oh, what a husband I have!"

"Catharine," said Jean gently, "there is nothing we can do. We live in this beautiful place . . . at least we live here for the time being. Let us enjoy it."

"To think that I could have married such a man! Does your kingdom, your family, your crown mean nothing to you?"

"The crown, as you have so often told me, was your wedding gift to me, my dear. It is not always comfortable to wear and if it were to be taken from me . . . well, then I should be plain d'Albret. It was the name I was born with."

Catharine narrowed her eyes. "Yes," she said, "you were Jean d'Albret from the time you were born, and it seems that so you may well die plain Jean d'Albret. Those who are not prepared to fight for their crowns would not arouse much sympathy if they lose them."

"But you, my dear, wish to fight for yours . . . fight an enemy ten times your size . . . fight to the death . . . and in death, my dear, of what use would the crown of Navarre be to you?"

Catharine turned from him in exasperation. Her grandmother Leonora, who had been Ferdinand's half-sister, had poisoned her own sister, Blanche, in order that she might take the crown of Navarre; Leonora had not lived long to enjoy that for which she had committed murder, and on her death her grandson, Catharine's brother, had become the King of Navarre.

Catharine now thought of her golden-haired brother Francis Phoebus, who had been so called on account of his wonderful golden hair and great beauty.

They had been a proud family, for Leonora's son, Gaston de Foix, had married Madeleine, the sister of Louis XI, and thus they were closely related to the royal house of France, and it was natural that they should look for protection to that monarch.

What an unlucky family we were! thought Catharine. My father, wounded by a lance in a tourney at Lisbon and dying long before his time. Francis Phoebus died only four years after he attained the crown, and so it had passed to Catharine, his only sister.

Ferdinand had desired a marriage between Catharine and his son Juan; that would have been one way—and by far the simplest—of bringing the Navarrese crown under Spanish influence, for then Ferdinand's grandchildren would have been the future kings and queens of Navarre; but Catharine's mother, the Princess of France, was determined that she would do nothing to aid the aggrandisement of Spain. So Juan had married Margaret of Austria and had died a few months after the marriage leaving Margaret pregnant with what had proved to be a stillborn child.

And Catharine had been married to Jean d'Albret—a match of her mother's making—because Jean was a Frenchman and the Princess Madeleine had been determined to keep Navarre a vassal state of France.

So this man is my husband! thought Catharine. And he does not care. All he wishes is that we should live in peace, that he may dance and make merry with those of the Court, ride through the country and speak with the humblest of his subjects, asking tenderly after the state of the vines, like the commoner he still is.

But the granddaughter of the murderess, Leonora, was not going to allow her crown to be taken from her if she could help it.

She cried out: "We must make the position known to the King of France. We must lose no time. Cannot you see how important that is, Jean, or are you still dreaming? Send for one of your secretaries and he shall prepare a letter for the King with all speed. Do you think Louis will allow Ferdinand of Aragon to walk into Navarre and take what is ours? He will see the folly of it. He will make a treaty with us which will let Ferdinand know that, if he should attempt to attack us, he will have to face the might of France as well as that of Navarre."

Jean rose and went to the door. Catharine watched him as he gave an order to one of the pages. His manner even towards the page lacked dignity. She felt exasperated beyond endurance because she was so afraid.

In a short time the secretary appeared.

He was a tall young man, with bold black eyes, a little over-dressed; Catharine guessed that he could on occasions be somewhat bombastic. He was a little subdued as he entered the apartment, she was pleased to notice, and that was due to the fact that the Queen was present.

Jean was very much mistaken in behaving in a free and easy manner with his subjects. It might make him popular, but it certainly did not make him respected.

"The King and I wish you to draft a letter to the King of France."

The Secretary bowed his head. It was as though he wished to hide his eyes, which were always lustful when he was in the presence of a woman; he could not help himself now, as a con-noisseur of the female body, studying the Queen and esti-mating the amount of pleasure the King derived from the relationship. He dared not allow the Queen to guess his thoughts, though it did occur to him that the King might. But the King would understand; he was easy-going and he would realize that a man of his secretary's virility could never keep the thought of sexual relationships out of his mind.

Jean was thinking exactly this. Poor young man, he

pondered, women plague him. If he were not perpetually concerned with plots and schemes to go to bed with this one and that, he would be a very good secretary.

The Queen was not thinking of the young man as a man; to her he was merely a scribe. He would draft the letter to the King of France and it should be sent off with all speed.

Navarre was in serious danger from Spain. Louis must come to their aid.

The Secretary, hurrying through the streets of the poorer quarter of Pamplona, slipped through an alley and, coming to a hovel there, stopped, looked over his shoulder and tried the door. It was open.

Before entering the house, he glanced once more over his shoulder to make sure that he was not being followed. It would never do for one of the King's confidential secretaries to be seen entering such a place.

Ah, thought the Secretary, who can say where love will strike?

He had a host of mistresses—some court ladies, some peasants. He was a man of wide experience and not one to go into the matter of birth and rank before embarking on a passionate love affair.

But this one . . . ah, this one . . . she was the best of them all.

He suspected her of being a gipsy. She had dark, bold eyes and thick crisply curling hair; she was wildly passionate and even he had felt a little overwhelmed and lacking in experience when they indulged in their love-making.

She would dance with her castanets, more Spanish than French; her skin was brown, her limbs firm and voluptuous; she was a cornucopia of pleasure. By a mere gesture she could rouse him to a frenzy of passion; a look, a slackening of the lips, were all that was necessary. She had said that he must come to this house, and he had come, although for anyone else he would have not done so. *He* would have decided the place of assignation.

He called her Gipsy. She called him Amigo. That was because he had accused her of being Spanish. A Spanish

Gipsy, he called her, and she had slapped his face for that. He smiled now to think how he had leaped on her then, how they had rolled on the ground together—with the inevitable conclusion.

He was pleased enough to be Amigo to her. A confidential secretary to the King of Navarre should not disclose his real name.

He called to her as he stood in the darkness of the house. "Gipsy. . . ."

There was a short silence and he was aware of the darkness. A feeling of foreboding came to him then. Had he been unwise to come? He was the King's secretary; he carried important documents in his pockets. What if he had been lured to this place to be robbed of those papers? What a fool he was to have brought them with him. He had not thought to clear his pockets. When he was on the trail of a woman he never thought of anything else but what he intended to do with that woman; and if that woman was one such as Gipsy, then the thoughts were all the more vivid, and completely all-absorbing, so that there was no room for caution or anything else.

Then as he hesitated he heard a voice say: "Amigo!" and his fears vanished.

"Where are you, Gipsy?"

"Here!" she was close beside him and he seized her hungrily.

"Wait, impatient one!" she commanded.

But there was to be no waiting. Here! Now! his desires demanded; and there and then it was, there in the darkness of this strange hovel, in one of the least salubrious byways of the town of Pamplona.

"There! Greedy one!" she cried pushing him away from her. "Could you not wait until I get a light?"

"I'll be ready again when you get the light, Gipsy."

"You . . ." she cried impatiently, "You want too much."

By the flickering light of a candle he saw the dark little room. So this was her home. He had seen her first near the castle, and he guessed that she came from the vineyards. There had been little time to discover much about each other, and all he knew was that she was a peasant girl who worked with the vines. All she knew was that he was employed at the Court. That made him rich in her eyes.

They had met many times in the vineyards at dusk; and even in daylight it had been easy enough to find a secluded spot. She knew that he carried papers in his pockets for they rustled when he threw off his doublet; he knew she carried a knife in the belt she wore about her waist.

"What is that for?" he had asked.

"For those who would force me against my will," she told him.

He had laughed triumphantly. She had never attempted to use the knife on *him*.

He was growing restive with passion again.

"Come up the stairs," she told him. "There we can lie in comfort."

"Come then," he said. "I pray you, lead the way."

She went before him carrying the candle. He caressed her bare thighs beneath her tattered skirt as they went.

She turned and spat at him: "Your hands stray too much."

"And how can I help that when I am near you?"

"And near others too!"

"What! You suspect me of infidelity to you?"

"I know," she answered. "There is one who works with me in the vineyards. She is small and fair and comes from the North."

He knew to whom she referred. The girl was a contrast to Gipsy; small, fair, almost reluctant, with a virginal air which was a perpetual challenge to him. It had challenged him only yesterday and he had succumbed.

"I knew her once," he said.

"You knew her yesterday," she told him.

So the girl had told! Foolish creature! Yet he was not displeased. He liked the women to boast of their connections with him.

Gipsy set down the candle. The room made him shudder. It was not what he was accustomed to. But there was always pleasure in novelty. And when Gipsy carefully unstrapped the belt containing the knife and laid it almost reverently on the floor and then began to take off all her clothes, he saw nothing but Gipsy.

"You also," she said.

He was more than willing to obey.

Naked she faced him, a magnificent Juno, her hands on her hips.

"So you deceive me with that one!" she spat out.

"It was nothing, Gipsy . . . over and done with . . . quickly forgotten."

"As with me?"

"You I will remember all my life. We shall never be parted now. How could any man be satisfied with another after Gipsy?"

"So you would marry me?"

He hesitated for half a second, and he could not help his mouth twitching slightly at the incongruity of the suggestion. Imagine Gipsy at Court—perhaps being presented to King Jean and Queen Catharine!

"Certainly, I would marry you," he said glibly.

"I told you once that if you went with another woman I would make you sorry for it."

"Gipsy . . . you couldn't make me anything but happy. You're too perfect. . . ."

He seized her; she eluded him; but he laughed exultantly; this was merely lover's play. He sensed her lassitude even as she struck out at him; in a matter of moments he forced her onto the straw.

Afterwards she lay supine beside him. He felt relaxed, the conqueror. She could not resist him, even though she was so frenziedly jealous.

He need not even bother to cover up his peccadilloes. He had been wrong to imagine that he would have to go carefully with Gipsy. Gipsy was like all the others—so filled with desire for a man of his unusual capabilities that she could not resist him.

She bent over him tenderly. "Sleep," she whispered. "Let us both sleep for ten minutes; then we will be wide awake again."

He laughed. "You're insatiable," he said . . . "even as I. Ah, they're a well matched pair, my Gipsy and her Amigo."

She bit his shoulder affectionately. And he closed his eyes.

Gipsy did not sleep, although she lay still beside him with her eyes closed. She was picturing him with that other one, and not only that one. There were many others. This faithful lover! she thought contemptuously.

She had told him that he would be sorry if he were not true to her. She had been true to him, yet he considered her so far beneath him that there was no need to keep his promises to her.

She was passionate; she had revelled in their intercourse; but he was only a man, and there were many like him in Pamplona who would be ready to come to Gipsy's bed when she beckoned.

She listened to his breathing. He was asleep. Perhaps he slept lightly. Perhaps he would wake if she stirred.

She moved quietly away from him. He groaned and vaguely put out a hand, which she avoided, carefully watching the flickering candlelight on his face as she did so.

His hand dropped; his eyes remained shut.

Gipsy stood for a second, watching him; then she picked up her belt. From it she took the knife.

"No man betrays me," she whispered. "Not even you, my fancy court gentleman. I warned you, did I not. I said you'd be sorry. But you'll not be sorry . . . because you'll not be anything after tonight."

Her eyes blazed as she lifted the knife.

He opened his eyes a second too late; he saw her bending over him; he saw her blazing eyes, but this time they shone with hate instead of love, with revenge, not with passion.

"Gipsy . . ." He tried to speak her name, but there was only a gurgle in his throat. He felt the hot blood on his chest . . . on his neck, before the darkness blocked out her face, the sordid room in candlelight, and wrapped itself about him, shutting out light, shutting out life.

* * *

Gipsy washed the blood from her naked body and put on her clothes. Then she blew out the candle and went down the stairs and out to the street.

She ran swiftly through the alley and through several narrow streets until she came to the house she wanted.

She knocked urgently on the door. There was no answer and again she knocked. At length she heard the sound of slow footsteps.

"Quickly, Father," she cried. "Quickly!"

The door was opened and a man stood peering at her; he was struggling into the robes of a priest.

She stepped inside and shut the door.

"What has happened, my child?" he asked.

"I need your help. I have killed a man."

He was silent in horror.

"You must help me. Tell me what to do."

"This is murder," said the priest.

"He deserved to die. He was a liar, a cheat and a fornicator."

"It is not for you to pass judgment, my child."

"You must help me, Father. It does not become any of us to prate of the sins of others."

The priest was silent. He had sinned with the woman, it was true. But what a provocation such a woman was, particularly to one who led the celibate's life on and off.

"Who is the man?" he asked.

"He is of the Court."

The priest drew a deep breath. "Fool! Fool! Do you imagine that murder of a noble gentleman can go unnoticed? If it had been one of your kind I might have helped. But a gentleman of the Court! There is nothing I can do, my child, but hear your confession."

"You will do more," she said. "Because you are wise, Father, and you have been my friend."

The priest fidgeted in his robes. He looked at her face in the candlelight. It was pale, and the eyes were enormous; there was no contrition there, only a contentment that vengeance had been wreaked on the faithless, only the determination that he

who had shared in her sin should now share in her crime. She
was a dangerous woman.

"It may well be that he was not in truth a gentleman of
the Court," said the priest. "It may be that that was a story he
told you."

"He was well dressed and he carried papers in his pockets."

"That's what he told you."

"I felt them . . . tonight. They were papers."

"Take me to where he lies."

They hurried back to the house wherein the murdered man
lay. The girl took the priest up to the room; it was not the muti-
lated body nor the blood-soaked straw which claimed the
priest's attention, but the papers which were in the pockets of
the man's garments.

"Hold the candle nearer," he commanded.

She did so and, as he read, the priest's hand shook with
excitement, for what he held in his hand was the draft of a
secret treaty between the Kingdoms of Navarre and France.

"Well?" said the girl.

"This could be worth a fortune," he said.

"You mean . . . papers? How so? But I shall sell his clothes.
They should fetch something."

"Yes, they should. But these papers are worth more than
clothes, I'll be ready to swear. I believe there are some who
would pay highly for them."

"Who would?"

"The Spaniards." The priest's mind became alert. Priests
were so poor in Pamplona—perhaps as they were all over
the world—and there were some who could not help being
attracted by riches even as they were by the voluptuous charms
of a woman.

The situation was full of danger. The man who lay on the
straw was one whose kind rarely came their way. His death
must not be traced to this house. The priest was now an accom-
plice of the woman and it was imperative to him to cover up
this murder.

"Listen carefully," he said. "I will leave at once on a
journey. I am going to Spain, and there I shall endeavour to see

the secretary of the King. He will, if I am not mistaken, be interested in this paper. But speed is essential. If what is written here comes to his knowledge before I reach him, then he will not be ready to pay me for what he already knows. But if he does not know . . . then he will be willing to pay me highly for what I can tell him."

"What is on the paper?" asked the girl.

"Matters of state. This man did not lie. He *was* one of the secretaries of the King. Now listen to me. There is one thing we must do before I leave. We must get him out of this house. And when he is gone you must clean away all signs of his having been here. Let us waste no time."

They worked feverishly. The priest had cast off his robes to prevent their being marked by blood, and worked in nothing but his drawers. The girl took off her clothes and put on only a light loose robe which could be washed immediately once she had rid herself of her victim.

They carried the body out of the house and through the alley. They then placed it against a wall and hurried back to the house, where the priest put on his robes and carefully secreted the papers about his person.

"I shall set out at once," he said, "for there is little time to lose. You must tell people that I have been called away to see my sick brother. As for you, wash the house so that there are no signs of blood, wash your clothes and do not try to sell his until at least three months have passed."

She caught his arm. "How do I know that when you have the money for the papers, you will come back?"

"I swear by my faith that I will."

She was satisfied. He was after all a priest.

"If you do not . . ." she said.

He shook his head and smiled at her. "Have no fear. I shall never forget you."

He would not. She knew too many of his secrets; and she was a woman who did not hesitate to plunge a knife into the body of a man who had deceived her.

And while the priest set out on his journey for Spain, the girl cleaned the house and her garments, so that when the sun rose there was no sign there that the King's secretary had ever been her guest.

Cardinal Ximenes arrived in Logroño on the banks of the river Ebro at the spot which marked the boundary between Castile and Navarre.

Ferdinand received him with such pleasure that the Cardinal guessed something unusual had happened to cause this. He dismissed all, so that they were alone together.

Ferdinand said: "Cardinal, you were opposed to my plans for attacking Navarre. The English are sending a force under the command of the Marquis of Dorset. It is my desire that they shall hold the French while I march on Navarre, which you have wished to leave untouched because you say it is a peaceful state."

The Cardinal nodded and then looked deep into Ferdinand's glowing eyes.

Smiling, Ferdinand reached for some papers which lay on the table at which he sat. He thrust them at Ximenes.

"Your Excellency should read this."

The Cardinal did so, and Ferdinand who was watching closely saw that almost imperceptible tightening of the thin lips.

"So you see," cried Ferdinand triumphantly, "while you were seeking to protect this *innocent* little state, its King and Queen were making a treaty with our enemy against us."

"So it would seem," replied Ximenes.

"Is it not clear? You see those papers."

"A rought draft of the treaty, yes. But how did they fall into your hands?"

"They were sold to me by a priest of Pamplona. I paid a high price for them—but not too high for their worth."

"A priest! Like as not this person was masquerading as such."

Ferdinand laughed slyly. "There are priests who do not regard their duty as highly as does your Eminence."

"I should distrust this person."

"So should I have done, but I am informed that one of the

King of Navarre's confidential secretaries was found stabbed
to death in a byway of Pamplona—stripped of all his clothes. It
is reasonable to suppose that he would carry such papers in his
pocket."

Ximenes nodded. He had no doubt of the authenticity of the
documents. And since the state of Navarre was making such a
treaty with France, there was only one course open to Spain:
attack.

Ferdinand leaned across the table. "Am I to understand that
Your Eminence now withdraws his opposition, and stands
firmly behind the attack on Navarre?"

"In view of these documents," answered Ximenes, who
never allowed personal pride to stand between him and his
duty, "I think we are justified in going forward against
Navarre."

CHAPTER VI

The French Disaster

At the headquarters of his army in San Sebastian Thomas Grey, second Marquis of Dorset, felt sick, dizzy and decidedly uneasy. He had long regretted the day when his King had put him in charge of ten thousand archers and sent him to Spain as the spearhead of an army which, when the country was ready would, with the King at its head, join Dorset.

From the first he had been bewildered. The help he had been led to expect from his Spanish allies did not come. Ferdinand's army had done little to help him. There had been scarcely any fighting except for a few clashes with isolated French troops; and his men roamed the countryside, drinking too much Spanish wine, eating too much garlic to which they were unaccustomed and which did not agree with them, catching diseases and vermin from the gipsy girls.

If, thought Dorset, I were not so ill myself that I fear I shall never leave this accursed country, I should feel alarmed, very alarmed.

Home seemed far away. The wrath of the King unimportant. The flies here were such a pest and the sight and smell of men, suffering from the continual dysentery, so repellent, that what was happening in England was of little importance.

He felt listless; that was due to the dysentery; he had ceased to long for home, only because he felt so tired. He believed that he had bungled his commission and that there would be trouble if he ever reached England; but he was too weary to care.

He had been chosen for this honour not because of his military skill but because the King had a fondness for him. Dorset excelled at the jousts and that was enough to make the King admire him. He had enough skill to come near to rivalling the King without quite matching him—a state which endeared Henry to a man and made him his friend.

"Why, Dorset," he had said, "I see no reason why you should not take the first contingent to Spain. These ministers of mine have now decided that they are in favour of war. Fox has given in at last—though the fellow was obstinate for so long. But you shall go, my friend, and show these Frenchmen the valour of our English archers."

The rosy cheeks had glowed and the eyes sparkled. "Would I were in your shoes, Dorset. Would I were going to lead an army into battle. But they tell me the time is not ripe for me to leave yet. In a year mayhap I'll be ready."

So it was Dorset who came to Spain, and Dorset who now lay sick of the maladies which sprang from a foreign land.

Life had not been easy for him; indeed he had lived in uneasy times. He was closely related to the royal family, and to the York branch, not that of Lancaster. His grandfather had been Sir John Grey, the son of Elizabeth Woodville (Queen of Edward IV) by her marriage with Lord Ferrers of Groby. Such a connection would be regarded somewhat cautiously by the Tudors; and although he had been received at Court he had quickly fallen under the suspicion of Henry VII and been confined to the Tower.

Dorset remembered now those days of imprisonment when he had lain in his cell and hourly expected the summons to the executioner's block. It would certainly have come had not Henry VII died; but, in those first months of power, his son had desired to show that he had escaped from the influence of his father. He had taken the heads of Dudley and Empson, his father's favourites, and given a pardon to Dorset.

The Marquis had done well in the service of the golden boy. Bluff, hearty, the young sportsman had given his father's prisoner the wardenship of Sawsey Forest; he made Dorset one of his companions, for such a figure was an ornament in the tilt-yard.

And after that, greater honours had been bestowed. How

happy Dorset would have been if he had been allowed to confine his battles to the tiltyard!

He was lying in his tent, turning from side to side, feeling too ill to care what happened to him, when one of his men entered to tell him that the English ambassador to Spain was without.

"Bring him in," said Dorset.

And the ambassador entered. Dorset made an attempt to rise but he was too weak to do so.

"Sir John Still," he said, "you find me indisposed."

"I am grieved that this should be so." The ambassador was frowning as though he too shared the uneasiness of all who were connected with this campaign. "I have come to see if there is anything you need beyond the two hundred mules and asses which I had sent to you."

Dorset smiled wryly: "What we need is a means of getting back to England," he said grimly.

Sir John Still looked startled, and Dorset went on: "The mules and asses which you sent were unable to work. They had been starved and many of them were dying when they arrived. Those which survived had never been exercised and were unable to work for us."

"But I paid the Spaniards a great price for those animals."

"Ah, another Spanish trick."

"A trick?"

"Sir John, surely you know why we are here. The Spaniards have no intention of being our allies and helping us to regain our territories in France. We are here that the French may be uncertain of our numbers and, expecting that we might be a great army, must needs protect their land. Thus they are kept occupied while the Duke of Alva, at Ferdinand's command, walks into Navarre."

"You mean . . . that we English have been tricked!"

"Do not look so surprised, ambassador. All are tricked when they attempt to deal with Ferdinand of Aragon."

"I bring you instructions from England," said the ambassador. "The army is to remain here throughout the winter. Next year the King will be ready to join you."

"Stay here during the winter!" cried Dorset. "It's impossible. Those men out there are half dead now with the sickness from which you see me suffering. They'll not endure it."

"These are the orders from England."

"They in England can have no notion of what is happening here. We are given garlic . . . garlic all the time. There is more garlic than real food. The men are unused to this; they suffer from it. The wines overheat their bodies. Eighteen hundred men have already died; if we stay here many more weeks there will not be a healthy man among us."

"You cannot return. To do so would mean you had failed. What have you achieved since you have been here?"

"Ferdinand has conquered Navarre. We have served the purpose for which we came."

"You speak like a traitor, my lord Dorset."

"I speak truth. These men will die if they stay here. If disease does not finish them, the French will. No good can come of their staying."

"Yet the King's order is that they should."

Dorset staggered to the door of the tent. "Come with me," he said. "I will tell these men of the King's command that they are to stay in Spain."

The fresh air seemed too much for Dorset. He swayed uncertainly like a man intoxicated, and the ambassador had to hold him to steady him. Bent double with the pain which distorted his yellow face, Dorset tried to shout, but his voice was feeble. "Men! News from home."

The word *home* acted on the camp like magic. Men crawled out of tents, dragging with them those who could not walk. There was a feverish joy in their faces. They believed that the horror was over, and their commander had summoned them to tell them to prepare to leave for home.

"The King's orders," said Dorset. "We are to stay here through the winter."

There was a growl of discontent.

"No!" cried a voice; and others took up the cry. "Home! We are going home!"

"The orders of our most Gracious Sovereign. . . ."

"To the devil with our most Gracious Sovereign. Let him fight his own wars. Home! England! We're going home to England."

Dorset looked at the ambassador.

"You see," he said; and he staggered wearily back into his tent.

Now he was afraid. He saw that he was caught between the desires of his King and those of his men. He was faced either with disobedience to the King or wholesale desertions.

"I must write to His Grace," he said. "I must make him aware of the true state of affairs."

The ambassador waited while he wrote; but meanwhile outside in the camp the cries of rebellion grew louder. Dorset knew, and the ambassador knew, that even the King's order to remain in Spain would carry no weight with those men out there.

The King was watching the return of his troops. He stood, legs apart, hands clenched at his side, his eyes so narrowed that they were almost lost in the flesh of his face.

Beside him stood the Queen, and she was ready to weep at the sorry plight of these men. They were in rags and many were still suffering from the fever; some had to be carried ashore. Yet as they came they were shouting with incoherent joy because the soil they trod was English, and the tears showed clearly on their poor sunken cheeks.

"What a sad sight," murmured the Queen.

"It sickens me!" the King growled.

But he did not see this return as Katharine did. He felt no pity. He had only room for anger. This was the army which he had sent to France and of which he had been so proud. "I have never seen a finer army!" he had written to John Still. And now . . . they looked like a party of vagabonds and beggars.

How dared they do this to him! He was the golden king, the darling of fortune. So far he had had everything he desired, except a son. He remembered this fleetingly and glared distastefully at his wife. There were tears in her eyes. She could weep for that band of scarecrows when she should be weeping because she had failed him and, although she could become pregnant, could not give birth to a healthy boy.

Katharine turned to him. "There is my lord Dorset, Henry. Oh, poor Dorset. How sick he is. See him. He cannot walk. They are carrying him on a litter."

The King followed her gaze and strode over to the litter on which lay the emaciated figure of the man who had once been a champion of the jousts. The sight of such sickness disgusted Henry.

"Dorset!" he cried. "What means this? I sent you out with an army and an order to fight for victory. You return with these . . . scarecrows . . . and dishonourable defeat."

Dorset tried to see who was towering over him, shouting at him.

He said: "Where am I? Is it night?"

"You are in the presence of your King," roared Henry.

"They'll mutiny," murmured Dorset. "They'll endure no more. Is it morning yet?"

"Take him away," cried the King. "I never want to see his treacherous face again."

The bearers picked up the litter and were passing on.

"He is sick, very sick," Katharine ventured to point out.

Henry looked at her, and she noticed that characteristic narrowing of the eyes.

"He will be far sicker when I have done with him!"

"You can't blame him for what has happened."

"Then whom else!" snarled Henry. He looked about him impatiently. "Put me up a gallows," he shouted. "Not one, but twenty . . . a hundred! By God and all his saints, I'll show these paltry cowards what I do to those who fail to carry out my orders."

His face was suffused with rage. The tyrant was bursting his bonds. The metamorphosis was taking place before the eyes of the Queen. The vain good-natured boy was showing signs of the brutal egocentric man.

Katharine, watching him, felt an apprehension which was not only for the men whom he had so carelessly condemned to death.

* * *

Katharine knelt before the King. The terrible rage which she had seen on his face had not altogether disappeared. There were signs of it in the over-flushed cheeks, the brilliant blue of the eyes.

He was watching her with interest, and she suddenly knew that she could change this tragedy into one of those situations which so delighted him in a masque.

"Henry," she cried, "I implore you to spare these men."

"What!" he growled. "When they have disgraced England! When our enemies are laughing at us!"

"The odds against them were too great. . . ."

It was a mistake. The faint geniality which she had perceived to be breaking through was lost, and the blue eyes were dangerous. "You would seek to enter our state counsels, Kate? You would tell us how to conduct our wars?"

"Nay, Henry. That is for you and your ministers. But the climate . . . and that disease which attacked them . . . how could you or your ministers know that such a catastrophe would befall them? That was ill luck."

"Ill luck," he agreed, somewhat mollified.

"Henry, I beg of you, show your clemency towards them. For this time forget the sneers of your enemies. Instead prepare to show them your true mettle. Let them know that England is to be feared."

"By God, yes!" cried the King. "They shall know this when I myself go to France."

"It will be so. Your Grace will go with an army, not as Dorset went, with only his archers. You will make great conquests . . . and so, in your clemency and your greatness, you can afford to laugh at your enemies and . . . spare these men."

"You have friends among them, Kate. Dorset is your friend."

"And a friend also to Your Grace."

He looked down at her head. Her hair fell about her shoulders—that beautiful hair; her eyes were lifted to his in supplication.

She was playing her part in the masque, but he did not know it; his masques were always real to him.

So he was pleased to see her thus, humble, begging favours. He was fond of her. She had failed so far but she was young yet. He would forgive her those miscarriages when she gave him a bonny son. In the meantime there was this game to be played.

"Kate," he said, his voice slurred with emotion, "I give you the lives of these men. Rise, my dear wife. They deserve to die for their treachery to me and to England, but you plead . . . and how could such as I deny a fair lady what she asked!"

She bowed her head, took his hand and kissed it. It was alarming when the masque had to be played out in stark realities.

CHAPTER VII

The Perfidy of Ferdinand

In his headquarters at Logroño, Ferdinand was in gleeful conference with Cardinal Ximenes. It appeared that the King had cast off his infirmities; he was as a young man again. Perhaps, thought the Cardinal, watching him, he congratulates himself that, although his body may be failing him, his mind is as shrewd and cunning as it ever was—and indeed, it may be more so, for his experience teaches him further methods of double-dealing, of plotting against his friends while he professes his regard for them.

Ximenes could have felt sorry for the young King of England if he had not been convinced that what had happened to him was due to his own folly. The King of England was clearly a braggart, seeking easy glory. He had certainly not found it in Spain; and one of the first lessons he would have to learn was that none but the foolish would enter into alliance with the most avaricious, double-dealing monarch in Europe—Ferdinand of Aragon.

Henry was as yet over-sentimental; he believed that because he was Ferdinand's son-in-law he would be treated with special consideration. As if Ferdinand had ever considered anything but his gold and his glory.

"So, Excellency, the campaign is over; it merely remains to consolidate our gains. Jean d'Albret and Catharine have fled to France. Let them remain there. As for me . . . I have no further wish for conflict, and I do not see why, if Louis is agreeable, I should not make a truce with him."

"And your son-in-law?"

"The young coxcomb must fight his own battles . . . if he can, Excellency. If he can!"

"He received little help from his allies, Highness."

Ferdinand snapped his fingers. "My son-in-law will have to learn that if he hopes to win battles he should not send an army into a foreign land without the means to maintain it."

"He relied too strongly on the promised help of his ally."

"It was not promised, I do assure you. But we waste our time. I hear he tried his gallant officers and that they were forced to give evidence on their knees! That must have been a sight, eh! He was trying them for the incompetence and lack of foresight of himself and his ministers. And it was my daughter who saved them from the gallows."

"It would seem that the Queen of England has not forgotten the teachings of her mother."

Ferdinand was sobered by the mention of Isabella; then he shrugged off the memory with the reminder that Isabella had worked unsparingly for Spain. She would surely have realized the importance of Navarre and have understood that the means of acquiring it were not so important as long as the deed was accomplished with the minimum of bloodshed and expense to Spain.

"I am sending despatches to my son-in-law, Excellency. Here they are. Glance through them and give them your approval!"

Ximenes took the proffered documents.

In these Ferdinand explained to Henry that the incompetence of Dorset's army had made conquest of Guienne impossible. He was not suggesting that Dorset was a true example of an Englishman; and it was his belief that English soldiers, if properly trained and armed, would make fair enough soldiers; perhaps then they would not show up so badly against those of Europe. At this time he could not ask Henry to send more men into Spain, even though he himself should lead them. He had been forced to conclude a six months' truce with Louis, as he feared that, if he had not, the French might feel—in view of the sad spectacle they had recently witnessed of English troops in action—that it would be an act of folly not to invade England, where they might—as they had seen a sample of English valour and fighting prowess—expect an easy victory. It was a great regret to Ferdinand that the English had failed to achieve their object—the conquest of Guienne—and if it was still the desire of his dear son-in-law that the province should be won for England, he, Ferdinand would, at the conclusion of the six months' truce, win it for England. He would need ten thousand German mercenaries to help him, for his dear son-in-law would readily understand that, in view of their recent capers, he could not ask for Englishmen. The cost of the mercenaries would be great, but it was not *money* his son-in-law lacked but men of valour and fighting spirit. Ferdinand would be hearing more of this through his ambassador, Don Luis Caroz, and more importantly and more intimately from his dearly beloved daughter who was also the wife of that dear and honoured son, the King of England.

Ximenes glanced up after reading the document.

"This will act as an irritant rather than balm to your dear son-in-law for whom you have such an affection," he said.

"It is what I intend," answered Ferdinand. "Do you not see, the young coxcomb will be so incensed that he will immediately plan to make war on Louis. It is exactly what we need to keep Louis engaged while we rest from battle and enjoy the spoils of victory."

Ximenes thought of Ferdinand's daughter. He could scarcely remember what she looked like as it was many years since he had seen her. Her mother had felt tenderly towards her, too tenderly, he had often said; for her devotion to her family had often come between herself and her duty to God.

Yet he was sorry for Isabella's daughter. He saw her as a helpless barrier between the youthful follies of her husband and the cruel ambition of her father.

How could he complain when Ferdinand was working for the glory of Spain? There could be no doubt that the recent conquest had brought glory to the country.

Ximenes handed the papers back to Ferdinand. He must approve; but how he longed for the peace of Alcalá, for that room in which the scholars sat with him working on the polyglot bible.

Ximenes believed then that he would have been a happier man if he had lived his hermit's life, free from power and ambition.

Happy! he reproved himself. We are not put on this Earth to be happy!

Smiling complacently, Ferdinand sealed his documents, forgetting as he did so encroaching old age, the pains which beset his body, the constant needs of ointments and aphrodisiac potions that he might in some measure wear the semblance of youth.

He could win battles; he could outwit his enemies, with even more cunning than he had shown in the days of his youth. Experience was dearly bought; but there were moments such as this one when he valued it highly and would not have exchanged it for the virility of his young son-in-law of England.

Katharine was seated before her mirror and her women were dressing her hair. Her reflection looked back at her and she was not displeased with it. Henry admired her hair so much; he liked her to wear it loose by night—which tangled it; but often she compromised by having it plaited into two heavy ropes.

Henry was ardent again. They were full of hope, he and she; the next time there was the sign of a child she was to take especial care, he had commanded. It was clear to him that he was dogged by ill luck. Witness the campaign in Spain for instance. Their inability to produce a child who could live was merely another example of their bad luck.

She smiled. If only I had a child, a son, she thought, I could be completely happy.

"Maria," she said to her maid of honour, Maria de Salinas, "you have a happy look today. Why is that?"

Maria was confused. "I, Your Grace? But I did not know. . . ."

"It is a look of contentment, as though something for which

you longed has come to pass. Does it concern my Lord Willoughby?"

"He intends to speak for me, Your Grace."

"Ah Maria, and since this has brought that look of happiness to your eyes, what can my answer be but yes?"

Maria fell to her knees and kissed Katharine's hand. When she lifted her face to the Queen's there were tears in her eyes.

"But you weep," said Katharine, "and I thought you were happy."

"It will mean that I can no longer remain in the service of Your Grace."

"He will wish to leave Court and take you away to the country then?"

"It is so, Your Grace."

"Well, Maria, we must accept that." And she thought: How I shall miss her! Of all the girls who came with me from Spain, Maria was the best, the most faithful. It was Maria whom I could trust as I could trust no other. Now she will be gone.

"I myself feel like shedding tears. Yet this must be a happy occasion, for you love this man, Maria?"

Maria nodded.

"And it is a good match. I know the King will willingly give his consent with mine, so there is naught to make us sad, Maria. Why, Lord Willoughby will not carry you off to a strange country. There will be times when you will come to Court, and then we shall be together."

Maria dried her eyes with her kerchief and Katharine, looking into the mirror, did not see her own reflection, but herself arriving in England, after saying an infinitely sorrowful farewell to her mother, with her the duenna Doña Elvira Manuel, who had proved treacherous, and her maids of honour who had all been chosen for their beauty. Maria had been one of the loveliest even of that lovely band. They were scattered now, most of them married. . . . Inez de Veñegas to Lord Mountjoy, and Francesca de Carceres, most unsuitably, to the banker Grimaldi.

"Maria, tell me, have you seen Francesca recently?"

"She still waits for an audience. Does Your Grace wish to see her? Perhaps, now that I am going. . . ."

Katharine's face hardened. "She left me once, because she felt it was to her advantage to do so. I would never take back one who has proved her disloyalty to me and to her family."

"I have heard, Your Grace, that the banker loves her truly."

"Then if she is so loved she should be content with that state of life which she deliberately chose. There will never be a place for her in my household."

When Katharine spoke as firmly as that Maria knew that her mind was made up.

Katharine changed the subject. "I hope that you do not intend to leave me at once, Maria."

Maria knelt once more at the Queen's feet and buried her face against Katharine's skirts.

"It is my only regret that I cannot be in constant attendance on Your Grace."

There was sudden commotion outside the apartment. The door was flung open and the King stalked in. His face was a deeper red than usual and his anger was apparent from the manner in which he strutted. In his hand he carried papers, and a quick glance at those papers, as she swung round from the mirror, told Katharine that it was news from Spain which had angered her husband.

Maria rose to her feet and dropped a curtsey with the other women in the apartment. The King did not bestow his usual smile of appreciation on some particular beauty who caught his eye. Henry was always single-minded and now his thoughts were on the papers he carried.

He waved his hand in an imperious gesture. It was eloquent. It meant: "Leave us." The women hastened to obey, and Maria's heart sank seeing those signs of anger in the King's face, because she, who was closer to Katharine than any of her companions, knew that the Queen was beginning to fear the King.

When they were alone Henry stood glaring at his wife, for the first few seconds too angry to speak. She waited, having learned from experience that when the King was in such a mood a carelessly spoken word could fan the flame of anger.

Henry waved the papers as though they were banners and he were advancing on an enemy.

"News from your father!" he spat out. "He seems determined to insult me."

"But Henry, I am sure this cannot be so. He has the utmost regard for you."

"So it would seem. He tells me here that my armies are useless. He is offering to fight my battles for me if I will pay him to provide mercenaries!"

"This cannot be so."

"You have eyes. Read this," he roared.

She took the papers and glanced at them. She could only see her father as her mother had taught her to look at him. Isabella had never complained to their children of Ferdinand's conduct; she had always represented him as the perfect King and father. Katharine had only heard by chance that her father had on many occasions been unfaithful to Isabella and that there were children to prove it. And even though she must accept him as an unfaithful husband—in her opinion to the greatest and most saintly woman who had ever lived—still she could not believe that he was anything but honourable; and she accepted in good faith what he had written.

"Well?" demanded Henry harshly.

"My father considered what happened to our men in Spain. He wishes to help you."

"So he casts a sneer at me and my armies."

"You read into this what is not intended, Henry."

"I . . . I? I am a fool, I suppose, Madam. I lack your perception. There is something you and your father forget." He came close to her, his eyes narrowed, and she shrank from the malice she saw in his face. "But for me, what would have happened to you? I brought you up to your present position. It would be wise not to forget that. There were many who were against our marriage. What were you then? A miserable outcast. Your father would not support you . . . you were living in poverty." Henry folded his arms behind his back and scowled at her. "I was told that a monarch such as I might choose my wife from all the greatest heiresses in the world. And what did I do? I chose you. You, Madam, who had been the wife of my brother, who were neglected by your father, who was living in miserable poverty in Durham House. I raised you up. I set you on the throne. And this is my reward. . . ."

She tried to fight the terror which such words inspired. She had grown pale and her twitching fingers caught at the cloth of her gown.

"Henry," she said, "this I know well. Even if I did not love you for your many qualities . . . I would be grateful and wish to serve you until the end of my life."

He was slightly mollified. She thought: Oh God, how easy it is to placate him, how easy to anger him.

" 'Tis as well you are aware of your debts," he growled. "And your father! What have you to say for him? He too should be grateful for what I did for you. This is an example of his gratitude!"

"Henry, he is offering to help you. . . ."

"With German mercenaries! Because we English are unable to fight our own battles!"

"He does not mean that, Henry. I am sure of this."

"Not mean it! Then why does he say it?"

"Because he believes you to be suffering a keen disappointment, because he is sorry our army did not achieve its end."

"He does not want English troops on Spanish soil! By God, would I had hanged the traitor Dorset. Would I had not listened to your woman's pleading for a worthless life."

"Nay, Henry, you must not blame Dorset." She was suddenly overwhelmed by her tenderness for this big man who, it seemed to her, at times had the heart and mind of a child. "Let us face the truth. We failed. We failed because we had not enough food for our men, and we sent them out ill-equipped. Certainly you cannot accept my father's offer—though he makes it in friendship; I do assure you of that. But there is an answer to those who have jeered at our failure. There is an answer to my father."

"What is this answer?"

"That you should prepare an army that will be invincible, that you should place yourself at the head of it and attack the French, not from the South but from the North. There you would find a climate not unlike our own; there would not be the same difficulties in feeding an army that was separated from England only by twenty-one miles of sea. And with you at the head of it. . ."

A slow smile was spreading across the King's face. He did not speak for a few seconds; then he burst out: "By God, Kate, we have the answer there. That is it. We shall start from Calais . . . and go on from there. And this time it will not be a Marquis who commands, but a King."

All ill humor had disappeared. He seized her in his arms and hugged her, but already his thoughts were far away from her; he was leading his men into triumphant battle. This would be a masque to outdo those merry exercises that had charmed the courtiers and the people at Windsor, Richmond and Westminister.

He was content—content with life, content with Kate.

He danced round the apartment with her, lifting her in his arms, pausing so that she should marvel at his strength, which she did—running his fingers through her hair and over her body.

"There's one thing that will not please me. I shall be separated from my Kate. And what will she be doing while she awaits the return of the conqueror, eh?" The little eyes were alight with laughter and confidence. "Mayhap she will be nursing the heir of England . . . the heir to all those lands which I shall bring back to the English crown!"

Katharine was laughing in his arms. The danger was over for a while; the King was happy again.

So it was to be war. Katharine was eager to show Henry how she could work for him and that he could rely on his Queen's being always at his side.

Henry was in high spirits. He was certain that he was going to win fresh honors and was already regarding the coming war as a glorified masque. It was a comfort to know that he could safely leave those matters of minor importance to Katharine, and he was pleased with her because she was so eager to be made use of.

He spent all his nights with her.

"There is one thing only I long for, Kate, and that is to leave you pregnant on my departure. What joy for me! I go forth to win honour for England, knowing you are at home nursing my seed within this comely belly of yours. I'll give England new dominions, Kate, and together we'll give her heirs. How's that?"

"Henry, if only it could be so I'd be the happiest woman on Earth."

"Of course it shall be so." He had no doubt.

Katharine summoned Thomas Wolsey to her presence; she was impressed by his efficient handling of his duties which now included the assembling of the materials to be used in the war.

She was glad one day when in conference with the almoner that the King joined them.

Henry's face glowed with bluff good humor.

"Ha, Master Wolsey," he cried. "Her Grace tells me that you are of great use to us."

"I do my humble best, Sire," answered Wolsey. "My regret is that I have not four pairs of hands and four heads with which to serve Your Grace the better."

Henry laughed and laid a great hand on Wolsey's shoulder. "We are well pleased with those two hands and that head, my friend. The Queen has shown me the value of your work. She regards you highly, and the Queen and I are of one mind on all matters."

"There is great joy in serving such a master . . . and such a mistress."

"And we are fortunate in our servant. Show me the list of supplies you have prepared."

"They are here, Your Grace."

"Fox tells me that you work with the vigor of two men. He too has a high opinion of you."

"The Bishop has always been a good friend to me."

"It pleases us. We like our ministers to work well together. Too often we hear of discord, so that it is pleasant to hear of harmony. Now, let me see. So many victuals, eh? So much conduct money. And you can raise it, Master Wolsey?"

"I have no doubt of it, Sire. I can explain in detail how I propose to make these arrangements."

"Enough, enough. We trust you. Bother us not with the how and the why and the where. Let us find that we have what we need. That is all we ask of you."

"It shall be so, Sire."

Henry once more patted Wolsey's shoulder and the almoner, who had always been a man to seize his opportunities, said with an air of impulsiveness which concealed a perfected rehearsal: "Your Graces, have I your permission to speak to you on a . . . somewhat delicate matter?"

Henry tried to look shrewd; Katharine was faintly alarmed. She was always afraid that someone whom she regarded highly would, by a carelessly spoken word, anger the King and so ruin a promising career.

"Speak," said Henry.

Wolsey lowered his eyes. "This is bold of me, Your Grace, but I was bold in the service of your most noble and honoured father, and thus found favour with him. I would serve Your Grace with all the zeal I gave to your father's cause."

"Yes, yes," said Henry impatiently.

"It concerns my lord of Surrey."

"What of my lord of Surrey?"

"I have noticed of late that he is failing. He plans to go to France with Your Grace. This is rash of me . . . but I shall not think of my own recklessness in speaking my mind—only of the service I could do Your Grace. Sire, the Earl of Surrey is too old to accompany Your Grace to France, and such men can do much to impede an expedition. If it is Your Grace's wish that the Earl of Surrey should accompany you to France, then it is my wish also, but . . ."

Henry nodded. "He speaks truth," he said. "Surrey is an old man. Do I want greybeards to march with me!"

The thought occurred to Katharine that the only reason he

could want them would be to call attention to his own radiant youth.

But they were going into battle. Henry wanted young men beside him. He also wished to show this man that he appreciated what he had done. Bishop Fox, who looked upon Wolsey as his protégé, had informed the King that the energy of Wolsey astonished even him. He had taken control of tanneries and smithies, of bakeries and breweries; so that they were all working for the state to enable Master Wolsey to provide everything that was needed for the expedition. He worked all hours of the day and far into the night; he scarcely stopped to eat; he was determined to please the King by his diligence, determined that this time the war should not fail through lack of equipment.

I like this Thomas Wolsey, the King told himself.

To throw Surrey to him in exchange for all his labours was a small thing. Surrey was old and arrogant and had passed from the King's favour. And Wolsey asked it, Henry believed, not out of enmity towards the old man, but in his zeal for the success of the cause.

"When we leave for France," said Henry, "Surrey shall stay behind."

Wolsey bowed his head in such humble gratitude that he might have been receiving a great honour for himself.

"I am greatly relieved, Your Grace; I feared my importuning . . ."

Henry slapped the almoner's back with a blow which made him stagger a little.

"Have no fear, Master Wolsey. Serve us well and you will find us a good master."

Wolsey took the King's hand and kissed it; there were tears in the eyes which he raised to Henry's face. "And the greatest, Sire," he murmured. "A master whom all men must delight to serve."

Henry's pleasure was apparent. He was thinking: When this war is won, I'll not forget Master Wolsey. Mayhap I'll keep him near me. He's a useful man, and a wise one.

* * *

Wolsey, coming from the royal apartment was smiling to himself.

This war was serving him well, for it had brought him closer to the King's notice. He was going to impress the young monarch with his worth, as he had his father on that occasion when the old King had believed he had not begun a mission and had then found it completed with efficiency and success.

"The way is clear for me," he whispered to himself. "There is nothing to fear."

He felt faintly regretful that he could not share his triumphs with his family. He would have liked to see Mistress Wynter and the boy and girl at Court. He would have liked to put honours in their way. Of course he *would* do so. Both his children would be well looked after. Yet it saddened him that they must remain hidden.

He wondered what the King would say if he knew that Wolsey escaped from Court now and then to a woman who had borne him two children. He could guess. The little eyes would show a shocked expression; the royal mouth would be prim. Henry would expect celibacy in his priests; and he would be harder than less sensual men on those who were incontinent. *There* was a man, thought Wolsey, who lusted after the personable women whom he encountered. Yet he did not know it perhaps. He feigned to have a kingly interest in his subjects; but the interest was greater when the subject was a woman and a fair one.

No, the matter must be kept secret; his enemies must never discover the existence of Mistress Wynter. And he had enemies—many of them. They were an essential part of a man's life when that man had determined to rise from humble beginnings to greatness.

There was one of them approaching him at this moment.

The Earl of Surrey was pretending not to see him, but Wolsey decided that he should not pass.

"Good day, my lord."

Surrey gave him a haughty stare.

"You did not see me," went on Wolsey. "My lord, is your sight failing then?"

" 'Tis as good as it was the day I was twenty."

"A long, long time ago, my lord. You were deep in thought; mayhap that was why you did not see me. You were thinking of the campaign in France."

Surrey's curiosity overcame his contempt for one of such humble origin.

"You have been with the King?" he asked. "What news of our leaving? Are the stores ready yet?"

"They will be by the time the King is ready to leave. There will be work for us who go with him to France, and for those of you who stay behind."

"I am prepared to leave whenever His Grace gives the word," said Surrey.

"*You* are prepared to leave, my lord?"

"Indeed I am."

"You are certain then that you are to serve with the King in France?"

"Of a surety I am certain. Am I not the King's general?"

Wolsey smiled knowledgeably and in a manner which replaced Surrey's bombast with fear.

He could have struck the man, but he did not wish to soil his hands by touching a tradesman's son. Wolsey murmured: "A merry good day to you, my lord," and passed on.

Surrey stood for a few seconds looking after the almoner; then as his rising rage smothered his good sense, he hurried to the royal apartments.

"I wish to see the King at once," he demanded.

The guards looked astonished; but this was after all the great Earl of Surrey, and it might well be that he had news of importance to impart to the King.

He strode past them and threw open the door of the King's apartment. Henry was leaning against a table where Wolsey had recently left him; Katharine was seated, and the King was twirling a lock of her hair in his fingers.

"Sire, I must have immediate speech with you!"

Henry looked up, rather peevishly. He did not expect people to burst in unannounced. Could it be that Surrey considered that he was of such nobility that he need not observe the laws of ordinary courtiers?

Henry let fall the lock of hair and fixed his gaze on Surrey. The Earl should have been warned by the glitter in the King's eye, but he was too alarmed to take notice of anything.

"Sire, I have just met that butcher's son, coming from your apartments. The insolence of the fellow is beyond endurance."

"If you speak of my good friend Wolsey," said Henry sharply, "I should warn you, my lord, to do so with more respect."

"Your Grace, the fellow hinted that I am too old to follow you in battle. The impertinent butcher's cur. . . ."

"Your face is an unhealthy purple, Surrey," said Henry, "and it would seem that you are forgetful of your manners." He turned to Katharine. "Could that be his age, do you think?"

Katharine said nothing. She dreaded such scenes. She wanted to warn Surrey, but there was no restraining the irate nobleman.

"The impudent jackanapes! I'd have his tongue cut out. I'd cut off both his ears. . . ."

"Which shows what a fool you are and how unfit for our counsels," retorted Henry. "You would rob us of the man who is doing more than any to make the expedition into France a success."

"He has bemused Your Grace with his sly ways."

There was nothing he could have said to rouse Henry's anger more certainly. To suggest that he, the astute and brilliant leader, was a dupe!

Oh Surrey, you *fool*! thought Katharine.

Henry stood up to his full height and his voice rumbled like thunder when he shouted: "Nay, my lord Earl, there is no room for you in my army. There is no room for you in my Court. You will leave it at once. Do not let me see you until I send for you."

"Your Grace. . . ."

"Are you so old then that you have lost your hearing!" roared Henry cruelly. "You heard me, sir. Go! At once. Leave the Court. You are banished from our sight. Will you go, or shall I have to call the guard?"

Surrey crumpled suddenly, so that he did indeed look like an old man.

He bowed stiffly and left the King's presence.

From a window of the Palace Wolsey watched the departure of Surrey. He wanted to laugh aloud in his triumph.

"Such disgrace shall befall all the enemies of Thomas Wolsey," he told himself. "No slight shall be forgotten."

He remembered then a certain gentleman of Limington in Somerset, a Sir Amias Paulet. In the days when Thomas had been rector of Limington he had not shown what Paulet considered adequate respect to this local bigwig; and Paulet had, on some flimsy pretext, caused Thomas Wolsey to be set in the stocks.

Even now Thomas could remember the indignity, and he told himself that when the time was ripe Paulet should deeply regret the day he had Thomas Wolsey set in the stocks.

An eye for an eye, a tooth for a tooth. Nay, thought Thomas, I am no ordinary man, and any who robs me of one tooth shall pay with two of his own.

So Surrey, who had called the King's almoner a butcher's cur, had lost his chance of following the King to France; he had also lost his place at Court.

That was meet and fitting, thought Thomas smiling. There would be many scores to settle on the way up, and they should be settled . . . settled in full.

It was some time since Ferdinand had felt so full of vigour. Hourly despatches were reaching him. He was playing the double game of politics which was so dear to his heart, and he never enjoyed it so much as when he was deluding those who thought themselves to be his allies, and coming to secret terms with those whom his allies thought to be a mutual enemy.

There was only one matter of moment to Ferdinand: the good of Spain. Spain's desire at this moment was for peace.

She had Navarre and, with the acquisition of that important little state, she was ready to consolidate her triumphs.

The English were clamouring for action. Katharine wrote naïvely from England. His dear innocent daughter, did she think that politics were arranged like rules in a convent? She was eager to please that handsome young husband of hers and her father at the same time.

She was invaluable.

Through her, it seemed, Ferdinand could set the young monarch dancing to his tune. He could let England work for Spain. What an excellent state of affairs it was when one had docile children to work for one.

He was a little sad, thinking of his lost youth and his inability to get Germaine with child. The times when he could go to bed with several women in one night were over. But he was still the sly fox of Europe.

He would forget the fear of impotence; forget the delights of love and think of wars instead.

He would allow Caroz to make a treaty for him in London with his son-in-law. He would give his promises . . . although he had no intention of keeping them. Promises were counters used in a game. If it was worthwhile redeeming them, you did so; if not, you forgot you had ever made them.

He sat down and wrote to Caroz. ". . . my armies to invade Guienne while the English are to attack from the North. I doubt not that the present Henry will be about to repeat the success of that other Henry in France, and we shall soon be hearing news of another battle of Agincourt. Let there be a treaty between our two countries, and assure my son-in-law that I am in this matter with him, heart and soul. . . ."

While he was writing a page entered to tell him that the friar for whom he had sent had arrived.

"Bring him to me," said Ferdinand.

And the man was brought.

Ferdinand was pleased with his appearance. He looked like a wandering friar; he could pass from Spain to the Court of France without attracting a great deal of notice.

"I have work for you," he said. "You are to leave immediately for France. Seek out King Louis and tell him from whom you come. Tell him that the English are preparing to make war on him and that I, through my daughter, have information of where they will attack and in what force they will come. Sound him well. Let him know that I am ready to make peace with him for a consideration . . . terms which we can later discuss if he is ready to consider this matter."

The friar listened eagerly to Ferdinand's instructions and, when he had left, Ferdinand returned to the letter which he was writing to Caroz.

"I would have my son-in-law know that France is the enemy of us both and that we must stand together to crush her. Let me know how far preparations have proceeded, and we will sign our treaty so that all the world shall know that we are of one family and together in this matter."

Ferdinand sealed his letters and sent for his messengers.

He stood at the window watching their departure, laughing inwardly.

I am no longer young, he chuckled, I cannot satisfy a wife, let alone a mistress. Yet I am still the slyest fox in Europe.

On a bright April day the King presided over the ceremony of signing the treaty with his father-in-law.

Luis Caroz, whose magnificence of person was only slightly less than that of the King, stood with Henry and Katharine; and a cheer went up from all those assembled, because they believed that with the help of Ferdinand they could not but be victorious against France.

The great days of conquest were about to begin. The triumphs of the warlike Henry V would be repeated. They looked at the glowing face of their twenty-two-year-old King and they told themselves that he would bring England to a new greatness.

Katharine felt content.

One of her dearest dreams was to make strong the friendship between her husband and father; that she believed she had achieved.

Surely that other—the bearing of a healthy son—must follow.

Katharine stared at the letters in consternation. This could not be true. Her father could not have made a truce with the King of France a few days before Caroz was signing one on behalf of his master with the King of England.

There had been some confusion, a mistake somewhere.

She sent at once for Caroz. The ambassador came to her in complete bewilderment. As he passed through to her apartments he met her confessor, Fray Diego Fernandez. Fray Diego greeted the ambassador without much respect, and Caroz was quick to notice the quirk of satisfaction about the priest's mouth.

Laugh, my little man, thought Caroz. Your days here are numbered. I am beginning to make Ferdinand understand that you work more for England than for Spain.

But Caroz had little time to spare for the impudent priest on this day, and hurried to the apartment where Katharine was eagerly waiting to receive him.

"You have heard this news?" she asked.

"Yes, Your Grace."

"There has been some mistake."

Caroz shook his head. He knew his master better than the Queen knew her father, and it seemed to him that such an act was characteristic of Ferdinand. What worried him was the action Ferdinand would take next, for Caroz guessed that he had already settled on a scapegoat, and that would very likely be his ambassador in England.

"It cannot be that my father was making an agreement with France while the treaty of alliance was being signed here in England!"

"It would seem so, Your Grace."

"How could such a terrible misunderstanding come about?"

"Doubtless your father will offer some explanation."

Henry strode into the apartment. He was in a violent rage.

"Ha!" he cried. "Don Luis Caroz! So you are here. What news is this I hear from Spain? Someone has lied to me. How could your master give his name to two such agreements at the same time!"

"Sire, I can no more understand than you can."

"Then it is time you did. I want an explanation of this conduct." Henry turned to Katharine. "It would seem, Madam, that your father has been mocking us."

Katharine shivered, for Henry looked as though he were ready to destroy all things Spanish, including Caroz and herself.

"It cannot be so," she answered as calmly as she could. "This news *must* be false."

"It's to be hoped so," growled Henry.

Caroz said: "Sire, have I Your Grace's permission to retire, that I may despatch a letter to my master with all speed?"

"Retire!" cried Henry. "It would be well for you to retire, Sir Ambassador. If you stay I may do to you what those who betray my trust deserve."

The ambassador hurried away with all speed, leaving Katharine alone with her husband.

Henry stood in his favourite position, legs apart, fingers playing with his dagger hilt, eyes glinting blue fire between the lids which almost met.

"My ally!" he shouted. "So this is Spanish honour! By God, I have trusted you Spaniards too much. And what has it brought me? An alliance which is no alliance . . . a barren wife."

"No . . . Henry."

"No! What of this treaty your father has signed with France? France! Our enemy! His and mine! I have served you royally. I brought you from your poverty and set you on a throne. And how do you repay me? Three births and not a child to show for it. It would seem that Spaniards seek to make a mock of the King of England."

"Henry, it is no more my fault than yours that we have no child. That matter has nothing to do with this treaty it is said my father has made with France."

"Has is not, Madam. Has it not!"

"Henry, how could I be blamed because our children did not live?"

"Perhaps," said Henry more quietly, "it is because it is not the will of God that you should bear children. Perhaps because you were my brother's wife. . . ."

"The Pope gave us the dispensation," she said, her voice trembling with a vague terror.

"Because he believed that you were a virgin when you married me."

"As I was."

While he looked at her the rage in his face subsided and it was replaced by a look which might have been one of speculation. "As you tell me, Madam," he said.

And with that he turned and left her—bewildered, unhappy, and numbed by a fear which was as yet vague and shadowy.

Ferdinand wrote to Henry and his daughter.

There had been a terrible misunderstanding. He was desolate because he feared he had been misrepresented. He had given no firm instruction that Caroz was to sign a treaty on his behalf with Henry. He was afraid that this matter had cast a slur on his honour; for even though he knew himself to be blameless, would others understand the truth?

It was a humiliating thing for a King to admit, but he feared that his ambassador in England was an incompetent fellow. He had misunderstood instructions . . . not deliberately. He would not believe that Don Luis was a rogue—but merely a fool.

"My dear daughter," he wrote, "you who were brought up in our Court know well the piety of your mother and that it was her wish that all her family should share that piety. I am a sick man, daughter. You would not recognize me if you saw me now. I believe myself to be very close to death. My conscience troubled me. When death is near, those of us who have striven to lead a religious life have an urgent desire to set our affairs in order. Make peace with your enemies—that is one of God's laws. So I looked about me and thought of my greatest enemy. Who could that be but Louis XII of France? So, believing that there should be reconciliation between Christians, I signed the truce with him. This was my reason. You, who are your mother's daughter, will understand my motives."

When Katharine read that letter her attitude towards her father began to change.

What loyalty do I owe to him now? she asked herself. It was the memory of her mother which had until this time made her wish to serve him; but her mother would never have agreed to the signing of these two treaties within a few days of each other.

It was not easy for one who had been brought up with the strictest regard for filial duty, to criticize a parent's action, but Katharine was beginning to do so.

The letter which Ferdinand had written to Henry was in the same strain.

He did not wish his son-in-law to think that he put friendship with the King of France on the same level with that which he bore to the King of England, he wrote. Nay, he had made peace with France because he feared he had but a short time to live and wished to die at peace with his enemies. But out of his love for his son-in-law, he would be ready to break the truce with France if necessary. There was a way in which this could be done. The province of Béarn was not included in the treaty and, if Ferdinand attacked Béarn and the King of France came to its defence—as he most assuredly would—then he would attack the Spanish, which would be breaking the treaty. And so it would be France which had broken faith, not Spain.

Henry scowled when he read this. He was beginning to believe that he was a fool to put any trust in such a double dealer. But it did not mean that he was not going forward with his plans for war.

Maria de Salinas came to the Queen's side and whispered: "Caroz is without. He is in a sorry state. An attempt has been made on his life."

Katharine, who had been sitting at her embroidery with two of her ladies, rose immediately and went with Maria into the adjoining ante-room.

"Bring him to me here," she said.

Maria returned in a short time with Caroz. His fine satin doublet was torn, and there was blood on his arm.

"Your Grace," he panted, "I was set upon in the street. I was attacked, but by a stroke of good fortune my attacker slipped just as he was about to thrust home his sword. It caught my arm and I ran . . . I ran for my life."

"Bring me water and bandages," said Katharine to Maria. "I will bind up the wound. I have a special unguent which is a wonderful healer."

As she spoke she cut the sleeve away from the wound and saw to her relief that it was not deep.

"I am submitted to insults on all sides." Caroz was almost sobbing. "Everyone here blames me for the treaty His Highness has made with the King of France. They have determined to kill me. It is unsafe for me to go abroad in the streets."

"You are distraught, Don Luis," said Katharine. "Pray calm yourself. This may have been nothing but the action of a cutpurse."

"Nay, Your Grace. The people are infuriated with me. They blame me, although Your Grace well knows. . . ."

Katharine said: "This may make you feel a little faint. Lie back and close your eyes."

As she washed the wound and applied the unguent, she thought: Poor Don Luis. He is the scapegoat. I must do all in my power to save him. I should not forgive myself if he, bearing the blame for my father's action, should also suffer the death wound which would be his should these people lay their hands upon him.

She bound the wound and made Don Luis lie down, setting two of her pages to watch over him.

Then she went to the King's apartment.

Henry frowned at her. He was still displeased with the Spaniards and he wished her to know that she was included in that displeasure. But she faced him boldly. She was certain that some of his friends had set an assassin to attack Don Luis, and she believed that Henry alone could save the ambassador from another attack. She felt sickened with humiliation because of her father's conduct and, although she had no great regard for

Don Luis, she was determined that his death should not be placed to her family's account.

"Henry," she said, "Don Luis has been attacked."

Henry growled his indifference.

"His murder would help us not at all."

"Us?" he demanded. "For whom do you work, Madam? Do you set yourself on the side of your father or your husband?"

Katharine drew herself to her full height and in that moment she looked magnificent, with her eyes flashing and the colour in her cheeks.

"I have made my vows to love, cherish and honour my husband," she said distinctly. "*I* do not break my vows."

Then Henry laughed exultantly. His Kate was a handsome woman. She was telling him clearly that she recognized her father's duplicity and that she was ranging herself on her husband's side against him. The woman adored him. That was easy to see.

"Why, Kate," he said, "I knew it well."

She threw herself into his arms and clung to him.

"Oh Henry, I am fearful that you should go to war."

He stroked her hair gently. "No harm will come to me, Kate. I'll give a good account of myself."

"Yet I shall fret if you are away."

"You are a good wife to me, Kate. But have no fear for me. I'll go to France and I'll come back . . . in triumph . . . and you shall share those triumphs with me."

"Come back safely . . . that is all I ask."

"Bah! You speak like a woman." But he was not displeased that she should.

It was then that she asked him to forbid further attacks on Caroz.

"The man is a fool," she said, "but no knave. Rest assured that he signed the treaty on my father's behalf in good faith."

"I'll order it, Kate . . . since you ask me. Caroz can live on without fear of losing his life. And if your father does not recall him, he shall keep his position at Court." His eyes narrowed. "The man is a fool. But sometimes it is not a bad thing when those who are set to work against us are fools."

Katharine did not answer. She had shown clearly that she would never completely trust her father again. Henry was satisfied.

And so the life of Caroz was saved.

The June sun shone on the walls of Dover Castle. From a window in the keep Katharine looked down on the fleet in the harbour, waiting to set sail. She knew most of the ships by name for she had taken the greatest interest in the preparations for this war. There lay the *Peter Pomegranate*—named in deference to her, whose device of the pomegranate had become so well known at the Court. There was the *Anne of Greenwich* side by side with the *George of Falmouth*; there was the *Barbara*, the *Dragon* and the *Lion*.

It had been a magnificent cavalcade which had passed along the road to Dover. The people had come out to cheer their King, and when they had seen him, so richly clad, so handsome, they had declared he was more like a god than a man. He was preceded by his Yeomen of the Guard in the Tudor colours, green and white; and the knights in armour and the gaily caparisoned horses were a colourful sight.

But it was the King who stood out in that glittering assembly. He was not in armour, but dressed as Supreme Head of the Navy of which he was very proud. There were four hundred ships waiting to set sail from Dover harbour, and he himself had superintended a great deal of the preparation for the journey. Thomas Wolsey was with him; he had learned more and more the value of that man.

And there rode Henry in his vest of gold brocade, his breeches of cloth of gold and his hose of scarlet. About his neck on a thick gold chain hung a whistle—the biggest any of the spectators had ever seen—and this was set with jewels which flashed in the sunlight. He blew on the whistle from time to time to the delight of all those who heard it.

Of all the pageants in which he had played his joyful parts there was not one which had delighted him as did this new game of going to war.

Katharine rode with him, applauding, admiring; and the glances he threw her way were full of love and tenderness.

There was a reason for this. As though to crown his happiness she had been able to give him, some few weeks before, the news which he had so wished to hear.

"Henry," she had said, her eyes alight with happiness, "there can be no doubt that I am with child."

Then he had embraced her and told her that there was only one regret in his life; that to make this holy war on France he must leave her.

"You must take care of yourself, Kate," he had said. "Remember in this fair body lies the heir of England."

She had sworn to take the utmost care.

Then he had requested her to be present at the meeting of the Council, and there he had announced that since he must go away he must appoint a Regent to govern the land in his absence.

"I have given this matter great thought. I have prayed for guidance, and I am leaving you the best and only possible Regent." There was the pause for dramatic effect; then the little eyes, shining with sentiment, were on Katharine.

"Gentlemen of the Council, your Regent during my absence will be Her Grace the Queen."

She had been overcome with joyful emotion, and she thought, as she did on all such occasions, If only my mother could be with me now!

So she was to be Regent during his absence. She was to have a Council to help her, should she need their help. The King had chosen the Archbishop of Canterbury, Thomas Lovell, and the Earl of Surrey. The Earl had been allowed to return to Court for Henry was in a mellow mood. Many of his most able statesmen were accompanying him to France, and Surrey who, in spite of his arrogance, was a man of experience, could be more useful at Court than skulking in the country, perhaps planning mischief. So back to Court came the Earl—although Thomas Wolsey had discreetly tried to advise the King against the old man's recall. Henry did not accept Wolsey's advice, and Wolsey was too clever to press it.

So they had ridden into Dover, up the steep hill to the Castle, there to rest awhile until the expedition was ready to sail.

The King was now ready to embark. Beside him were the most courageous of his knights, men such as Brandon, Compton, Sir John Seymour, Sir Thomas Parr and Sir Thomas Boleyn. There was the indefatigable Thomas Wolsey determined to keep a wary eye on food supplies and equipment, not forgetting to glance with the faintest hint of triumph at the Earl of Surrey who was with those who remained behind.

There on Dover strand the King had decided a ceremony should take place. He wanted all his subjects to know in what affection he held his Queen; and when before them all he took her into his arms and kissed her loudly on both cheeks, a cheer went up, for the people never loved their King so much as when he, sparkling with the glitter of royalty, showed them that he was at heart an ordinary family man.

Then he took Katharine's hand and addressed the assembly.

"My subjects, my friends, you see me about to depart on a holy war. I grieve to leave my country but it is God's will that I should cross the sea to bring back to you that of which the French have robbed us. On this fine day you can see the coast of France; my town of Calais lies across the sea and I am now about to set out for that town. From there I shall seek to win back my rights and your rights. But while I am engaged on this duty I do not forget my people at home, so I leave you one who, I hope, is almost as dear to you as she is to me—my wife, your Queen. My friends, when I go aboard, when I set sail, Queen Katharine becomes the Governor of this Realm and Captain General of the forces for home defence."

As he took Katharine's hand and kissed it, another cheer went up.

He looked into her face and his eyes were glazed with tenderness and the pleasure he felt in scenes such as this.

"Farewell, my Kate. I will return with rich conquests. Guard yourself well . . . and that other."

"I will, my King," she answered.

A last embrace, and to the fanfares of trumpets he went abroad.

Katharine stood, with those who were remaining behind, on Dover strand, watching the glittering fleet as it set sail for France.

She was praying for Henry's safety, for divine guidance that she might carry out her duties in a manner worthy of the daughter of Isabella of Castile.

She determined to surprise the King with her ability to govern; she was going to show him that if at one time she had sought to win advantages for Spain, she no longer did so; for there was only one country which she now called her own; and that was England.

Yet the real reason for her exultation lay within her own body. The child! This child must come forth from her womb, strong and healthy; and when he did come he must not be allowed to die.

There must not be another disaster. If such a calamity should befall her, all the affection of the last weeks, all the love and devotion which the King had sworn he bore her, would be as lightly swept away as the gaudy paper decorations after a masque.

CHAPTER VIII

Henry at War

By the time the King's fleet had reached Calais the rain had begun to fall. This was disappointing as the cloth of gold and rich brocade trappings lost some of their dazzle in the downpour.

Henry was cheerful, however, determined to show his men that he was ready for any adversity, so certain of success that he was not going to be downcast by a little rain.

Then tents were set up; the army encamped; and on that first night, the King, his garments soaked, made the rounds of the camp like a practised commander. He laughed at the rain and he made his men do the same.

"We are not the men to let a wetting disturb our spirits. We'll snap our fingers at the weather as we will at that old rogue, the King of France."

The men were cheered by the sight of him—pink cheeked, ruddy haired and full of health and high spirits.

Nor was the end of his endeavours for when he returned to his tent he did not take off his clothes.

"If this rain continues to fall," he told his companions, "the Watch will be in poor spirits as the night progresses. I have heard how Henry V before Agincourt went among his men to comfort them. I will show my soldiers that they have as good a leader in me as the victors of Agincourt had in that other Henry."

It was three o'clock when the King, still in his damp clothes, made the rounds of the camp.

He found the Watch disconsolate. In the darkness they did not recognize the figure on horseback immediately and Henry heard them, cursing the weather and talking of the warm beds in England which might have been theirs.

"Ay," said the King, "warm English beds sound even more inviting than they are in reality—when remembered under the rain of other lands."

"Your Grace!"

"Have no fear," said Henry. "I myself was thinking of my own bed and the comforts and pleasures I might have been enjoying there. We are of a kind, my friends. Men, all of us. It is understandable that our thoughts turn to the comforts of home. But be of good cheer. You see, I, like you, am damp from the rain. I suffer all that you suffer. That is how I would have it. My men and their King are together in this war. He never forgets it; nor should you; and if we have been made to suffer in the beginning, fortune promises us better things, God willing."

"Amen," murmured the men. And then: "God bless Your Grace!" Smiling, Henry rode back to his own tent. He was not displeased with the rain which had enabled him to show his men that he was with them to take part in their misfortunes and give them a share in his triumphs.

In the morning the rain was over and the sun shone brilliantly. The King was in high spirits and he told himself that he could not leave his good people of Calais before he had made them gay with certain masques and joustings, so that they might see something of the skill which their King and his men would display in battle.

So there in Calais there was jousting and tilting; and the King won the admiration of all by his skill with the bow.

Henry, however, was impatient to be done with mock battles and begin the real fighting, but it was necessary to await the arrival of his ally against the French, the Emperor Maximilian.

There was much talk of Maximilian who was known as one of the greatest soldiers of Europe. Henry was delighted to have him as a friend in this struggle against the French. With the help of Maximilian he could afford to snap his fingers at the other dubious ally, Ferdinand.

It was while he was showing his skill at archery that a message came to him from Maximilian.

He discarded his bow and read it immediately.

The Emperor believed that the first steps in the conquest of France should be the taking of those two towns, Thérouanne and Tournai. Once these were in the hands of the allies, Maximilian pointed out, there would be no difficulty in pouring men in from Flanders. He wanted the King of England to know that he merely proffered the advice of an old campaigner and he was the happiest general in Europe to serve under the banner of the King of England.

Henry, whose plans had been not to go so far from the main object—Paris—as towns on the Flemish border, was so charmed by the Emperor's last words that he succumbed immediately to his suggestions and set out for Thérouanne.

The Emperor Maximilian—that hardened old campaigner—had been in communication with Ferdinand concerning the aspirations of the King of England.

"This young colt will become a menace to all if he is not curbed," wrote Maximilian. "I am mindful of his recent expedition as your ally. He has a conceit which makes it unnecessary to deceive him because he so obligingly is ever ready to deceive himself."

The Emperor had no great desire to make war on the King of France, but rather to make an alliance with him as Ferdinand had done; he was, as was Ferdinand, in secret negotiations with Louis.

The three great European rulers—Louis, Ferdinand and the Emperor—did not take very seriously the cavortings of the young King of England, who had too much money to squander; but they were all ready to make use of him, and Maximilian had offered a bargain which was irresistible. His treasury was empty and he desperately needed to fill it; therefore he was eager to come to terms with the English King. He would place at Henry's service the cavalry of Burgundy and as many German *Lanzknechts* as he wanted. It would be necessary of course for Henry to pay for the hire of these men, because, while the Emperor had the men, he had not the means to keep them on the battlefield.

As for the Emperor himself, he would place himself under the command of Henry. "I shall be honoured to serve under such a banner. . . ." were words calculated to bring such satisfaction to the King of England that he would leap at the bargain without considering the cost. Such a general as the Emperor Maximilian must be paid for, and the King of England must understand that his personal expenses would be considerable. But all he would ask was a hundred crowns a day; and the King would naturally be expected to shoulder the expenses of the Emperor's household guards.

"We are invincible," Henry had cried, "now we have one of the greatest soldiers in Europe fighting under our banner."

The three experienced old warriors now prepared to watch the antics of the young cockerel who believed that war was a superior—though more expensive—kind of masque.

Cynically Ferdinand waited. Louis was preparing to make peace with Maximilian and Ferdinand. Maximilian was telling himself that the conquest of Thérouanne and Tournai were all he needed, and he saw no reason why Henry should not pay him for winning them for himself.

Louis had given his instructions that his soldiers were to avoid battle with the English. They were merely to harry them and make their stay in France mildly uncomfortable.

Dorset's campaign was remembered; so nobody took the English seriously . . . except themselves.

What a glorious moment when the Emperor, simply dressed in black—because he was mourning the death of his second wife—rode into the camp to pay homage to the dazzling young King.

Henry embraced the Emperor and would not let him kneel; but the glitter of triumph was in his eyes for all to see.

Maximilian, who cared not at all for cloth of gold but only for making his Empire great, was quite ready to kneel if by so doing he could deceive this young man.

There were tears in Henry's eyes. "This is the greatest

moment of my life," he declared, "to fight side by side with your Imperial Highness."

"Who is happy at this time to be your general," answered the Emperor glibly.

"The capture of these towns should be an easy matter," Henry told him. "And then . . . to Paris!"

"My daughter Margaret has written to me urging me to insist on your visiting her before you leave this land. She has heard of your fame and says that she will hold it hard against me if I allow you to depart without being her guest for a while."

Henry smiled. He had heard that Margaret of Savoy was not uncomely, and the thought of shining in feminine company was very attractive.

"I desire to see the lady as much as she does to see me," he declared.

"Then we must insist on that visit. My grandson has also heard of you. Charles—as you know he is being brought up by his aunt, my daughter Margaret—has said he wishes to see the King of England because he has heard that he is a young King possessed of all the virtues; and as he himself will be a ruler over great dominions he feels that to study the grace and prowess of great Harry of England would be a lesson to him."

"I have heard excellent reports of that boy."

"Ay, he'll make a good King. He's a serious young fellow."

"I can scarce wait to see him . . . and his aunt. But first there is a war to be won."

The Emperor agreed, and turned the conversation to plans for the first battle.

The battle was of short duration. The French, who had not taken their enemy seriously and had been ordered by Louis not to join in a pitched battle, put into effect a mock retreat before Thérouanne; but the English were very serious; and for that matter, so was Maximilian, as this town, with Tournai, was at a strategic point on the border of the Netherlands, and Maximilian's object in joining this campaign was to win them.

The mock retreat soon became a retreat in real earnest; the small French forces were put to flight; and because they had been instructed not to fight, they were overcome by panic when they saw the weight of English and German forces; they galloped from the battlefield with the cavalry of the enemy in hot pursuit.

Henry was exultant; he had taken as prisoner the famous Chevalier Bayard, that knight who was known to be *sans peur et sans reproche*, and he felt that he was indeed making up for the disgrace which Dorset's army had brought upon his country.

The battle was derisively called by the French: The Battle of the Spurs; and shortly afterwards, with the Emperor beside him, Henry had taken Tournai.

When these two towns, the taking of which had been his reason for entering the war, were in his hands, Maximilian had had enough of war. Not so Henry.

He burst into Maximilian's tent and cried: "Now the way is clear. Now it is for us to go straight through to Paris to complete the victory."

Maximilian was thinking quickly. The date was August 22nd. It was hot but the summer was almost at its end and in a few weeks the rains would start. Henry could have no notion what the Flanders mud could be like.

The idea of marching on Paris, even if it was possible to defeat Louis, would only mean, if they were successful, that this conceited young man would become more overbearing than ever. The English were becoming too powerful already, and Maximilian had no intention of helping them at the expense of Louis, who was already preparing to make a treaty with him as he was with Ferdinand.

He must be kept in Flanders until the winter set in; then he would have to return to England, for he could not stay where he was through the winter. He could spend the winter in England preparing for a fresh onslaught next spring if he liked; that was of little concern to Maximilian since he had achieved what he wanted: These two towns which jutted into the Hapsburg dominions and which were therefore a menace to Netherlands trade.

"Have I your permission to speak frankly to Your Grace?" he asked.

Henry was always so delighted when the Emperor addressed him in humble fashion that he was ready to give what was asked even before the request was made.

"You have indeed."

"I am an old man. I have fought many battles. If we marched on Paris now, we could be defeated."

"Defeated! Standing together as we do. Impossible!"

"Nay, Your Grace, if you will forgive my contradiction. Louis has not put all his forces into the field for the protection of these two insignificant towns. He would fight to the death for Paris. Our men need rest, and a little gaiety. It is always wise in war to consolidate one's gains before one passes on to fresh conquests. I am under your command but it is my duty to give you the benefit of my experience. My daughter Margaret is impatient to see you. She is eager that the proposed marriage between Charles and your sister Mary may be discussed more fully. We have won these towns from the French. Let us fortify them and then go to my daughter's court. There she will entertain you right royally . . . the King of England, conqueror of Thérouanne and Tournai."

Henry wavered. He longed for conquest, yet the thought of being entertained and flattered by Margaret was growing more and more inviting.

When Maximilian had left him Henry sent for Thomas Wolsey.

He looked affectionately at the almoner, of whose worth he had become daily more and more aware. When he needed anything, it was Thomas Wolsey who always seemed to be at his side to supply it. The Emperor had congratulated him on the excellence of his equipment. All this he owed to Wolsey.

He had even come to the point when he spoke to him of matters far beyond the man's duty; and, moreover, listened to his advice which had always seemed to him sound.

When Wolsey came to the King he saw at once the indecision in the King's eyes and he was alert. It was his policy to give the King the advice he hoped for and then allowed him to think that he had taken his, Wolsey's.

The King put his arm through that of Wolsey and proceeded to walk with him about the tent . . . a habit of Henry's when he was deep in thought and with one whom he wished to favour.

"Friend Thomas," he said, "we have won a victory. These two towns are in our hands. The Emperor is of the opinion that this victory should be consolidated and that we should now proceed to his daughter's court at Lille, there to rest awhile. Now you are in charge of our supplies. Is it your opinion that we need this time to make ready for further attacks?"

Wolsey hesitated. He could see that the King was torn between two desires and he was not certain which course the King had made up his mind to follow. Wolsey must be on the right side.

"Your Grace is tireless," he said. "I know full well that it would be no hardship for you to continue in fierce battle." He paused significantly. Then went on: "For others, who lack Your Grace's powers. . . ."

"Ah!" said the King, and it was almost a sigh of relief. "Yes, I owe something to my men, Thomas. I need them beside me when I ride into battle."

Wolsey went on triumphantly now that he had received his cue. The King wished to go to the court of the Duchess of Savoy, but it must be a matter of duty not of pleasure.

"Therefore, Sire," Wolsey continued, "I would say, since you command me to give you my humble advice, that for the sake of others—though not your august self—it would be desirable to rest awhile before continuing the fight."

Wolsey's arm was pressed; the King was smiling.

"I must perforce think of those others, Thomas. Much as it irks me to leave the field at this stage . . . I must think of them."

"Your Grace is ever thoughtful of his subjects. They know this, and they will serve you with even greater zeal remembering Your Grace's clemency towards them."

The King sighed deeply but his eyes were glittering with delight.

"Then, my friend, what must be, must be. We shall be leaving ere long for Lille."

Wolsey felt gratified; he had once more gracefully leaped what might have been a difficult hurdle.

The King was also gratified, for he went on: "The bishopric of Tournai was fallen vacant, I hear. Louis has put forward a new Bishop. I venture to think, now that Tournai is no longer in French hands, it is not for Louis to appoint its Bishop and my nomination will more readily receive the blessings of His Holiness."

"Sire!" Wolsey's gratitude shone from his eyes as he knelt and kissed his sovereign's hand.

Henry beamed on him. "It is ever our wish," he said, "to reward a good servant."

Bishop of Tournai! pondered Wolsey. A further step along the road.

Bishop! he thought, and he kept his head lowered over Henry's hand lest his eyes should betray the ambition which he felt was so strong that it must be obvious.

Bishop! Cardinal? And then: Pope himself!

CHAPTER IX

The Flowers of the Forest

At home in England Katharine took her responsibilities very seriously. She was eager that when he returned Henry should be satisfied with the manner in which she had governed the realm during his absence. She attended meetings of her Council and impressed them with her good sense; she spent any time she could spare from these duties with her ladies who were busily working, stitching standards, banners and badges. She prayed each day for the strength to do her duty and that the child she carried would not suffer because of her activities.

She felt well and full of confidence. The news from France was good. Henry was in high spirits; she had heard of the successful conclusion of the Battle of the Spurs; and she wondered now and then whether Henry was learning soldiers' habits, for she knew that there would be women to haunt the camp. Would he remain faithful? She must remember how stoically her own mother had accepted Ferdinand's infidelities; and Isabella had been a Queen in her own right. Ferdinand had ruled Castile as her consort, and Isabella never forgot that; and yet she meekly accepted his unfaithfulness as something which women, whose husbands are forced to spend long periods from their marriage beds, must regard as inevitable.

She was thankful that there was so much with which to occupy herself. There was always the child to comfort her, and she thanked God daily that she had become pregnant before Henry had left.

This one must live, she told herself again and again. It would not be possible to go on having such disappointments.

145

One day, when she sat stitching with her women, Surrey came into the apartment without ceremony.

"Your Grace," he cried, "forgive this intrusion. You will understand when you hear the news. The Scots are gathering and preparing to swarm over the Border."

She stared at him in horror. "But the King made a treaty with his brother-in-law . . ." she began.

Surrey snapped his fingers. "Treaties, Your Grace, it would seem are made to be broken. This is no surprise to me. When the English army is overseas the Scots always attack."

"We must meet this attack," said Katharine quickly.

"Ay, Your Grace. I've men enough to meet the beggarly Scots."

"Then go to it. There's little time to waste."

Katharine went with him to the Council chamber. The time for stitching was over.

As she did so she was aware of the child moving within her and she felt exultant because of its existence and a certain apprehension because of the anxieties to come.

She thought of Margaret, Henry's sister, who was wife to James IV of Scotland, and it saddened her because sister must surely be working against brother.

She listened to Surrey, addressing the Council. His eyes gleamed and he seemed to have thrown off twenty years. It was as though he were saying, I was considered too old to join the French frolic. Now the King and the butcher's cur shall see how real victories are won.

I pray God that Surrey may succeed, thought Katharine. His victory would be hers, and if they could defeat the Scots Henry would be well pleased with her.

And yet . . . nothing would please him long, she knew, unless she brought forth a healthy son.

She spoke to the Council.

"There is little time to lose," she said. "Let us gather all our available forces and move at once to the Border. The Scottish King has broken his treaty and seeks to strike us in the back while the King with our armies is on foreign soil. Gentlemen, we must defeat him. We must show His Grace that there are as good men in England this day as there are in France."

"We'll do it," cried Surrey; and everyone in the Council chamber echoed his words.

But this was no occasion for words only. Action was needed. No one and nothing must be spared in the great endeavour.

The days were filled with a hundred anxieties. How could she raise the money to supply an army in France and another on the Border? There was only one answer: New taxes must be levied. Surrey was already in the North, fortifying the Border, raising an army to subdue the Stuart, and she herself was in continual correspondence with Wolsey. The amount of money and goods which were needed for the French war was staggering; yet somehow she must raise it.

There was no time now to indulge in those restful hours of sewing with her ladies. Disastrous news came from the North, where James had mustered an army of, some said, one hundred thousand men and was crossing the Tweed determined on battle.

She saw panic in certain faces about her. The King abroad on his French adventure, his country undefended and only a woman in control. Was this to be the end of the Tudor dynasty? Were the Stuarts going to do what they had longed to do for generations—join the two countries under Stuart rule?

It was unthinkable. She was riding about the country rousing the people to a realization of their danger because that army must be raised somehow. Surrey could not be expected to drive back a hundred thousand warlike Scots unless he had an army to match them.

But she knew she should rest more. There were times when she threw herself on her bed too exhausted to take off her clothes. In this national danger she forgot even the child because there seemed only one goal: to save England.

As she passed through the various towns and villages she stopped to talk to the people who flocked to see her. She looked magnificent on her horse, her eyes alight with purpose.

"God's hand is over those who fight for their homes," she cried. "And I believe that in valour the English have always surpassed all other nations."

The people cheered her and rallied to her banner, and when she reached Buckingham she had raised a force of sixty thousand men.

"I will lead them to York," she said, "and there join up with Surrey."

When she dismounted she could scarcely stand, so exhausted was she. But she was triumphant because she had achieved that which had seemed impossible and had surely proved herself to be a worthy Regent.

Tired as she was she found time to write to Henry before she slept. She also sent a note to Wolsey—that most able man—who in the midst of all his exertions never failed to find time to write to the Queen, although often Henry was too busy to do so.

She feared that Henry might be too rash on the battlefield; she was worried about his tendency to catch cold; she was having new linen sent for him as she knew how fastidious he was in such matters; and she asked good Master Wolsey, on whom she relied, to look after the King and keep him well, and advise him against over-rashness.

She sealed the letters and sent them off before she dropped into a deep sleep.

In the morning she was unable to leave her bed; her limbs were cramped, and there were frightening pains in her womb.

She felt sick with apprehension but she said to Maria de Salinas: "I rode too long yesterday. My condition is making itself felt."

"Your Grace should abandon the idea of riding North, and stay here for awhile," said Maria anxiously. "You have raised the men. They can join Surrey and his army while you rest a little."

She protested but even as she did so she knew that however much she wished to ride on she would be unable to do so.

She spent that morning in bed after giving orders that the army was to march on without her. And as she lay, racked by periodic pains, she remembered how her mother had told her that she had once sacrificed a child to win a war.

That night her pains had increased and she could no longer feign not to understand the cause. The time had not come and the child was about to be born.

"Oh God," she murmured, "so I have failed again."

Her women were about the bed. They understood.

"Why, Maria," she said, her mouth twisted bitterly, "it has come to be a pattern, has it not. Why . . . why should I be so forsaken?"

"Hush, Your Grace. You need your strength. You are young yet. All your life is before you."

"It is the old cry, Maria. Next time . . . next time . . . And always this happens to me. Why? What have I done to deserve this?"

"You have exhausted yourself. You should never have left Richmond. It is easy to understand why this has happened. My dearest lady, rest now. Do not take it too hard. There will be another time. . . ."

Katharine cried out in pain, and Maria called to those who were waiting: "The child is about to be born."

It had been a boy. She turned her face into the pillows and wept silently.

She would meet Henry on his return and her arms would be empty. He would look at her with those blue eyes, cold and angry. So you have failed once more! those eyes would say. And a little more of his affection would be lost.

They brought news to her as she lay in bed mourning for the lost boy.

"Your Grace, the Scots attacked Surrey's men six miles south of Coldstream. They fought there on Flodden Hill and it is victory, Your Grace, with the King of Scots dead and his men slain or in retreat. It is such a victory that warms the heart. They can never rally after this."

She lay still. So her efforts had not proved in vain. She had helped to save England for Henry, and she had lost him his child.

But how could she rejoice whole-heartedly? A Kingdom for the life of a child! Her mother had paid the same price. But how different had been the position of Isabella of Castile from that of Katharine of Aragon!

In the streets they were singing of victory. The battle of Flodden Field would be remembered down the ages, because it would be years before the Scots would be in a position to rise again. And this had been achieved with the King away from home and the Queen in control of the Kingdom.

"Long live Queen Katharine!" cried the people.

And she smiled and thought: How happy I should have been if I could have stood at the windows holding my child in my arms.

The people were singing Skelton's song:

> "Ye were stark mad to make a fray,
> His Grace being then out of the way.
> Ye wanted wit, sir, at a word
> Ye lost your spurs and ye lost your sword. . . ."

And on the other side of the Border they were mournfully bewailing their dead.

But it was victory, thought Katharine, even though the child was lost. Had the Scots triumphed the kingdom might have been lost. As for the child—she was telling herself what so many others had told her: You are young yet. There is still time.

She sat down to write to Henry.

"Sir,

My lord Howard hath sent me a letter open to Your Grace within one of mine by which you shall see the great victory which our Lord hath sent your subjects in your absence. . . . To my thinking this battle hath been to Your Grace and all your realm, the greatest honour that could be and more than should you win all the crown of France. Thanked be God for it and I am sure Your Grace forgetteth not to do so."

She went on to say that she was sending him the coat of the King of Scotland for his banner. She would have sent the body of the King of Scots himself, but those about her had persuaded her against this. She wished to know how the dead King's body should be buried and would await Henry's instructions on this matter.

"I am praying God to send you home shortly, for without this no joy here can be accomplished. I am preparing now to make my journey to our Lady of Walsingham."

She did not mention the death of the child. As yet she could not bring herself to do so.

CHAPTER X

Bessie Blount

As Henry rode with Maximilian to the court of the Duchess of
Savoy in the town of Lille he felt completely happy.

The townsfolk had come out to see him and, as he rode
among them, they shouted greetings; and when he asked Maximilian what they said, the Emperor answered him: "But this is
not a King, this is a God."

His own subjects could not have been more appreciative
and, when some of the beautiful women placed garlands about
his neck, he took their hands and kissed them and even went so
far, when the girls were pretty, to kiss their lips.

He came as a conqueror and he could never resist such
homage.

Margaret of Savoy greeted him with pleasure. He thought
her fair enough but she seemed old to him, twice widowed, or
one might say three times if her first betrothal to the Dauphin
of France were counted. Henry found some of the pretty girls
of Lille more to his taste.

As for Margaret herself, she seemed mightily taken with that
seasoned charmer, Brandon, and Henry, amused, made a point
of bringing them together on all occasions.

So this was Charles, he mused, studying the fourteen-year-
old boy, who was to be his brother-in-law. He could not help
feeling complacent at the sight of him for, when Ferdinand and
Maximilian died, this boy could be heir to their dominions
which constituted a great part of Europe not to mention those
lands overseas which their explorers had discovered and
brought under their sway.

This boy would therefore be one of the rivals with whom

152

Henry would juggle for power in Europe. It was an amusing
thought. The boy's somewhat bulging eyes suggested that he
needed great concentration to understand what was being said;
he seemed to find difficulty in closing his mouth; his hair was
yellow and lustreless; his skin so pale that he looked unhealthy.

His mother's mad, thought Henry. And, by God, it seems
that the boy too could be an idiot.

Charles, however, greeted his grandfather and the King of
England in the manner demanded by etiquette and he appeared
to be endeavouring to take in everything that was being said.

He's far too serious for a boy of that age, Henry decided.
Why, when I was fourteen, I looked eighteen. I was already a
champion at the jousts and I could tire out a horse without a
hint of fatigue to myself.

So it was comforting to discover that this future ruler was
such a puny, slow-witted young fellow.

"My grandson," said Maximilian, "may well inherit the
dominions on which the sun never sets. 'Tis so, is it not,
Charles?"

Charles was slow in replying; then he said: " 'Tis so, Imperial Highness, but I trust it will be long ere I do so."

"And what's your motto, Grandson? Tell the King of England that."

Again that faint hesitation as though he were trying very
hard to repeat a lesson. " 'More Beyond', Grandfather."

"That's right," said Maximilian.

Then he put an arm about the boy and held him against him,
laughing.

"He's a good fellow, my grandson. He's a Fleming all
through. None of your mincing Spaniards about Charles. And
he works hard at his lessons. His tutors are pleased with him."

"We're all pleased with him," said Henry, laughing at his
own subtlety.

Those weeks spent at Lille were delightful ones for Henry. He
had changed since coming to France. Previously he had been
more or less a faithful husband. Often he wished to stray, and
in the case of Buckingham's sister had been prepared to do so;

but he had always had to fight battles with his conscience. He was possessed of deep sensual appetites and at the same time wished to see himself as a religious and virtuous man. He wanted to be a faithful husband; but he desperately wanted to make love to women other than his wife. The two desires pulled him first in one direction, then in another; and always it seemed that he must come to terms with his conscience before indulging in his pleasures.

He had persuaded himself that when he was at war and far from home, he could not be expected to eschew all sexual relationships. The same fidelity must not be expected of a soldier as of a man who was constantly beside his wife. He reckoned that all monarchs of Europe would have laughed at what they would call his prudery.

He is young yet, they would say. He believes it is possible to remain faithful to one woman all his life. What a lot he has to learn!

His conscience now told him that it was no great sin, while he was abroad, to make a little light love here and there.

The women expected it.

"By God," he told himself on the first lapse. "I could not so have disappointed her by refusing to grant that which she so clearly desired."

And once the first step was taken, others followed and thus the King of England was finding the life of a soldier a highly interesting and exhilarating one.

With each new love affair he thought less kindly of Katharine. She was his wife; she was the daughter of a King; but, by God, he thought, she knows less of the arts of loving than the veriest tavern wench.

Brandon was his closest companion, and Brandon's reputation, he had always known, was a none too savoury one.

He watched Brandon with the women and followed his example even while he shook his head over the man and was shocked by his conduct.

I am King, he excused himself. The woman will remember all her life, what she and I have shared. It was but a kindness on my part. But Brandon!

Always Henry saw his own acts shrouded in mystic glory. What he did was right because he was the King; it was entirely different if another did the same thing.

He was a little worried about Brandon because his sister Mary was so fond of the fellow, and he was afraid that one day she would be so foolish as to ask to be allowed to marry him. What would she say if she could see that bloodless boy to whom she was betrothed—and side by side with handsome, wicked Brandon!

Brandon was now even daring to carry on a flirtation with the Duchess Margaret; and such was the fascination of the man that Margaret seemed nothing loth.

He had watched the exchange of glances, the hands that touched and lingered.

By God, he thought, that fellow Brandon now has his eyes on the Emperor's daughter.

He thought about the matter until some hot-eyed wench sought him out in the dance and, when they had danced awhile, found a quiet room in which to explore other pleasures.

Each new experience was a revelation.

What did we know—Katharine and I—of making love? he asked himself. Was our ignorance the reason for our lack of children?

It behoved him to learn all he could.

There must be children, so what he did was really for England.

Charles Brandon was hopeful. Was it possible that he could marry Margaret of Savoy? The prospects were glittering. He could look into a future which might even lead to the Imperial crown, for this crown was never passed to a hereditary heir. The Empire was composed of vassal states and Emperors were elected from a few chosen candidates.

The Emperor's grandson was a feeble boy who, Brandon was sure, would never win the approval of the electors. But Margaret was powerful and rich. Votes were won through bribery and the husband of Margaret would stand a very fair chance.

It was a dizzy prospect, and he brought out all his charm to dazzle the woman. He did not even have to make a great effort for she was attractive and he could feel real affection for her. Poor woman, she had been unfortunate first to have her betrothal to the Dauphin ruthlessly terminated by an ambitious King of France; then her marriage to the heir of Spain was short-lived, her child, which came after her husband's death, still-born; then had followed the marriage with the Duke of Savoy who had soon left her a widow.

Surely she was in need of such solace as one of the most glittering personalities of the English Court—or any Court for that matter—could give her.

Brandon had for some time been thinking a great deal of another Princess who he was sure would be delighted to be his wife. This was none other than the King's own sister, young Mary. Mary was a girl of great determination and too young to hide her feelings; Brandon had been drawn to her, not only because of her youthful charms and the great glory which would surely come to the King's brother-in-law, but because there was an element of danger in the relationship, and he was always attracted by danger.

But Mary was betrothed to the pale-eyed anaemic Charles, and she would never be allowed to choose her husband; but Margaret of Savoy was a widow, and a woman who would make her own decisions.

That was why he was growing more and more excited and blessing the fate which had brought him to Lille at this time.

He was elated because he believed that the King was not ill-disposed to a marriage between himself and Margaret. Henry knew how his sister felt towards him, and Henry was fond of young Mary. He would hate to deny her what she asked, so it would be helpful to have Brandon out of her path, to let Mary see she had better be contented with her fate, because Brandon, married to the Duchess Margaret, could certainly not be the husband of the Princess of England.

So Brandon made up his mind that he would take an opportunity of asking Margaret to be his wife.

When they walked in the gardens, Margaret allowed herself

to be led aside by Brandon, and, as soon as they were out of earshot of their companions, Brandon said to her familiarly: "You spoil that nephew of yours."

Margaret's eyes dwelt fondly on young Charles who was standing awkwardly with his grandfather and Henry, listening earnestly to the conversation.

"He is very dear to me," she answered. "I had no children of my own so it is natural that I should care for my brother's son."

"It is sad that you never had children of your own. But you are young yet. Might that not be remedied?"

Margaret saw where the conversation was leading and caught her breath in amazement. Would this arrogant man really ask the daughter of Maximilian to marry him as unceremoniously as he might—and she was sure did—invite some peasant or serving woman to become his mistress?

She was amazed and fascinated at the project; but she sought to ward it off.

"You have not a high opinion of my young nephew," she said. "I see that your King has not either. You do not know my Charles; he is no fool."

"I am sure that any child who had the good fortune to be under your care would learn something to his advantage."

"Do not be deceived by his quiet manners. There is little he misses. He may seem slow of speech, but that is because he never makes an utterance unless he has clearly worked out what he is going to say. Perhaps it would be well if others followed his example."

"Then there would never be time to say all that has to be said in the world."

"Perhaps it would not be such a tragedy if much of it was left unsaid. Charles' family has been very tragic. As you know his father died when he was so young, and his mother. . . ."

Charles Brandon nodded. Who had not heard of the mad Queen of Spain who had so mourned her unfaithful husband that she had taken his corpse with her wherever she went until she had been made more or less a prisoner in the castle of Tordesillas where she still remained.

But Brandon did not wish to talk of dull Charles, his philandering father or his mad mother.

He took Margaret's hand in his. Reckless in love had always been his motto, and he was considered a connoisseur.

"Margaret," he began, "you are too fair to remain unmarried."

"Ah, but I have been so unfortunate in that state."

"It does not mean you always will be."

"I have had such experiences that I prefer not to risk more."

"Then someone must try to make you change your mind."

"Who should that be?"

"Who but myself?" he whispered.

She withdrew her hand. She was too strongly aware of the potent masculinity of the man for comfort.

"You cannot be serious."

"Why not? You are a widow who can choose your husband."

She looked at him. He was indeed a handsome man; he had the experience of life which was so missing in his young King.

Margaret asked herself: Could I be happy again with him?

He saw her hesitation and, taking a ring from his finger, slipped it on hers.

She stared at it with astonishment.

They were then joined by Henry, Maximilian and young Charles, and as the young boy stared at the ring on his aunt's hand there was no expression in his pallid eyes, but Margaret, who knew him so much better than everyone else, was aware that he understood the meaning of that little scene which he had witnessed from afar—understood and disapproved.

By the beginning of October Henry, tired of play, now hoped to win fresh laurels; but the rainy season had started and when he sought out Maximilian and demanded to know when they would be ready to start on the march to Paris, the Emperor shook his head sagely.

"Your Grace does not know our Flanders mud. It would be impossible to plan an offensive when we have that to contend with."

"When then?" Henry wanted to know.

"Next Spring . . . next summer."

"And what of all the troops and equipment I have here?"

"That good fellow Wolsey will take charge of all that. You can rely on him to get them safely back to England for you."

Henry hesitated. He remembered the disaster which Dorset had suffered when he had stayed a winter in Spain.

He saw now that this was the only course for him to take. He was disappointed, for he had hoped to return to England, conqueror of France. All he had to show was the capture of two French towns and certain prisoners, whom he had sent home to Katharine, and who were causing her some anxiety because she had to feed them and treat them as the noblemen they were, because as the war with Scotland had proved costly and the war with France even more so, there was little to spare for the needs of noble prisoners.

Katharine had the victory of Flodden Field to set side by side with the conquest of Thérouanne and Tournai, and Henry felt piqued because he had to admit that she had scored the greater victory.

He felt angry towards her, particularly as he had now heard of the loss of the child. "Lost, that your kingdom might be held, Henry." Grudgingly he agreed that all she had done had been necessary. But, he had said to himself, it seemed that God's hand was against them; and since he had known many other women in France his satisfaction with Katharine had diminished.

Oh, it was time he went home; and he could go as a conqueror. The people of England would be eager to welcome him back.

He sent for Brandon.

"How goes the courtship?" he asked slyly.

Brandon shook his head. "I need time."

"And that is something you cannot have. We are returning to England."

Brandon was downcast. "Have no fear," said Henry, "we shall return and then ere long I doubt not you'll have swept the Duchess Margaret into marriage."

"She has returned my ring and asked for the one I took from her," said Brandon.

"Is that so? The lady is coy."

"One day she seems willing enough, and the next she holds back. She talks of previous marriages and says that she is afraid she is doomed to be unfortunate in that state. Then she talks of her duty to her nephew. 'Tis true that young fellow looks as though he needs a keeper."

Henry laughed. "I rejoice every time I look at him," he said. "Max can't last forever. Nor can Ferdinand . . . and then . . . it will not be difficult to dupe that little fellow, what think you? And who will take over from old Louis . . . for he too must be near his death-bed? Francis of Angoulême." Henry's eyes narrowed. "I hear he is a young braggart . . . but that he excels in pastimes."

"A pale shadow of Your Grace."

Henry's mouth was prim suddenly. "That fellow is a lecher. His affairs with women are already talked of . . . and he little more than a boy! Brandon, have you thought that one day, and that day not far distant, there will be three men standing astride Europe . . . three great rivals . . . the heads of the three great powers? There will be Francis, myself and that young idiot Charles." Henry laughed. "Why, when I think of those two . . . and myself . . . I have great reason for rejoicing. God will not favour a lecher, will He, against a virtuous man? And what hope has young Charles, whose mother is mad and who seems to have been born with half his wits? Oh, Brandon, I see glorious days ahead of me and I thank God for this sojourn in Europe where my eyes have been opened to all that, with His help, may come to me."

"Your Grace stands on the threshold of a brilliant future."

Henry put his arm about Brandon's shoulder. "In which my friends shall join," he said. "Why, Charles, I might even win for you the hand of Margaret, eh, in spite of the fact that she returns your ring and demands hers back; in spite of the snivelling little nephew who doubtless cries to his aunt that her duty lies with him."

The two men smiled, drawn together by a joint ambition.

Henry was placated. He sent for Wolsey and told him to make arrangements to return to England.

Katharine was deep in preparations for the return of the King.

Surely, she thought, he cannot but be pleased with me. It is true I have lost the child but, much as he longs for an heir, he must be satisfied with what I have done.

She had Margaret, widow of dead James IV, remain Regent of Scotland; after all, was she not the King's sister? It would have been too costly to have taken possession of the Scottish crown. She trusted Henry would approve of what she had done.

She had recovered from the last miscarriage, and felt well in body if a little uneasy in mind.

Maria de Salinas, now married to Lord Willoughby, was not at this time separated from her, and she talked to her about the masque she was planning to celebrate the King's return.

"It must be colourful," said Katharine. "You know how the King loves colour. Let there be dancing, and we will have the King's own music played. That will delight him."

While they sat thus Maria ventured: "Your Grace, Francesca de Carceres, realizing that there is no hope of regaining her place in your household, now has hopes of joining that of the Duchess of Savoy. She believes that if Your Grace would speak a word of recommendation to the Duchess on her behalf she would have her place."

Katharine was thoughtful. It would be pleasant to be rid of Francesca's disturbing proximity. While she was in England she would continue to haunt the ante-chambers, hoping for an interview with the Queen. Any mention of the woman brought back unpleasant memories . . . either of the old days when she had suffered such humiliation, or of that other unfortunate affair of Buckingham's sister.

Francesca was an intriguer. Was it fair to send her to the Court of the Duchess with a recommendation?

It was not just, she was sure of it.

No, much as she longed to be rid of Francesca she was not going to send her with a recommendation to someone else.

"No," said Katharine, "she is too perilous a woman. I shall not give her the recommendation she requires. There is only one thing to be done for Francesca; that is that she should be sent back to her own country. When Thomas Wolsey returns I will put this matter before him, and I doubt not he will find some means of having her sent back to Spain."

"It is where she longed to go in the past," said Maria. "Poor Francesca! I remember how she used to sigh for Spain! And now . . . when she does not want to return, she will go back."

"My dear Maria, she is an adventuress. She wanted to go to Spain because she thought it had more to offer her than England. Remember how she wanted to come to England, when I left Spain, because she thought England would have greater opportunities for her. Such as Francesca deserve their fate. Waste no sorrow on her. You have achieved happiness, my dear Maria, with your Willoughby, because you did not seek to ride over others to reach it. So be happy."

"I shall be so," said Maria, "as long as I know that Your Grace is too."

The two women smiled at each other then. Their gaiety was a little forced. Each was thinking of the King—on whom Katharine's happiness depended. What would happen on his return?

Henry came riding to Richmond.

As soon as he had disembarked, he had called for a horse, declaring that he was not going to wait for a ceremonial cavalcade.

"This is a happy moment," he cried. "Once more I set foot on English soil. But I cannot be completely happy until I am with my wife. So a horse . . . and to Richmond where I know she eagerly awaits me."

He had been unfaithful a score of times in Flanders but that made him feel more kindly towards Katharine. Those affairs had meant nothing to him, he assured himself. They were not to be given a moment's thought. It was Katharine, his Queen, whom he loved. There was no other woman who was of any importance to him.

Such peccadilloes were to be set at naught, merely to be mentioned at confession and dismissed with a Hail Mary and a Paternoster.

Katharine heard the commotion below.

"The King is here."

"But so soon!" Her hands were trembling, as she put them to her headdress. Her knees felt as though they were giving way beneath her.

"Oh, Maria, how do I look?"

"Beautiful, Your Grace."

"Ah . . . you say that!"

"In my eyes Your Grace is beautiful."

"That is because you love me, Maria."

And how shall I look to him? she wondered. Will he, like Maria, look at me with the eyes of love?

She went down to greet him. He had leaped from his steaming horse. How dramatic he was in all he did.

His face was as smooth as a boy's, flushed with exercise, his blue eyes beaming with good will. Thank God for that.

"Kate! Why Kate, have you forgotten who I am?"

She heard his laughter at the incongruity of such a suggestion, saw the glittering arms held out. No ceremonial occasion this. Now he was the good husband, returning home, longing for a sight of his wife.

He had swung her up in his arms before those who had come riding ahead of the cavalcade, before those who had hastened from the Palace to greet him.

Two audible kisses. "By God, it does my heart good to see you!"

"Henry . . . oh my Henry . . . but you look so wonderful!"

"A successful campaign, Kate. I do not return with my tail between my legs like some licked cur, eh! I come as conqueror. By my faith, Kate, this time next year you'll be with me in Paris."

"The news was so good."

"Ay, the best."

He had his arm round her. "Come," he said, "let's get within walls. Let's drink to conquest, Kate. And later you and I will talk together . . . alone, eh . . . of all that has been happening there and here."

His arm about her they went into the great hall where the feast was waiting.

He ate while he talked—mainly of those great victories, Thérouanne and Tournai—and from his talk it would appear that he and he alone had captured them. Maximilian had been there, yes . . . but in a minor role. Had he not placed himself under Henry's banner; had he not received pay for his services?

"And you looked after our kingdom well in our absence, Kate. You and Surrey together with the help of all those good men and true I left behind me. So Jemmy the Scot is no more. I wonder how Margaret likes being without a husband. 'Tis a sad thing, Kate, to be without a husband. You missed me?"

"Very much, Henry."

"And we lost the child. A boy too. Alas, my Kate. But you lost him in a good cause. I have heard how you worked for England . . . when you should have been resting. . . ." His eyes were slightly glazed; he was remembering past experiences in Flanders. That sly court Madam, lady to the Duchess; that kitchen girl. By God, he thought, I have profited more than my Kate realizes by my Flanders campaign.

"Well, Kate, it grieves me. But we are young yet. . . ."

She thought: He has learned soldiers' ways in Flanders.

His eyes were warm, his hands straying to her thigh. But she was not unhappy. She had been afraid that he would blame her for the loss of the child as he had on other occasions.

He was drinking freely; he had eaten well.

"Come," he said, " 'twas a long ride to Richmond. 'Tis bed for us, Kate."

His eyes were warm; so that all knew that it was not to rest he was taking her.

She did not object; she was filled with optimism.

There would be another time, and then it should not fail.

The Court was gay that Christmas. There was so much to celebrate. Henry was looking forward to the next year's campaign.

His sister Margaret was looking after his interests in Scotland; and at the Palace of Richmond masques, balls and banquets were arranged for Henry's delight.

One day Lord Mountjoy, when talking to the Queen, mentioned a relative of his whose family were eager that she should have a place at Court.

William Blount, Lord Mountjoy, was one of Katharine's greatest friends. He was her chamberlain and one of the few seriously inclined men of the Court; Katharine had a great regard for him and had tried to influence the King in favour of this man. Mountjoy's friends were the learned men on the fringe of the Court—men such as Colet, Linacre, Thomas More.

So far the King had shown little interest in the more serious-minded of his subjects. His greatest friends were those men who danced well or excelled at the joust, men such as William Compton, Francis Bryan, Nicholas Carew, Charles Brandon.

But it sometimes seemed to Katharine that Henry grew up under her eyes. He had remained a boy rather long, but she was convinced that eventually the man would emerge and then he would take an interest in the scholars of his Court.

"I'm thinking of this relative of mine," Mountjoy was saying. "She is fifteen or sixteen . . . a comely child, and her parents would like to see her enjoy a place in Your Grace's household."

"You must bring her to me," said Katharine. "I doubt not we shall find room for her here."

So the next day Mountjoy brought little Bessie Blount with him to the Queen's presence.

The girl curtseyed, and blushed at Katharine's scrutiny, keeping her eyes modestly downcast. A pretty creature, thought Katharine, and one who, if she could dance, would fit well into the Christmas masque.

"Have you learned the Court dances?" asked Katharine.

"Yes, Your Grace."

"And you wish to serve in my household. Well, I think that can be managed."

"Thank you, Your Grace."

"Can you play a musical instrument or sing?"

"I play the lute, Your Grace, and sing a little."

"Then pray let me hear you."

Bessie Blount took the instrument which one of Katharine's women offered her and, seating herself on a stool, began to pick out notes on the lute and sing as she did so.

The song she sang was the King's own song:

> "Pastance with good company
> I love, and shall until I die.
> Grudge who will, but none deny;
> So God be pleased, this life will I
> For my pastance
> Hunt, sing and dance."

And as she sat there singing, her reddish gold hair falling childishly about her shoulders, the door was burst open and the King came in.

He heard the words of the song and the music; he saw the child who sang them; and the words he was about to utter died on his lips. He stood very still, and those who were with him, realizing the command for silence in his attitude, stood very still behind him.

When the song came to an end, the King strode forward.

"Bravo!" he shouted. " 'Twas well done. And who is our performer?"

Bessie had risen to her feet and the flush in her cheeks matched her hair.

She sank to her knees, her eyes downcast, her long golden lashes, a shade or two darker than her hair, shielding her large violet-coloured eyes.

"Ha!" cried Henry. "You should not feel shame, my child. 'Twas worthy of praise." He turned to the company. "Was it not?"

There was a chorus of assent from those who stood with the King, and Katharine said: "This is little Bessie Blount, Your Grace, Mountjoy's relation. She is to have a place in my household."

"I am right glad to hear it," said Henry. "An she sings like that she will be an asset to your court, Kate."

"I thought so."

Henry went to the girl and took her chin in his hands. She lifted her awestruck eyes to his face.

"There is one thing we must ask of you, Mistress Bessie, if you belong to our Court. Do you know what it is?"

"No, Your Grace."

"Then we'll tell you, Bessie. 'Tis not to be afraid of us. We like our subjects who play our music and sing it well, as you do. You've nothing to fear from us, Bessie. Remember it."

"Yes, Your Grace."

He gave her a little push and turned to the Queen.

Mountjoy signed to the trembling girl that she should disappear. She went out quickly and with relief, while Henry began to talk to the Queen about some item of the pageantry. But he was not really thinking of that; he could not dismiss the picture of that pretty child sitting on the stool, so sweetly singing his own music.

Never had the King seemed so full of vigour as he did that Christmas. That year the pageants were of the gayest, the banquets more lavish than ever before. Katharine hid her weariness of the continual round of pleasure which lasted far into the night, for it seemed that the King never tired. He would hunt through the day, or perhaps joust in the tiltyard, a splendid figure in his glittering armour inlaid with gold which seemed not to hamper him at all. His laughter would ring out at the splintering of lances as one by one his opponents fell before him.

Often he tilted in what was meant to be a disguise. He would be a strange knight from Germany, from Flanders, from Savoy; even from Turkey. The massive form would enter the tiltyard in a hushed silence, would challenge the champion, and, when he had beaten him would lift his visor; then the people would go wild with joy to recognize the well-known features, the crown of golden hair.

Katharine never failed to display a surprise which she was

far from feeling. He would come to her, kiss her hand and tell her that his exploits were all in her honour. At which she would kiss him in return, thank him for the pastance, and then chide him a little for risking his life and causing her anxiety.

Henry enjoyed every moment. There was nothing he desired more than to be the popular, dazzling, god-like King of England.

It seemed, thought Katharine, that he had become a boy again. But there was a difference.

On occasions he would sit pensively staring before him; the music he played on his lute was plaintive. He was kinder, more gentle than he had ever been to Katharine and seemed to take great pains to please her.

Henry was changing subtly because he was falling in love.

She was a slip of a girl of sixteen with hair of that red gold colour not unlike his own; but shy and innocent as she was, she could not remain long in ignorance of his interest and its significance. In the dances which were arranged for the Queen's pleasure she would often find herself as his partner; their hands would touch and a slow smile would illumine the royal features. Bessie smiled shyly, blushing; and the sight of her, so young, so different from the brazen members of his Court, increased the King's ardour.

He watched her at the banqueting table, at the masques, in the Queen's apartments, but he rarely spoke to her.

He was surprised at his feelings. Previously he had believed that, if he desired, it was for him to beckon and the girl to come willingly. It was different with Bessie. She was so young, so innocent; and she aroused such tender feeling within him.

He even began to question himself. Should I? It would be so easy . . . like plucking a tender blossom. Yet she was ready for the plucking. But she was fragile and strangely enough he would not be happy if he hurt her.

Perhaps he should make a good match for her and send her away from Court. It was astonishing that he, who desired her so ardently, should think of such a thing; but it was his conscience which suggested this to him, and it was significant that it should never have worried him so insistently as it did over this matter of Elizabeth Blount.

During the masque they danced together.

He was dressed in white brocade of the Turkish fashion and he wore a mask over his face, but his stature always betrayed him, and everyone in the ballroom paid great deference to the unknown Turkish nobleman.

The Queen was seated on a dais with some of her women about her, splendidly clad in cloth of silver with many coloured jewels glittering about her person. She was easily tired, although she did not admit this: so many miscarriages were beginning to take their toll of her health. Often after supper she would make an excuse to retire and in her apartments her women would undress her quickly so that she might sink into an exhausted sleep. She was aware that meanwhile Henry capered and danced in the ballroom. It was different for him. He had not suffered as she had from their attempts to get children; she was nearly thirty; he was in his early twenties, and she was beginning to be uncomfortably aware of the difference in their ages.

Now she watched him leaping, cavorting among the dancers. Did he never tire? He must always remind them of his superiority. She imagined the scene at the unmasking; the cries of surprise when it was seen who the Turkish nobleman really was—as if everyone in the ballroom was not aware of this. She herself would have to feign the greatest surprise of all, for he would surely come to her and tell her that it was all in her honour.

How much more acceptable would a little peace be to me, she thought.

Henry wound his way among the dancers because he knew that she was there and he must find her. No mask could hide her from him. She was as delicate as a flower and his heart beat fast to think of her.

He found and drew her towards an embrasure. Here they could feel themselves cut off from the dancers; here Katharine could not see them from her dais.

"Mistress Bessie," he began.

She started to tremble.

His big hand rested on her shoulder then strayed down her back.

"Your Grace . . ." she murmured.

"So you have seen through the mask, Bessie."

"Anyone must know Your Grace."

"You have penetrating eyes. Can it be because you have such regard for your King that you know him, however he tries to hide himself?"

"All must know Your Grace. There is none like you."

"Ah . . . Bessie."

He seized her hungrily and held her against him for a few seconds.

He put his face close to her ear and she felt his hot breath on her neck. "You know of my feelings for you, Bessie. Tell me, what are yours for me?"

"Oh . . . Sire!" There was no need for more; that was enough.

His pulse was racing; his desire shone in the intense blue visible through the slits of the mask. He had abandoned all thought of restraint. Only this evening he had been thinking of a good match for her. A good match there should be, but this was for afterwards.

"I have sought to restrain my ardour," he said, "but it is too strong for me, Bessie."

She waited for him to go on, her lips slightly parted so that she appeared breathless; and watching her, his desire was an agony which demanded immediate satisfaction.

But they were here in the ballroom, barely hidden from the rest of the company.

Tonight? he thought. But how could he leave the ball? Oh, the restraint set upon a King! All his actions watched and commented upon; too many people were too interested in what he did.

There must be no scandal, for Bessie's sake as well as his own.

He made a quick decision. For the sake of propriety his desire must wait . . . for tonight.

"Listen, Bessie," he said. "Tomorrow I shall hunt, and you must join the hunt. You will stay close beside me and we will give them the slip. You understand?"

"Yes, Sire."

He let his hand caress her body for a few seconds, but the emotions this aroused startled him, so he gave her a little push and murmured: "Back to the dance, girl." And she left him to stand there in the embrasure, trying to quell the rising excitement, trying to steel himself to patience.

He rode with Compton and Francis Bryan beside him, the rest falling in behind. He had caught a glimpse of her among the party. She rode well, which was pleasing.

He said to Compton: "We must not forget this day that we have ladies with us. The hunt must not be too fierce."

"Nay," answered Compton, "since Your Grace is so considerate of the ladies, so must we all be."

It was impossible to keep secrets from Compton. He was one of those wise men who seemed to read the King's secrets before Henry had fully made up his mind to share them. Bryan was such another. His friends had often hinted that the King should live less virtuously. "For," Compton had said, "if Your Grace sinned a little the rest of us would feel happier about our own sins."

He could rely on their help and, as they already guessed his feelings towards Bessie and were waiting for the culmination of that little affair, Henry decided that he would use their help.

"When I give the sign," he said, "I wish you to turn aside from the rest of the party with me . . . keep about me to cover my retreat."

Compton nodded.

"And see that Mistress Blount is of our party."

Compton winked at Bryan knowing Henry could not see the signal. There was scarcely a man in the party who would not understand. But Henry always believed that those about him only saw that which he wished them to see.

"Your Grace," said Compton, "I know of an arbour in the woods which makes an excellent shelter."

"He has dallied there himself," put in Bryan.

"Well, Sire, it is an inviting arbour. It calls out to be of use."

"I would like to see this arbour and perhaps show it to Mistress Blount."

"Your humble servants will stand guard at a goodly distance," said Compton. "Near enough though to prevent any from disturbing Your Grace and the lady."

Henry nodded. Alas, he thought, that love must be indulged in thus shamefully. If I were but a shepherd, he thought, and she a village maid!

The thought was entrancing. To be a shepherd for an hour's dalliance one afternoon! And such was his nature—he who was more jealous of his rank and dignity than any man—that when he sighed to be a shepherd he really believed that it was his desire.

He saw her—his village maiden—among the women. Gracefully she sat her horse; and her eyes were expectant. It is a great honour I do her, Henry assured himself. And I'll make a goodly match for her. It shall be a complaisant husband who will be happy to do this service for his King.

It was easily arranged under the skilful guidance of Compton and Bryan; and even the sun shone its wintry light on the arbour; and the lovers did not feel the chill in the air. They were warmed by the hunt—not only of the deer but for the quenching of their desire.

Henry took her roughly into his arms; kissed her fiercely; then expertly—for he had learned of these matters in Flanders—he took her virginity. She wept a little, in fear and joy. She was overcome with the wonder that this great King should look her way. Her modesty enchanted him; he knew too that he would teach her passion and was amazed by the new tenderness she discovered in his nature.

He wanted to dally in the arbour; but, he said, even a King cannot always do as he wishes.

He kissed his Bessie. He would find means of coming to her apartments that night, he promised. It would not be easy, but it must be done. He would love her for ever; he would cherish her. She had nothing to fear, for her destiny was the King's concern and she would find him her great provider.

"Nothing to fear, my Bessie," he said running his lips along the lobe of her ear. "I am here . . . I your King . . . to love you for evermore."

During the weeks that followed Henry was a blissful boy. There were many meetings in the arbour; and scarcely anyone at Court did not know of the King's love affair with Elizabeth Blount, except Katharine. Everyone contrived to keep the matter from her, for as Maria de Salinas, now Lady Willoughby, said on her visits to Court, it would only distress the Queen, and what could she do about it?

So Katharine enjoyed the company of a gentler Henry during those weeks; and she told herself that his thoughtfulness towards her meant that he was growing up; he had come back from Flanders no longer the careless boy; he had learned consideration.

He was a gentler lover; and he frequently said: "Why, Kate, you're looking tired. Rest well tonight. I shall not disturb you."

He even seemed to have forgotten that desperate need to get a child. She was glad of the rest. The last miscarriage together with all the efforts she had put into the Scottish conflict had exhausted her more than anything that had gone before.

One day the King seemed in a rare quiet mood, and she noticed that his eyes were over-bright and his cheeks more flushed than usual.

She was sewing with her ladies when he came to her and sat down heavily beside her. The ladies rose, and curtseyed, but he waved his hand at them, and they stood where they were by their chairs. He did not give them another glance, which was strange because there were some very pretty girls among them, and Katharine remembered how in the past he had been unable to prevent his gaze straying towards some particular specimen of beauty.

"This is a charming picture you're working," he said, indicating the tapestry, but Katharine did not believe he saw it.

He said after a slight pause: "Sir Gilbert Taillebois is asking for the hand of one of your girls, Kate. He seems a good fellow, and the Mountjoys, I believe, are eager enough for the match."

"You must mean Elizabeth Blount," said Katharine.

"Ah yes . . ." Henry shifted in his seat. "That's the girl's name."

"Your Grace does not remember her?" said Katharine innocently. "I recall the occasion when Mountjoy brought her to me and you came upon us. She was singing one of your songs."

"Yes, yes; a pretty voice."

"She is a charming, modest girl," said Katharine, "and if it is your will that she should make the match with Taillebois, I am sure we shall all be delighted. She is after all approaching a marriageable age, and I think it pleasant when girls marry young."

"Then so be it," said Henry.

Katharine looked at him anxiously. "Your Grace feels well?"

Henry put his hand to his brow. "A strange thing . . . Kate, when I rose this morning I was a little dizzy. A feeling I never remember before."

Katharine rose quickly and laid a hand on his forehead.

"Henry," she cried shrilly, "you have a fever."

He did not protest but continued to sit slumped heavily on his chair.

"Go to the King's apartments at once," Katharine commanded the women who were still standing by their chairs. "Tell any of the gentlemen of the King's bedchamber . . . any servant you can find, to come here at once. The King must go to his bed and the physicians be called."

The news spread through the Palace. "The King is sick of a fever."

The physicians were about his bedside, and they were grave. It seemed incredible that this healthy, vital young King of theirs could be so sick. None knew the cause of his illness, except that he was undoubtedly suffering from high fever. Some said it was smallpox; others that it was another kind of pox which was prevalent in Europe.

Katharine remained in his bedchamber and was at his side through the day and night; she refused to leave it even when her women told her that she would be ill if she did not do so.

But she would not listen. It must be she who changed the cold compresses which she placed at regular intervals on his burning forehead; it was she who must be there to answer his rambling questions.

It was clear that his mind wandered. He did not seem to be sure whether he was at the court of Lille or in some arbour in a forest—presumably, thought Katharine, some place he had seen when he was on the Continent. Patiently she sat beside his bed and soothed him, superintending his food, making special healthgiving potions, conferring with his physicians and keeping everyone else from the sick room; and in less than a week his magnificent health triumphed over the sickness and Henry was able to sit up and take note of what was going on.

"Why, Kate," he said, "you're a good wife to me. It was not such an unhappy day, was it, when I said I'd marry the King of Spain's daughter, in spite of the fact that they were all urging me not to."

That was her reward. But as she sat beside his bed smiling she did not know that he was thinking how old and pale she looked, how wan, how plain. That was because he was comparing her with one other, whom he dared not ask to be brought to his sick room, but who was nevertheless continually in his thoughts.

He had come near death, he believed, and he was a little alarmed to contemplate that he might have died at a time when he was actually in the midst of an illicit love affair, committing what the priests would tell him was a cardinal sin.

But was it so? He began to wrestle with his conscience, a pastime which, since the affair with Bessie, he had indulged in with greater frequency.

But, he mused, she was so enamoured of me, that little Bessie. She would have broken her little heart if I had not loved her. It was for Bessie's sake, he assured himself. And I found her a husband.

Taillebois would be a good match for her, and she would

have reason to be grateful to her King. As for himself, how far had he wronged his wife? She was ageing fast. There were dark shadows under her eyes; her once firm cheeks and neck were sagging; all the red seemed to have gone out of her hair and it was growing lustreless and mouse-coloured. She needed rest; and while he had Bessie abed Katharine could rest, could she not? She was grateful for the respite. Let her recover her health before they tried for more children.

So he had done no harm. How could he when he had made Bessie happy and Katharine happy? It was only himself who must fight this persistent conscience of his. He was the one who suffered.

He said: "My good Kate, you have nursed me well. 'Tis something I shall not forget. Now tell me. Before I went to bed with this sickness I had given my consent to Taillebois' marriage with that girl of yours. What's done about it?"

Katharine looked shocked. "There could be no marriage while Your Grace lay so ill."

"But I'm well again. I'll not have my subjects speaking of me as though I'm about to be laid in my coffin. Tell them to go on with that marriage. Tell them it is their sovereign's wish."

"You must not bother about weddings, Henry. You have to think about yourself."

He took her hand and fondled it. "I am a King, Kate, and a King's first thoughts must be for his subjects."

She kissed him tenderly, and in that moment of happiness she seemed to regain much of her lost youth.

He could not ask for Bessie to be brought to him, so he determined to be out of his sickroom within a day or so. He could, however, receive his old friends; and Bryan, Compton, Brandon and Carew all visited the sickroom and there were soon sounds of laughter coming from it.

Henry had become interested in illness for the first time in his life, and wanted to try his hand at making potions. During his sickness he had been tormented by certain ulcers which appeared on various parts of his body and that one which was on his leg had not healed like the others. This was treated with liniments and pastes, and he took a great interest in the prepa-

ration of these; something which, Katharine knew, he would
have laughed to scorn a few months previously.

Compton disclosed a similar ulcer of his own and this made
an even greater bond between those two. One day Katharine
came into the sickroom to find Compton with his bare leg
stretched out on the King's bed while Henry compared his
friend's affliction with his own.

Under the treatment Henry's ulcer began to heal and he, full
of enthusiasm, determined to heal Compton's. To take his
mind from Bessie, he made ointments with Compton, into
which he believed that if he added ground pearls he could con-
struct a cure. He was determined to wait until he was strong
before he returned to public life, because at the balls, and the
masque, and banquets he must be as he had ever been; the King
must leap higher in the dance; he must never tire.

So passed those days of recuperation, and during them
Henry continued to think longingly of his Bessie who had
become Lady Taillebois.

Spring had come and, now that the King was well again, he had
two great desires: to be with Bessie and to prepare for the war
against France.

He had sent Charles Brandon over to Flanders—after be-
stowing upon him the title of Duke of Suffolk—for two pur-
poses: to continue with his wooing of Margaret of Savoy and
to make plans for the arrival of the army in spring or early
summer.

Henry was relieved to see Charles out of the way, for the
infatuation of young Mary for that man was beginning to alarm
him. Mary must be prepared to accept that other Charles,
Maximilian's and Ferdinand's grandson, and when Henry
thought of that pale-faced youth with the prominent eyes and
the seemingly sluggish brain, he shuddered for his bright and
beautiful sister. But he would have to remind her that royal
marriages were a matter of policy. I married my wife because
she was the daughter of Spain, he often reminded himself, and
he relished the thought because it was another excuse for infidelity. How could Kings be expected to be faithful when they

married, not for love, but for state policy? He had already forgotten that it was he himself who had determined to marry
Katharine, and that he had done so in spite of opposition.

It was a sad augury—but as yet Katharine continued in
ignorance.

The days were full of pleasure and Henry's kindness and
gentleness towards his Queen continued.

Often he and Bessie met, and their favourite meeting place
was a hunting lodge which Henry called Jericho. This was in
Essex near New Hall Manor which belonged to the Ormonde
family. Henry stayed occasionally at New Hall, which pleased
him because of its proximity to Jericho. Thomas Boleyn, who
was eager for the King's favour, was the son of one of the
Earl of Ormonde's daughters, and the ambitious Boleyn was
always ready to make arrangements for the royal visit and to
ensure secrecy for the King's visits to Jericho with Lady
Taillebois.

So the days passed pleasantly and, when Katharine was able
to tell Henry that she was once more pregnant, he declared that
he was full of joy and there must be a masque to celebrate this
happy news.

CHAPTER XI

The French Marriage

In the bed, about which the elaborate curtains had been drawn, Thomas Wolsey felt shut away from the world with Mistress Wynter.

He talked to her more freely than he could to any other person because he trusted her completely. It was his pride—that integral part of his nature which in its way was responsible for his rise to power and against which he knew he must continually be on guard, because as it sent him soaring, so could it send him crashing to disaster—which made these sessions so sweet to him. He must hide his brilliance from the rest of the world, how he was always a step in front of the rest, how he always knew what could happen and must wait . . . patiently, ready to leap into the right position at that half second before others saw the leap, so that it appeared that he had always stood firmly there.

Only his Lark knew how clever he was, only to her could he be frank.

They were both sad because his visits to the little house were less frequent now.

"Matters of state, sweetheart," he would murmur into that pretty ear; and she would sigh and cling to him and, even while she listened to the tales of his genius, she still longed for him to be an ordinary man, like the merchants who were her neighbours.

They had eaten and drunk well. The table in this house was more lavish than it had been a year before; the garments his wife and children wore, more splendid. He had talked to his children, listened to an account of their progress; had dismissed them; and had brought Mistress Wynter to this bed-chamber where they had made love.

Now was the time for talk; so he lay relaxed and spoke of all that was in his mind.

"But when you are Pope, Thomas, how shall I be able to see you then?"

"Why, 'twill be easier then, my love," he told her. "A Pope is all-powerful. He does not have to fight his petty enemies as a Bishop does. Roderigo Borgia, who was Pope Alexander the Sixth, had his mistress living near the Vatican; he had his children living with him and none dared tell him this should not be done . . . except those who lived far away. The power of the Pope is as great as that of the King. Have no fear. When I am Pope our way will be made easier."

"Then Thomas, how I wish you were Pope!"

"You go too fast. There are a great many steps, I can tell you, from tutor to King's almoner, from King's almoner to . . . My love, I have a piece of news for you. I have heard that I am to receive the Cardinal's hat from Rome."

"Thomas! Now you will be known as Cardinal Wolsey."

She heard the ecstasy in his voice. "The hat!" he whispered. "When it is brought to me, I shall receive it with great ceremony so all may know that at last we have an English Cardinal; and that is good for England. Cardinal Wolsey! There is only one more step to be taken, my love. At the next conclave . . . why should not an English Pope be elected to wear the Papal Crown?"

"You will do it, Thomas. Have you not done everything that you have set out to do?"

"Not quite all. If that were so I should have my family with me."

"And you a churchman, Thomas! How could that be?"

"I would do it. Doubt it not."

She did not doubt it.

"You are different from all other men," she said, "and I marvel that the whole world does not know it."

"They will. Now I will tell you of the new house I have acquired."

"A new house! For us, Thomas?"

"No," he said sadly. "It is for myself. There I shall entertain the King; but perhaps one day it will be your home . . . yours and the children's."

"Tell me of the house, Thomas."

"'Tis on the banks of the Thames, well past Richmond. The Manor of Hampton. It is a pleasant place and belongs to the Knights of St. John of Jerusalem. I have bought the lease of this mansion and now I intend to make it my very own, for as it stands it suits me not. There I shall build a palace and it shall be a great palace, my sweetheart . . . a palace to compare with the palaces of Kings, that all the world shall know that if I wish to have a palace, I have the means to build me one."

"It will be some time before this palace is built as you wish it."

"Nay. I shall have them working well for me, sweetheart. I am setting the most prominent members of the Freemasons to work for me, and who now would care to displease Cardinal Wolsey? I have decided that there shall be five courts about which the apartments will be built. I tell you, they will be fit for a King."

"Does the King know of this, Thomas? I mean, what will he say if a subject builds a palace to match his own?"

"He knows and shows great interest. I am well acquainted with our King, sweetheart. He likes not the display of wealth of certain noblemen who have the temerity to fancy themselves more royal than the Tudors, but with one whom he believes he has brought out of obscurity, it is a different matter. In Hampton Court Palace, my love, he will see a reflection of his own power. So I talk to him of the palace and he is of the opinion that I take his advice. But it is he, you know, who always takes mine."

Wolsey began to laugh, but Mistress Wynter trembled slightly and when he asked what ailed her, she said: "You have come so high, Thomas, perilously high."

"And you think—the higher the rise the greater the fall? Have no fear, my Lark, I am sure-footed enough to remain perilously high."

"I was fearing that you might be too high to remember us . . . myself and the children."

"Never. You shall see what I will do for our son . . . for you all. Remember, my prosperity is yours."

"And soon you will be leaving England again for France."

Wolsey was thoughtful. "I am not sure of that."

"But the King is going to war this year as last. The whole country talks of it."

"There are certain matters which set me wondering, my dear. When we were in Lille we made a treaty with Maximilian and Ferdinand to attack the French. We won two towns which were of the utmost importance to Maximilian, and we paid him thousands of crowns to work with us. It seemed to me at the time that Maximilian came very well out of that campaign—as Ferdinand did out of the previous one. What was in it for England? But the King was pleased, so it was necessary for his servant to be pleased. One thing I have learned: a man must never go against his King. So, because Henry is pleased, so must I seem to be. But I am uncertain. I believe that Henry will soon discover that Maximilian and Ferdinand are not the friends he believes them to be."

"Then there would be no war in France?"

"It might well be so. My dear one, imagine these two wily old men. They have great experience of statesmanship. Remember that Maximilian's son Philip, and Ferdinand's daughter, mad Juana, were married. Their sons are Charles and young Ferdinand. They have their eyes on Italy, not on France. They want Italy for young Ferdinand because Charles will have the whole of Spain and possibly the Austrian Empire, which includes the Netherlands. The King of France also has his eyes on Italy. 'Tis my belief that the English invasion of France is being planned by Ferdinand and Maximilian to put fear into Louis' heart, and that if they can make favourable terms with him regarding Italy they will be ready to leave their English allies to fight France alone. It was significant that after the capture of Thérouanne and Tournai Maximilian was very eager that hostilities should cease. He knew further battles would mean bitter losses and he did not wish to impoverish himself, but to be in a strong position to bargain with the French."

"And our King does not know this?"

"As yet he is a happy boy; he thinks with the mind of a boy. He trusts others because he is frank himself. He has had warning of Ferdinand's perfidy; yet he is prepared to trust him as ever."

"It is because Ferdinand is his father-in-law, perhaps."

"The Queen is a clever woman, I believe, but she is fast losing her influence. The King is enamored of Lady Taillebois but Katharine does not know this. Lady Taillebois does not interest herself in politics. But she might not please the King for ever, and if there were a woman who made great demands on the King and sought to influence him . . . who knows what would happen."

"Thomas, I am alarmed by all this. It seems so dangerous."

"You have nothing to fear, my love. I will always protect you and our children."

"But Thomas, what if . . . ?"

She did not say it. It seemed sacrilege even to think of it. Thomas would always maintain his place. There was no man in England who was as clever as her Thomas.

The King paced up and down his apartment and with him was Charles Brandon, the newly created Duke of Suffolk. Suffolk, recently returned from Flanders, looked grim.

"So she'll not have you," Henry was saying.

"She was adamant in her refusals. You can be sure Maximilian has had a hand in this."

"An English Duke is match enough for a Duchess of Savoy!" growled Henry.

"Alas, Your Grace. She—or perhaps the Emperor—would not agree. And there is another matter."

Henry nodded. "Say on, Charles."

"There was a hesitancy in the Emperor's manner when, on your instructions, I tried to bring the negotiations for the Princess Mary's marriage to completion."

"Hesitation! What do you mean?"

"He was evasive. He seemed unwilling to make the final arrangements. Your Grace, it appears to me that the Emperor is one such as Ferdinand. He makes plans with us, and at the same time with others elsewhere."

Henry's brows were drawn together; he was thinking of the man who had placed himself under his banner and declared his willingness to serve the King of England.

"I cannot believe this," he shouted. "He served me well."

"He was paid well for doing so, Your Grace."

Henry's face darkened; but he could take more from Brandon than almost any other man.

"What means this change of front?"

"I know not, Your Grace, but let us be prepared."

Henry stamped angrily from the apartment, but he gave orders that preparations for war were to go on apace.

It was a week or so later when an envoy from France arrived to negotiate for those prisoners whom Henry had taken at the battles of Thérouanne and Tournai and who still remained in England.

The envoy asked if he might speak in private with the King and, when Henry received him—in Wolsey's presence—the envoy said: "I have words for Your Grace's ears alone."

Wolsey retired with dignity, knowing that the King would immediately pass on the news to him, and indeed having a shrewd notion as to what it must be.

When they were alone the envoy said to Henry: "Your Grace, I have a message from my master, the King of France. He wishes to warn you that King Ferdinand has renewed the truce he made with France, and that the Emperor Maximilian stands beside him in this."

"Impossible!" cried Henry. "This must be untrue."

"Your Grace will soon hear confirmation of this," said the envoy. "But my master, wishing to prepare you and to show you that he is willing to be your friend, determined to let you know of it as soon as the truce had been signed."

The veins stood out at Henry's temples; his face was purple and he cried: "The traitors! By God, I'll be revenged for this.

My friends indeed! Base traitors both. They'll be sorry if these words you speak are truth. And if they are lies . . . then shall you be."

"I speak truth, Your Grace."

"By God!" cried Henry, and strode from the apartment; storming into Wolsey's quarters, he told him the news.

Wolsey, who was already prepared for it, received it calmly enough.

"What now?" demanded Henry.

"We know our false friends for what they are."

"That will not conquer France for us."

"A project which Your Grace will doubtless decide must be set aside for a while."

The King's eyes were glazed with anger, and in those moments he looked like a petulant boy who has been deprived of some much desired toy.

"Your Grace, what else had the envoy to say?"

"What else? Was that not enough?"

"Enough indeed, Sire. But I thought mayhap the King of France, showing his friendship in this way, might have further signs of friendship to show us."

Henry looked bewildered.

"Would Your Grace consider recalling the envoy? Perhaps a little delicate questioning with Your Grace's usual subtlety might reveal something of the mind of the King of France."

"What is this you are saying? Do you believe it possible that I might become the ally of the King of France!"

"Your Grace, the other powers of Europe have proved themselves no friends of yours."

"'Tis true enough, by God."

"And Your Grace is now telling yourself, I know, that there can be no harm in hearing what this Frenchman has to say."

"Send for him," growled Henry.

In a short time the envoy stood before them.

Wolsey said: "Is it Your Grace's wish that I speak of those matters which you have explained to me?"

"Speak on," said Henry.

"It would seem," said Wolsey, "that the motive of the King of France is friendship towards his brother of England."

"That is my master's desire, Your Grace, Your Excellency."

"Then how would he show this friendship?"

"By making a peace with the English who shall be his friends, and forming an alliance which could not but bring dismay to those who have so clearly shown themselves the enemies of both countries. He says that to show his good faith he would be happy to make a marriage between France and England. As you know, Your Grace, Your Excellency, the King is without a wife. He is still of marriageable age. The marriage of the Princess Mary with the treacherous Hapsburg surely cannot now take place. The King of France would be happy to take the Princess as his bride."

Wolsey caught his breath. The King was astounded. This was a complete volte-face. But the treachery of Ferdinand and Maximilian rankled; and what better revenge could possibly be achieved than such a treaty, such a marriage? It would be France and England against Austria and Spain. Henry saw now that those two wily old men had wanted to set him fighting France while they turned their attention to Italy—thus widening the dominions of their grandsons.

It was all startlingly clear. And the revenge: this alliance, this marriage.

Wolsey was looking cautiously at the King. "His Grace will wish to have time to consider such a proposal," he said.

"That is so," said Henry.

The envoy was dismissed, and, placing his arm through that of Wolsey, Henry began to pace the apartment with him while they talked.

The news was out and Katharine was bewildered. So once more her father had shown his treachery. He and Maximilian together had been profiting by the inexperience of the King of England and had used him shamelessly: Ferdinand in the conquest of Navarre, Maximilian for the capture of those two towns which were important to Netherlands trade. In addition Maximilian had received many English crowns as payment for his double dealing. They had endeavoured to win concessions from the King of France by informing him of imminent invasion by England so that he would be ready to make peace with them, almost at any price in order to be free to tackle the English invaders.

Louis however had had a plan of his own to outwit them: the French and English should forget old enmities and stand together as allies.

Caroz was bewildered; he did not know which way to turn; and, as on a previous occasion he saw that he would be in the position of scapegoat. He hurried to see Katharine and was met by Fray Diego Fernandez who informed him haughtily that the Queen was in no way pleased with his conduct of Spanish affairs.

Caroz, angry beyond discretion, pushed aside the priest and forced his way into the Queen's apartment.

Katharine met him coolly.

"Your Grace," he stammered, "this news . . . this alarming news. . . . The English are incensed against us."

"Against you and your master," said Katharine coldly.

"My . . . master . . . your Grace's father."

"There is nothing I have to discuss," said Katharine. "I dissociate myself from the instructions of the King of Spain."

Caroz was astonished, because he sensed the coldness in Katharine's voice when she spoke of her father.

"Do you understand," stormed Caroz, "that there is a possibility of a treaty of friendship between England and France?"

"These are matters for the King and his ministers," said Katharine.

"But our country. . . ."

"Is no longer my country. I count myself an Englishwoman now, and I put myself on the side of the English."

Caroz was shocked. He bowed and took his leave.

As he went from the Queen's apartments he saw Fray Diego who smiled at him insolently.

His recall to Spain shall be immediate, Caroz decided. It is he who has poisoned the Queen's mind against her father.

* * *

The Princess Mary came hurrying into Katharine's apartments, her lovely eyes wild, her hair in disorder.

"Oh Katharine," she cried, "you have heard this news?"

Katharine nodded.

"I!" cried Mary. "To marry with that old man! He is fifty-two and they say he looks seventy. He is old, ugly and mean."

"I wish I could help you," said Katharine, "but I know of nothing I can do."

Mary stood clenching her hands. She was of a deeply passionate nature and had been greatly indulged by her brother. Her youth and beauty aroused his tenderness; and the fact that he was her guardian had always made him feel sentimental towards her, so that she had had her own way in all other matters and was furious that in this, the most important of all, she could not.

"I will not be used in this way. I will not!" she cried.

"Oh Mary," Katharine tried to soothe her, "it happens to us all, you know. We are obliged to marry the person who is chosen for us. We have no choice in the matter. We must needs obey."

"I'll not marry that old lecher," cried Mary.

"You'll be Queen of France."

"Who cares to be Queen of France! Not I . . . if I have to take the King with the crown."

"He will be kind to you. He has heard of your beauty and is very eager for the match."

"Lecher! Lecher! Lecher!" shouted Mary, and Katharine thought how like her brother she was in that moment.

"He will be gentle, perhaps kinder, more gentle than a younger man."

"Do I want gentleness! Do I want an old man drooling over my body!"

"Mary, I pray you be calm. It is the fate of us all."

"Did *you* have to marry a rheumaticky old man?"

"No, but I came to a strange land to marry a boy whom I had never seen."

"Arthur was handsome; he was young. And then you had Henry. Oh you fortunate Katharine!"

"You may be fortunate too. I am sure he will be kind to you, and kindness means so much. You were prepared to marry Charles, yet you did not know him."

"At least he is young." Mary's eyes blazed afresh. "Oh, it is cruel . . . cruel. Why should I, because I am a Princess, not be allowed to marry the man of my choice?"

Katharine knew that she was thinking of Charles Brandon. The whole Court knew of her feelings for that handsome adventurer; none more than Brandon himself who would dearly have liked to match her passion with his own. And now that it seemed he was not going to get Margaret of Savoy, he would doubtless be very happy to take the Princess of England.

Mary's defiance crumbled suddenly; she threw herself onto Katharine's bed and began sobbing wildly.

Wolsey was directing the King's thoughts towards the French alliance. He could see great advantages there. He believed the King was willing enough; Henry had counted on the help of Ferdinand and Maximilian to enable him to win territories in France; he had memories of Dorset's disastrous campaign, and he had begun to see the dangers of tackling the conquest of France alone.

Wolsey was for ever at his ear, explaining without appearing to do so; carefully, skilfully planting those thoughts in the King's mind which he wished him to have.

Contemplating an expedition to France gave Wolsey nightmares. What if they should fail to maintain supplies? What if there should be disaster for the English? There had to be a scapegoat, and that might well be the almoner who had won such praise for his conduct of the previous campaign. No, Wolsey was determined that there should not be an expedition to France this year.

There was something else which made him long for the French alliance.

He had received information from the Vatican to the effect that the Holy Father would be pleased to see an alliance between France and England and trusted his newly created Cardinal would work to that end. It was very necessary to please the Pope. It was important that the Holy Father and his Cardinals in the Vatican should feel they had a good friend in Cardinal Wolsey. It would be remembered when the time for the next conclave arrived.

So each day Henry began to see more clearly the advantages of the suggested alliance; and one of the most important clauses would be the marriage treaty between the Princess Mary and Louis XII.

In vain did Mary storm; Henry was sorry, but England must come before his sister's whims.

He was truly sorry for her and his eyes were glazed with tenderness when she flung her arms about his neck and sought to cajole him.

"I would do what you ask, sister, if I could," he cried, "but it does not rest with me."

"It does. It does," she cried vehemently. "You could refuse this day, and that would be an end to the matter."

"Then there would be no alliance with the French."

"Who cares for alliance with the French?"

"We all must, sweet sister. It is a matter of policy. We have to stand against those two scoundrels. You cannot see how important this is because you are yet a girl, but it is a matter of state. Were it not, willingly would I give you what you ask."

"Henry, think of me—married to that old man!"

"I do, sweetheart, I do. But it must be. It is the duty of us all to marry for the good of our country."

"He is old . . . old . . ."

"He is no worse than Charles. Charles looked to me like an idiot. By God, were I a maiden I'd as lief take Louis as Charles."

"Charles is at least young. Louis is . . . ancient."

"So much the better. You'll be able to twirl him round your pretty fingers. Ah, you'll get your way with the King of France, my sister, as you do with the King of England."

"But do I? When he will not grant me this one little thing?"

"'Tis the one thing I cannot grant my dear sister. Be good, sweeting. Marry the man. He'll not live long."

Mary drew away from him and looked long into his face. He saw the new hope spring up in her eyes.

"Henry," she said slowly, "if I make this marriage, will you grant me one request?"

"That's my good sister," he said. "Have done with your tantrums—for if news of these reached Louis' ears he would not be pleased—and I'll grant whatsoever you request."

Mary took her brother's face between her hands.

"Swear this," she said.

"I swear," he answered.

Then she went on, speaking very slowly and distinctly: "I will marry old Louis; but when he dies, I have Your Grace's promise that I shall marry wheresoever I like for me to do."

Henry laughed.

"You have my promise."

Then she threw her arms about his neck and kissed him heartily on the lips.

Henry was delighted; she could always charm him, for his pride in this pretty sister—all Tudor, as he was fond of saying—was great.

Now the Court noticed that the Princess Mary had become resigned to the French marriage. There were no more displays of temper, no more tears of rage.

She allowed herself to be drawn into the preparations, and her manner was quiet and calculating yet a little aloof, as though she were looking far ahead, well into the future.

The summer was progressing. Henry was as deeply involved with Bessie as ever; he delighted in her, and familiarity did not pall.

He hated all Spaniards, he told himself; and he could not entirely forget that Katharine was one of them. She seemed to grow less attractive and, had it not been for the fact that she was pregnant, he could have come near to hating her at this further revelation of her father's treachery.

It was comforting to see Mary quieter and even showing an interest in the preparations for her wedding.

One day in the early autumn, when he was told that Caroz

wanted to see him, he agreed to give the audience although he disliked the Spanish ambassador and had scarcely spoken to him since he had discovered that he had been betrayed by Ferdinand a second time.

Caroz came into his presence and Henry nodded briefly to him, without warmth.

"Your Grace is indeed kind to receive me. I have sought this interview for many days."

"I have been occupied with state matters which do not concern your master," the King answered coldly.

"It is a great grief to me that we are excluded from Your Grace's favour."

"It is a greater grief to me that I ever trusted your master."

Caroz bowed his head sorrowfully.

"My master seeks to recall the Queen's confessor, Fray Diego Fernandez."

Henry was about to say that this was a matter for the Queen, but he changed his mind. His conscience had been worrying him lately. He was spending a great deal of time in Bessie's company, and after a passionate night with her he often felt uneasy. During one of these uneasy periods he had told himself that Katharine had worked for her father rather than her husband, and this was another reason why she had forfeited the right to his fidelity.

Now he asked himself why he should consult Katharine about the return of her confessor. He did not like the man. He did not like any Spaniards at this time.

Bessie had been particularly enchanting last night and consequently the burden of his guilt this day was heavier.

He stuck out his lower lip petulantly.

"Then let the man be sent back to Spain," he said sullenly.

Caroz bowed low; he was exultant. The Queen could not countermand the King's order; and he had the King's word that Fernandez should be sent back to Spain.

Katharine was distraught. She had sent for her confessor and had been told that he was no longer at Court.

In desperation she summoned Caroz to her presence.

"What does this mean?" she demanded. "Where is Fray Diego?"

"On his way to Spain," replied Caroz, unable to restrain a smirk.

"This is impossible. I was not told of his departure."

"The orders were that he was to leave immediately."

"Whose orders?"

"Those of the King of Spain."

"The King of Spain's orders are invalid here at the Court of England."

"Not, I venture to point out, Your Grace, when they are also the orders of the King of England."

"What do you mean?"

"The King, your husband, ordered that Fray Diego should be sent back to Spain with all speed. He had no wish for him to continue to serve you as confessor."

Katharine hurried to the King's apartment with as much speed as she could, for her body was now becoming cumbersome.

Henry, who was with Compton mixing an ointment, turned with the pestle in his hand to stare at her.

She said curtly to Compton: "I would speak to the King alone."

Compton bowed and retired.

"What is the meaning of this?" demanded Henry.

"I have just heard that my confessor has been dismissed."

"Is that so?" said the King in a deceptively light tone.

"Dismissed," went on Katharine, "without any order from me."

"It is my privilege," Henry told her, and so disturbed was she that she did not see the danger signals, "to decide who shall and who shall not remain at my Court."

"My own confessor. . . ."

"A Spaniard!" Henry almost spat out the word. "May I tell you, Madam, that since I have had dealings with your father I do not trust Spaniards."

"He has been with me many years. . . ."

"All the more reason why he should return to his own country."

Katherine felt the tears in her eyes. Pregnancies were becoming more trying than they had been in the beginning, and her weakness often astonished her; usually she was not one to give way to tears.

"Henry . . ." she began.

"Madam," he interrupted, "do not seek to dictate to me. There have been spies enough at my Court. I would like to rid it of all Spaniards."

She caught her breath with horror.

"You have forgotten that I am . . ." she began.

But he cut in: "I do not forget. I know full well that you have been in league with your father, whispering in my ear, tempting me to this or that project . . . knowing all the while that it was to your father's benefit . . . and not to mine."

"Henry, I swear this to be untrue."

"Swear if you will. But who trusts a Spaniard?"

"You talk to me as though I were a stranger . . . and an enemy."

"You are a Spaniard!" he said.

She reached for the table to steady herself.

Evil rumours had been in the air of late. She had disregarded them as mere gossip: If the Queen does not give the King a child soon, he may decide that she is incapable of bearing children and seek a divorce.

She had thought at the time: How can people be so cruel? They make light of our tribulations with their gossip.

But now she wondered what had set such rumours in motion. When his eyes were narrowed like that he looked so cruel.

She turned away.

"I must go to my apartment," she said. "I feel unwell."

He did not answer her; but stood glowering while she walked slowly and in an ungainly manner from the apartment.

She was waiting now—waiting for the birth of the child which would make all the difference to her future. If this time she could produce a healthy boy, all the King's pleasure in his marriage would return. It was merely this run of bad luck, she told herself, which had turned him from her. So many failures. It really did seem that some evil fate was working against them. No wonder Henry was beginning to doubt whether it was possible for them to have a family; and because he was Henry, he would not say, Is it impossible for *us* to have children . . . but, for her? He would not believe that any failure could possibly come from himself.

She prayed continually: "Let me bear a healthy child. A boy, please, Holy Mother. But if that is asking too much, a girl would please, if only she may be healthy and live . . . just to prove that I can bear a healthy child."

In her apartments the device of the pomegranate mocked her. It hung on embroidered tapestry on the walls; it was engraved on so many of her possessions. The pomegranate which signified fruitfulness and which she had seen so many times in her own home before she had understood the old Arabic meaning.

How ironic that she should have taken it as her device!

She dared not brood on the possibility of failure, so she tried to prove to Henry that she was completely faithful to his cause. When the French ambassadors arrived she received them with outward pleasure and the utmost cordiality; she gave a great deal of time to the sad young Mary, helping her to live through that difficult time, cheering her, recalling her own fears on parting from her mother, assuring her that if she would meekly accept her destiny she would eventually triumph over her fears.

She was invaluable at such a time. Even Henry grudgingly admitted it and, because he knew that she was telling him that she had cut off her allegiance to her own people and was determined to work entirely for his cause, he softened towards her.

With the coming of that July the negotiations for the French marriage were completed and the ceremony by proxy was performed.

Mary, her face pale, her large eyes tragic, submitted meekly enough; and Katharine, who was present at the putting to bed ceremony, was sorry for the girl. Quietly she looked on while

Mary, shivering in her semi-nakedness, was put to bed by her women, and the Duc de Longueville, who was acting as proxy for the King of France, who was put to bed with her, he fully dressed apart from one naked leg with which he touched Mary. The marriage was then declared to be a true marriage, for the touching of French and English body was tantamount to consummation.

In October of that year Mary was taken with great pomp to Dover, there to set sail for France. Katharine and Henry accompanied her, and Katharine was fearful when she saw the sullen look in Mary's eyes.

It was a sad occasion for Katharine—that stay at Dover Castle while they waited for storms to subside, for she could not help but remember her own journey from Spain to England and she understood exactly how Mary was feeling.

How sad was the fate of most Princesses! she thought.

She was eager to comfort her young sister-in-law, and tried to arouse Mary's interest in her clothes and jewels; but Mary remained listless except for those occasions when her anger would burst out against a fate which forced her to marry an old man whom she was determined to despise because there was another whom she loved. The marriage had done nothing at all, Katharine saw, to turn her thoughts from Charles Brandon.

They seemed long, those weeks at Dover. Henry strode through the castle, impatient to have done with the painful parting and return to London, for there could be no real gaiety while the Queen of France went among them, like a mournful ghost of the gay Princess Mary.

Again and again Katharine sought to comfort her. "What rejoicing there will be in Paris," she said.

But Mary merely shrugged her shoulders. "My heart will be in England," she said, "so I shall care nothing for rejoicing in Paris."

"You will . . . in time."

"In time!" cried Mary, and her eyes suddenly blazed wickedly. "Ah," she repeated, "in time."

There were occasions when she was almost feverishly gay;

she would laugh, a little too wildly; she would even sing and dance, and the songs were all of the future. Katharine wondered what was in her mind and was afraid.

Her women doubtless had a trying time. Katharine had noticed some charming girls among the little band who were to accompany Mary to France. Lady Anne and Lady Elisabeth Grey were two very attractive girls and she was sure they were helping in upholding Mary's spirits.

One day when she went to Mary's apartments she saw a very young girl, a child, there among the women.

Katharine called to her and the little girl came and curtsied. She had big, dark eyes and one of the most piquantly charming faces Katharine had ever seen.

"What are you doing here, my little one?" she asked.

"Your Grace," answered the child with the dignity of a much older person, "I am to travel to France in the suite of the Queen. I am one of her maids of honour."

Katharine smiled. "You are somewhat young for the post, it would seem."

"I am past seven years old, Your Grace." The answer was given with hauteur and most surprisingly dignity.

"It would seem young to me. Do you travel with any member of your family?"

"My father is to sail with us, Your Grace."

"Tell me the name of your father, my child."

"It is Sir Thomas Boleyn."

"Ah, I know him well. So you are his daughter . . . Mary, is it?"

"No, Your Grace. Mary is my sister. My name is Anne."

Katharine, amused by the precocity of the lovely little girl, smiled. "Well, Anne Boleyn," she said, "I am sure you will serve your mistress well."

The child swept a deep and somewhat mannered curtsey, and Katharine passed on.

CHAPTER XII

The Open Rift

When Mary had sailed for France the Court returned to Richmond, and with the coming of the winter Katharine felt that she had regained a little of her husband's esteem which she had lost through the treachery of her father.

December was with them and plans for the Christmas festivities were beginning to be made. There were the usual whisperings, the secrets shared by little groups of courtiers, plans, Katharine guessed, for a pageant which would surprise her; there would doubtless be a Robin Hood or a Saracen Knight to startle the company with his prowess and later disclose himself to be the King. No round of gaiety would be complete without that little masquerade.

She felt old and tired, contemplating the excitement going on about her—like a woman among children. How was it possible for her to feel excitement about a pageant when she was so concerned with her own all-important and most pressing problem. Is it true, she asked herself, that I am growing old, far in advance of the King?

It was a cold day and she awakened feeling tired. This was proving a difficult pregnancy and she wondered whether she was less robust than she had been; an alarming thought, because she foresaw many pregnancies ahead of her, and if her health failed, how could she go on attempting to bear children? And if she did not, of what use was she to her King and country? The word Divorce was like a maggot in her brain.

Because she felt too tired to talk she dismissed her women and sat alone. She went to her prie-dieu and there she prayed, remaining on her knees for nearly an hour, begging, pleading that this time she might have a healthy child.

She rose and stood for some time before the embroidered tapestry on the wall, which portrayed her device of the pomegranate.

This time all will be well, she promised herself.

She thought she would take a walk in the gardens, and as she wished to be alone she went down by a rarely frequented spiral stone staircase.

As this part of the Palace was seldom used, it was very quiet here. She felt a curiosity about it and wondered why it had been neglected. She paused on the staircase to open a door, and saw a pleasant enough room. Entering, she found that the windows looked out on a courtyard in which grass grew among the cobbles. There was little sun in this part and she idly supposed that was why it was so rarely used.

She shut the door quietly and went on. Halfway down the staircase was another door and, as she passed this, hearing the sound of voices, she paused and listened. Surely that was Henry's voice.

She must be mistaken, for she had heard that he had gone off with the hunt that day. Impulsively she opened the door, and thus discovered what most members of the Court had known for many months. There could be no mistake. Bessie Blount, Lady Taillebois, was lying on a couch and Henry was with her. There could be no doubt whatever what they were doing: rarely could any have been discovered so completely *in flagrante delicto*. Katharine gave a gasp of horror.

Henry turned his head and looked straight at her, and in that second of time shame, fury, hatred flashed from his eyes.

Katharine waited for no more; she turned, shut the door, and stumbled back the way she had come. As she missed her footing and fell, the cold stone struck into her body, and she felt a sharp pain that was like a protest from the child; but she picked herself up and hurried on.

When she reached her own apartments she shut herself in.

One of her women came to her and asked if she were ill.

"I am merely tired," she said firmly. "I wish to be alone that I may rest."

Henry came into the room; his face was scarlet and his eyes sparkled with anger.

He had been caught by his wife in an extremely compromising situation with another woman, and he was deeply ashamed of the figure he had cut in her eyes. When Henry was ashamed of himself he was angry, and because he had always come to terms with his conscience before he indulged in what might be considered sinful, he was always prepared to defend his virtue. Thus he was doubly angry when he was shamed, and as he could never be angry with himself the flood of that anger must be allowed to flow over someone else.

He stood glowering at her as she lay on her bed.

She did not attempt to rise as she would have done on any other occasion. For one thing she felt too ill and there was a dull nagging pain in her womb which terrified her.

He said: "Well, Madam, what have you to say?"

She was suddenly too tired to placate him, too weary to hide her anger. She was no longer the diplomatic Queen; she was the wronged wife.

"Should I have anything to say? Should not you be the one to explain?"

"Explain! Do you forget I am the King? Why should I be called upon to explain?"

"You are also my husband. What I saw . . . horrified me."

Henry was thinking of what she had seen and he grew hot with indignation—not with himself and Bessie for being thus together, but with Katharine for shaming them.

"Why so?" he asked, battling with the rage which threatened to make him incoherent.

"You ask that! Should I be delighted to see you behaving thus . . . with that woman?"

"Listen to me," said Henry. "I brought you to your present eminence. What were you when I married you? Daughter of the King of Spain. A man who neglected you and used you to trap me. Yet I married you. Against the advice of my ministers

I married you . . . because I pitied you . . . because I thought
you would make me a good wife . . . would give me children.
And what have you given me? Still-born children! One son
who lived for a few days! Madam, I am beginning to wonder
whether you are incapable of bearing children."

"Is it for this reason that you dally thus shamelessly in daylight with the women of your Court?"

"This is but one woman," he said, "and her I love dearly.
She gives me such pleasure, Madam, as is beyond your ken. I
have given you the chance to bear me sons; I have considered
your health; I have not disturbed your nights. And because, in
my consideration for you, I have found another to allay those
desires which methinks are natural to all men, you play the
shrew."

"I see," said Katharine, "that I have been mightily mistaken.
I thought you a virtuous man. I did not know you."

"Find me one more virtuous in this Court! I hear Mass regu-
larly each day . . . and more than once a day. I have sought to
please God and his saints. . . ."

"They must be delighted by such spectacles as I have just
witnessed."

"You blaspheme, Madam."

"You commit adultery—by far the greater sin."

Henry's face was purple with rage.

"You forget your position, Madam."

Katharine rose from her bed and came to stand before him.

"I have never forgotten my position," she said. "I was ready
to show my gratitude. I have spent long hours on my knees
praying for a healthy child. Has it occurred to you that our
failure might in some measure be due to yourself?"

"I understand you not," he said coldly.

"The sensual appetites of men when indulged, so I have
heard, may make them sterile."

Henry was purple with rage. He was so furious that he could
not speak for some seconds, and Katharine went on: "I know
you have blamed me for our inability to get healthy children;
knowing what I now know I am of the opinion that the cause
may well come from you."

"This . . . is monstrous!" cried the King.

She turned away from him, for in that moment the pain of her body was greater than the pain of her mind. Her face was twisted with the effort to keep back her cry of agony.

Henry watched her and, guessing that the shock she had suffered might have brought about a premature birth, he swallowed his anger and going to the door began bellowing for her women.

When they came running, he said: "The Queen is ill. See to her."

Then he strode back to his own apartments; all who saw him scuttled away; even his dogs were aware of his moods and, instead of bounding towards him, they slunk after him keeping a good distance between themselves and that glittering angry figure.

It was over—yet another failure.

It was no consolation to know that the child was male.

"Oh God," moaned Katharine, sick and weak in her bed, "have You deserted me then?"

She was ill for several weeks and when she rose from her bed the Christmas festivities were in full progress.

She joined them and the King was cool to her, but now there was no longer anger between them. His attitude implied that she must accept with a good grace whatever she found in him; and since she was his Queen he would be at her side on public occasions.

But change had come to the Court. The Queen had aged visibly. Her body was no longer that of a young woman; it bore the marks of several pregnancies and had lost its shapeliness; her hair, still long and plentiful, was without that bright colour which had been so attractive and had done so much to lighten the somewhat heavy nature of her face; now that it was dull mouse-colour she looked much darker than before, and as her skin had become sallow she was thought of as a dark woman.

The King had changed too. He would never be so easily duped by his political enemies in future. He was still the golden, handsome King, but he was no longer a boy; he was a young man in the very prime of life. A certain bloom of innocence had been rubbed off. Now he led Bessie Blount in the dance and caressed her openly before his courtiers, no longer attempting to conceal the fact that he spent his nights with her. Often they would ride together to Jericho with a little company of friends and stay there, while Katharine remained behind at Richmond, Westminster or Greenwich.

Bessie was accepted as the chief mistress, and although there were others—little lights-o'-love who amused him for a while—none took Bessie's place.

The courtiers smiled. "It is natural," they said. "And since the Queen is so dull and has lost what beauty she had, and as she is fast becoming an old woman, who can blame young Henry?"

It was hurtful to Katharine, but she hid her feelings; yet she wondered whether she would be able to get a child now.

So much had happened in a year.

Now she spent most of her time sewing with her women, hearing Mass, praying in her own apartments, making pilgrimages to such places as the shrine at Walsingham.

Often she thought of those days when Henry had seemed contented with his wife. But it was not only the husband whom she had lost. She often remembered how, at one time when he had received foreign despatches, he brought them to her and they read them together. He never did this now.

There were two others who had supplanted her.

There was Cardinal Wolsey in state affairs, and in his bed there was Bessie Blount.

CHAPTER XIII

A Venetian Embassy and a Cardinal's Hat

It was New Year's night and there must be entertainment at the Court to celebrate such an occasion; so the great hall of Westminster had been decorated with cloth of gold, and at night, by torchlight, it was a beautiful sight indeed.

The people had crowded in to watch the royal sport; and on such an occasion Henry liked to show his people that he lived in the splendour expected of a King.

Katharine was seated on a dais at one end of the great hall as she had sat so often before. About her were her ladies, and she was glad to have with her her dear Maria de Salinas who, with her husband, was paying a visit to the Court. Maria had heard of the King's open liaison with Elizabeth Blount and had condoled with Katharine about this. It was the way of Kings, she said, and not to be taken seriously. Why, even the people accepted the fact that the King must have his mistress.

Katharine was considerably comforted by Maria and, perhaps because of that, looked more like her old self on that night. She was magnificently dressed in rich blue velvet, and diamonds, sapphires and rubies glittered about her person.

While she sat there a messenger came to her in the costume of Savoy and begged to be allowed to speak to her. Katharine recognized one of the gentlemen of the Court and knew at once that this was part of the entertainment.

"Pray speak on," she said.

There was silence in the hall, and the Savoyard said in loud ringing tones but using a foreign accent: "Your Grace of England, there are without a band of dancers from Savoy. They have travelled far that they may enchant you with their dancing on this first night of the New Year. Have they your permission to enter and dance for the pleasure of the Court?"

"I beg you bring them in at once. They must perform for us."

Katharine sat back on her throne while the party were brought in. There at the head of them were two tall figures—whom she knew well. One was Henry, the other Brandon. They were masked, but beneath the mask it was possible to see the King's golden hair.

"Welcome, Gentlemen," said Katharine.

They bowed low; and as they did so Katharine's eyes began to sparkle, for this was as it had been in the old days, and it might mean that Henry was going to forget their differences and treat her once more as his wife.

When Henry spoke—and who could not recognize his voice—he said: "Most beautiful Queen of this fair land, we are strolling dancers from the land of Savoy. We would fain dance before you so that Your Grace may judge whether there are not as good dancers from Savoy as live in this fair land."

Katharine threw herself into the game. "You may try," she said, "but I must warn you, we have most excellent dancers in this land, and they are led by the King himself whom all agree none has ever equalled. If you would care to try your skill against us, do so. But I dare swear you will be dismayed when you see the King dance."

"We are happy, Your Grace, to put our skill to the test, and you shall be our judge."

Katharine signed to the musicians then and by the light of the torches the little party took its place before her. There were four men and four women, all in blue velvet and cloth of silver and their costumes were fashioned after the manner of Savoy.

The dancing began. It was a beautiful ballet outstanding on account of the high leaping of the leader.

There were murmurs in the crowd. "Can it be? Does he in truth out-jump the King? Where is his Grace? He should see the unusual skill of these men and in particular the leader."

Sitting back Katharine marvelled at the ability of all to enter so whole-heartedly into the game and to show such seeming innocence of the masquerade which all must have seen so many times before.

At length the dancing ceased and the dancers were all on their knees before the Queen's throne.

"I pray you," said Katharine, "unmask, that we may see your faces."

The dancers rose to their feet and Katharine kept her eyes on the leader while he, with a dramatic gesture, drew off his mask.

There was a gasp throughout the Court and then loud bursts of applause. Henry bowed to the Queen and turned about so that none should be in doubt as to his identity.

He has not grown up at all, thought Katharine; and she felt a little happier, for it was more pleasant to see the naïve boy taking the place of the brutal man.

He then stepped to the Queen's side and taking her hand kissed it, which drew more lusty cheers from the people.

Holy Mother of God, murmured Katharine to herself, can we really go back to the beginning? Can it really be as though our troubles never happened?

She was more than ready to meet him halfway.

She said so clearly that all might hear: "So it was Your Grace. I could not believe there was one to rival you, and yet it seemed that Savoyard could do so. I thank Your Grace for my good pastance."

Then boldly she rose and putting her hands to his face drew him down to her and kissed him.

For a few seconds she held her breath with apprehension, but he had returned her kiss, and the people cheered.

"Good Kate," he whispered, "'tis all done in thy honour."

It seemed to the watchers then that something of the Queen's youth returned, as Henry sat beside her and they talked amicably.

That night they slept together. The need to get a child was as urgent as ever. It was a return to the old pattern; and there was, after all, to be another chance.

* * *

It was shortly after the New Year revels when a messenger from France came to Westminster with an urgent despatch for the King.

Henry read the news and let out an exclamation of dismay. He had the messenger taken to the kitchens to be refreshed and sent at once for Wolsey.

"News!" he cried. "News from France. Louis is dead. He died on New Year's day."

Wolsey took the news calmly; he had not expected Louis to live long; a new bride, such as Mary, would not act as an elixir to such as he was, for Louis was Gallic and as such would ape the gallant no matter at what cost.

Wolsey smiled secretly thinking of the old man trying to play lover to that young and passionate girl.

"This means, Your Grace, that Francis of Angoulême will now be King of France unless. . . ."

"Exactly," said the King, "unless my sister is with child by the King; then Francis' long nose will be a little out of joint. I'll warrant the sly fellow is beside himself with anxiety. Imagine! For years he and his mother and doting sister have watched old Louis . . . waiting for him to die. Then the old man marries my sister. 'Is she with child?' 'Is she not with child?' This is a fine joke."

"Let us hope, Your Grace, that the Queen of France *has* conceived. With one sister Queen of France and another Queen of Scotland, Your Grace would be most fortunately placed."

"'Tis so. 'Tis so."

Henry smiled at Wolsey. He appreciated this servant, being fully aware that Wolsey possessed something which he himself lacked. He called it seriousness. He would come to it in time; but at this stage he did not want to devote all his energies to state affairs. He had discovered that he was not as completely devoted to war as he had imagined he would be. When he entered into a game he liked to know what the outcome would be. He wanted the shouts of wonder at his prowess. These did not always come in war. Even Ferdinand and Maximilian—those great warriors, who, all would admit, had had their share of victories—frequently suffered defeat and humiliation. Henry had not been prepared to go to war alone with France, and the reason was that he feared defeat.

He was indeed growing up and it was unfortunate for his peace of mine that, in spite of his vanity and frequent displays of naïvety, he was also intelligent. And this intelligence kept asserting itself—even as his conscience did—to disturb his peace.

Therefore he was grateful to Wolsey. That man had genius, and while he could place state affairs in those capable hands he could be at peace. He was ready to show his appreciation to Wolsey who must be well on the way to becoming one of the richest men in England—next to himself. Henry rejoiced in Wolsey's advancement; he was ready to abet it. His face soft-ened at the sight of the man; he would put his arm about his shoulders as they walked in the gardens, so that all might realize the esteem in which he held his new Cardinal.

So now he said: "Well, Thomas, what's to be done?"

"There is nothing we can do but wait, Sire. All depends on whether the Queen of France carries the heir."

Henry nodded. "My poor sister! There she is, all alone in that country. And she will have to endure the period of mourning as a widow, shut into her darkened apartments where she will be most unhappy. I must send my envoy at once to France to convey my condolences ... to my sister, to Francis ..."

"And we will not add, Sire," said Wolsey with a smile, "that here we are praying that the Queen is with child."

The King laughed aloud and slapped Wolsey's shoulder.

"Nay, Thomas, we'll not mention the matter. I had thought that Suffolk might be the envoy on this occasion."

Wolsey was silent for a moment, and Henry's expressive mouth tightened. Wolsey was grateful for that mobile counte-nance which so often gave a hint of the King's desires before Henry uttered them.

Suffolk! pondered Wolsey. The Queen of France would be an excellent pawn in skilful hands. Were they going to throw her to Suffolk merely because her wanton body lusted after that man?

He followed Henry's thoughts. This was his sister Mary, his favourite sister who was gay and pretty; knowing how to flatter her brother she fostered his sentimentality towards her, and had lured him into a promise. "If I marry the King of France, when he is dead I shall marry whom I please." And Henry knew who pleased her.

He wanted to comfort her now, to say: Look, little sister, you are a widow in a foreign land; so I am sending you a gift to cheer you. And the gift was Suffolk.

Henry was telling himself that Brandon was a worthy envoy; and as he was ardently courting the Duchess of Savoy, in these circumstances sending him would merely be a gesture; no harm could come of it. Mary would have enough sense to know that there must be no dalliance with Suffolk while she might be carrying the heir of France within her.

In any case Henry had made up his mind.

So must it be, thought Wolsey, who was not going to commit the folly of going against the King in this matter and mayhap through it lose control of other and more important affairs.

"If Your Grace is satisfied with Suffolk as your envoy to the Court of France, then so I am," he said.

The Cardinal read the letter from Suffolk. He was gratified because the Duke had written to him. It indicated that this man understood that the one most likely to influence the King was Thomas Wolsey.

His Cardinal's hat had not yet arrived, but that was coming. He was growing more and more certain that one day he would gain the Papal crown; in the meantime he was content to govern England.

Suffolk had written that he and Mary had married.

Wolsey laughed aloud at the folly of the man. Then he thought of his own folly with Mistress Wynter, and his laughter faded a little.

But to marry with the Princess so soon after the death of her husband! Moreover, was Brandon in a position to marry? There were some who maintained that he was already married;

and he had certainly been involved in matrimonial tangles with three other women. The first was Elizabeth Grey, daughter of the Viscount of Lisle, who had been made his ward and whom he had contracted to marry. This lady had refused to marry him and the patent was cancelled. Later he had contracted to marry a certain Ann Brown, but before the marriage was celebrated he obtained a dispensation and married a widow named Margaret Mortymer, who was a relative of his. When he was weary of this woman he acquired a declaration of invalidity from the Church on the grounds of consanguinity, and it was said that later he went through a form of marriage with Ann Brown by whom he had had a daughter. Certainly his past did not bear too close a scrutiny and it was questionable whether he was in a position to marry again. Yet such was his fascination that not only had he charmed Mary but to some extent Henry as well.

Wolsey read the letter:

"The Queen would never let me be in rest until I had granted her to be married; and so now, to be plain with you, I have married her heartily, and have lain with her in so much I fear me lest she be with child. I am like to be undone if the matter should come to the knowledge of the King, my master."

He was asking Wolsey to break the news gently and to convey loving messages from Mary to Henry in the hope that he might be softened towards them and allow them to return home, which they longed to do.

Wolsey considered the matter. The King had provoked this situation. He had known how headstrong his sister was, and he had promised her that if she married Louis she should choose her next husband. Henry, Wolsey was sure, would feign anger at the news, but he would not be greatly disturbed. He loved his sister dearly and missed her, so would be glad to have her home. He missed Suffolk too, for that gay adventurer was one of the most amusing of his friends.

Therefore it was without much trepidation that Wolsey sought an audience and showed Henry the letter which he had received from Suffolk.

"By God's Holy mother!" ejaculated Henry. "So they are married—and she, like as not, with child. What if . . ."

"We should know, Your Grace, if the King of France was its father. I fear that is not so. Poor Louis, he could not get his wife with child."

For a moment there was a deep silence, and to Wolsey's consternation he saw the healthy flush in the King's cheeks darken.

So, thought Wolsey, he is already beginning to wonder whether *he* is capable of begetting children. Is it so? One would have thought Elizabeth Blount might have shown some signs by now; and the Court was becoming so accustomed to Katharine's failures that they expected her miscarriages before they occurred.

Wolsey said quickly: "The King of France was too old to beget children."

The King breathed more easily. The danger was past, and Wolsey went on: "What are Your Grace's wishes in this matter?"

"I am deeply shocked," said Henry. "Punishment there must be. I am displeased with them . . . both."

But indeed he was not. He was already wishing they were at the Court. He indulged his pleasures so much that he put their gratification before matters of state. While Wolsey thought of the grand marriages which might have been arranged for Mary, Henry was thinking: Mary will be happy; and I shall be happy to have my sister with me again.

But as ever he was ready to listen to Wolsey's advice; and, when later Suffolk wrote to Henry begging to be allowed to come home and offering his body, knowing that he might be "put to death, imprisoned, or destroyed" for this great sin he had committed, Henry left it to Wolsey to suggest on what terms the erring couple might be allowed to return.

"Let them return to Your Grace the gift you made the Princess Mary of plate and jewels," suggested Wolsey; "let Suffolk undertake to pay by yearly instalments the expenses you incurred by the French marriage. Then it would seem that they had been adequately punished. All would know that none dares flout your Grace's wishes with impunity, and at the same time these two, for whom we all have great affection, could—after a short period—return to Court."

Henry was delighted with the solution.

Once again he was realizing how much he could rely upon his dear friend Wolsey.

That young gay amorist, Francis of Angoulême, had leaped happily into the position which he and his family had coveted for himself for so long.

With what great joy he discovered that Mary Tudor was not with child; and, although he himself had cast lascivious eyes on this attractive English girl, the Suffolk marriage seemed a happy enough conclusion to that affair.

He was ambitious and energetic, and in the first weeks of his accession he was turning his eyes towards Italy.

It was during March of that year that a Venetian embassy arrived in England with the blessing of Francis.

The position of the Venetians in Europe was dictated by their trade. They were first and foremost traders and asked only to be allowed to continue to sell those goods for which they were famous. Since Maximilian had captured Verona, he had proved a serious handicap to Venetian trade, and the people of Venice believed that an alliance with France would enable them to regain Verona; and as France was aware that her power in Lombardy depended on Venetian friendship there was a *rapprochement* between the two.

It seemed important to Venice that England should strengthen her alliance with France, which should have been cemented by the marriage between Louis XII and the Princess Mary; but with Louis dead and his widow already the wife of English Brandon it seemed necessary to send an embassy to England.

So on a sparkling March day the Venetian embassy arrived, having been entertained most lavishly on the way by the new King of France.

Henry was on his mettle. He believed that Francis would have made a great effort to impress the Venetians with his grandeur and elegance, and was determined to outdo the King of France whom he had always believed to be his especial rival ever since he had heard that Marguerite of Angoulême—who had once been suggested as a bride for Henry—had declared her brother to be the handsomest, wittiest and most charming man in the world and one whom she would always love beyond any other.

So he was prepared. He was a sight so dazzling on that morning that even those who were accustomed to his splendour were astonished.

The Venetians had sailed up the Thames to Richmond in a barge which was gaily decorated with cloth of gold and silver. Before they entered the King's presence they were given bread and wine to sustain them, and then they were taken to the King's chapel to hear Mass.

When this was over they were led into the presence of the King. The Palace had been decorated to receive them, and gold and silver cloth and tapestries had been hung in each apartment. In these rooms three hundred halberdiers, wearing silver breast plates, stood at attention, in order to impress the newcomers with the might of England. They were astonished because the halberdiers, who were chosen for their height, towered above the little Venetians, their fresh faces glowing in striking contrast to the swarthy ones of the men of Venice.

Then to the King's chamber where Henry waited to receive them. He was standing when they entered, leaning against his throne. He wanted them to receive an immediate impression of his great height, which they could not do if he sat. Henry was indeed an impressive figure; his purple velvet mantle was lined with white satin, and fell behind him in a train four yards long; this mantle was fastened across his massive chest by a thick chain made entirely of gold; his doublet was of satin, crimson and white in colour; and on his head was a cap of red velvet decorated with a white feather. About his neck was a gold collar with St. George picked out in fine diamonds; and below that another collar from which hung a round diamond the size of a big walnut; and from this diamond hung a large flawless pearl.

The Venetians blinked. Francis had been elegantly splendid, but Henry was more colourfully so.

Henry was delighted with the impression he so obviously created; the blue eyes, under the red hair which was combed straight about his head, sparkled; he held out a hand, the fingers of which seemed entirely covered by dazzling gems.

Henry welcomed the newcomers warmly, telling them how happy he was to have them at his Court. They would be in need of refreshment, so he had a banquet prepared for them, and when they had eaten they should see the joust which Henry believed had been perfected by his countrymen.

The Venetians, overwhelmed by the friendliness and the hospitality of the King, were then graciously received by members of the King's Council at the head of whom was the new Cardinal Wolsey whom they well knew to be the most important man in the realm.

They met the Queen—herself gorgeously attired and glittering with jewels; but they had heard rumours of the King's feelings towards his wife and they did not believe her to have any real influence with him now.

Henry led the way to the banquet where he surrounded himself by the leaders of the embassy and delightedly watched their incredulity at the dishes produced by his cooks and the ability of the English to consume large quantities of food.

He had no intention of talking of state matters; that would come later with Wolsey; but he was eager to know whether the newcomers were comparing him with Francis in their minds.

He was soon asking questions about his great rival.

"You have recently left the King of France; tell me, is he as tall as I am?"

"There can be very little difference in the height of the King of France and the King of England," was the answer. "Your Grace is a big man; and so is Francis."

"Is he a fat man, this young King of France?"

"No, Your Grace. He could not be called a fat man. Far from it. He is lean and lithe."

"Lean and lithe." Henry caressed his own plump thigh.

"What are his legs like?" demanded Henry.

The Venetians were puzzled; they looked at each other. What sort of legs had the King of France? To be truthful they had not taken particular note of his legs; but they recalled that they must be spare because of the leanness of the King's body.

"Spare legs, eh!" cried Henry. "Look at mine." He held up his legs to display the fine calf, well shaped, firm, the leg of an athletic man. "Has he a leg like that, eh?"

The Venetians were certain that the King of France had not a leg like that.

Henry laughed, well pleased. Then he threw open his doublet. "Look at this thigh," he said. "'Tis every bit as firm and well shaped as my leg. Has the King of France a thigh like that?"

When the Venetians assured Henry that the thigh of the King of France could not be compared with the thigh of the King of England, he was delighted and felt full of affection towards them and Francis.

"Methinks," he said, "I am very fond of this King of France."

After the banquet Henry retired to prepare himself for the joust; and later this was held in the Palace courtyard.

Henry excelled even his previous exploits on that day, shivering many a lance; which was as it should be; and one by one his opponents went down before him.

He was extremely happy.

When he joined the Venetians to be congratulated he said: "I should like to joust with the King of France as my opponent."

But even as he spoke there was a shadow on his face. He was alarmed by this King on the other side of the water; he had heard so many tales of him, of his bravery, his wit and his lechery. He had scarcely been on the throne a week when he was talking of leading his armies to victory; and Henry had discovered that he himself had no great desire to place himself at the head of his armies.

What if he were to joust with Francis and Francis should win? Did Compton, Kingston and the rest go down before their King because they knew it was wise to do so?

"So," he growled, "the King of France thinks to make war

on Italy. He will cross the Alps. Will his people love him; think you, since he plunges them into a war at the very beginning of his reign?"

Then he was angry because he had longed to bring conquests to his people; and this he had failed to do. He burst out: "He is afraid of me. Why, were I to invade his kingdom he would not be able to cross the Alps into Italy, would he? So you see, all depends on me. If I invade France, Francis cannot make war on Italy. If I do not, he can. You see, my friends, in these hands I hold the future of France."

The thought pleased him, and he was once more in good spirits.

Now to forget war and plan new entertainments to impress the visitors.

That May was a happy month. Katharine rejoiced in the coming of spring which she had always loved in England. The dark winter was over; there were buds on the trees and wild parsley and stitchwort shone white in the hedges mingling with the blue of speedwell and ground ivy.

The season of renewal, she thought; and this year she had been happier than she had for some time, for it seemed to her that her relationship with Henry had been renewed and it was like the return of spring. She too had become wiser.

She had learned that she must accept her husband for the lusty young man he was, five years her junior; she must turn a blind eye on those flirtations which took place without too much secrecy; she must accept Elizabeth Blount as her maid of honour and her husband's chief mistress, and not care that he shared the bed of one because of his great desire to do so and of the other in order to serve the state and produce an heir.

She was full of hope that May. He visited her often; he was kind to her; she rarely saw an outburst of anger. She had learned how to avoid them.

This then was May Day, and Henry was happy because the occasion called for one of those ceremonial pageants in which he delighted.

He came to the Queen's apartment early and he was already

clad in green velvet—doublet, hose and shoes; and even his cap, which was sporting a jaunty feather, was of the same green.

"A merry good day to Your Grace," he called blithely. "I come to see if you will venture a-maying with me this morn."

"There is none with whom I would wish to go a-maying but Your Grace."

"Then Kate, your wish is granted. We leave at once. Come."

She was dressed in green velvet to match the King's, and because she was happy she had regained some of that youthful charm which had attracted him in the early days of their marriage.

So from the Palace of Greenwich they rode out to Shooter's Hill surrounded by members of the Venetian embassy and nobles of the Court, all gaily dressed to share in the maying.

When they reached the hill a party of men dressed as outlaws, led by one who was clearly meant to be Robin Hood, galloped up to them.

"Ho!" cried Henry. "What means this, and who are you who dare molest the King and Queen of England?"

Robin Hood swept off his hat; and Katharine recognized him through the mask as one of Henry's courtiers.

"Molest His Grace the King! That we would never do. The outlaws of the Forest respect the King even as do the gentlemen of the Court. Would Your Grace step into the good green wood and learn how the outlaws live?"

Henry turned to Katharine.

"Would Your Grace venture into the forest with so many outlaws?"

"My lord," answered Katharine, "where Your Grace ventured there would I fearlessly go."

Henry was delighted with her answer and Katharine thought: I begin to play his games as well as he does himself.

So into the forest they rode, and there they were taken to a sylvan bower made of hawthorn boughs, spring flowers and moss, where a breakfast of venison and wine was laid out.

"All for the pleasure of Your Graces," said Robin Hood.

The King expressed his delight and watched Katharine

closely to see if she appreciated this surprise. She did not disappoint him.

They sat close like lovers and the King took her hand and kissed it.

He was happy; he knew that his sister Mary and her husband were on their way to England, and that pleased him. He was going to enjoy being very displeased with them and then forgiving them; and he was going to be very happy to have them near him once more.

The sun shone brilliantly, and after the feast when they left the wood, several beautiful girls in a vehicle which was decorated with flowers and drawn by five horses were waiting for them. The girls represented Spring and they sang sweetly the praise of the sweetest season of all, not forgetting to add a few paeans of praise to their goodly King and Queen.

And so the May Day procession rode back to Greenwich.

That was a happy day. The King was like a young lover again.

Within the next few days Katharine conceived once more; and this time she was determined that her child should live.

That summer was a happy one. The knowledge that she was once more pregnant delighted Katharine and the King.

"Why, this time, sweetheart," said Henry, "our hopes shall not be disappointed. You have a goodly boy within you and he'll be the first of many."

Katharine allowed herself to believe this. She would not think of possible bad luck. This was her year.

In September there came news of Francis's victory. The King of France was hailed already as one of the greatest soldiers in history. Young, intrepid, he set out to perform the impossible and prove it possible.

Contrary to Henry's assertion that it depended on him whether or not France went into Italy, Francis—indifferent as to whether or not Henry made an attempt to invade France—had crossed the Alps with twenty thousand men, going from Barcelonnette to Salazzo, crossing passes which were no more than narrow tracks, accoutred as he was for war. That was not all. He had fought and won the resounding victory of Marignano.

Henry's anger when this news was brought to him was too great to hide.

He looked, said those who watched him at the time, as though he were about to burst into tears.

"He will have to face Maximilian," snapped out Henry.

"Nay, Your Grace. Maximilian now seeks friendship with my master," the French envoy answered.

"I assure you he is not seeking that friendship," snapped Henry.

The envoy lifted his shoulders, smiled and remained silent.

"How many of France's enemies have fallen in battle?" demanded Henry.

"Sire, it is some twenty thousand."

"You lie. I hear from sources which I trust that it was but ten thousand."

Henry dismissed the envoy and sulked for several hours.

News of Francis's success with the Pope was brought to him. Leo hailed the young conqueror and when Francis had attempted to kiss his toe had lifted him in his arms and embraced him.

Leo, it was said, had promised to support Francis, and when Maximilian died—and there must then be an election to decide who should be the next Emperor—he promised to give Francis his support.

It was intolerable.

"Ha," cried Henry. "They will learn that wise men do not trust Frenchmen."

But even these events worked favourably for Katharine, for Ferdinand, knowing that the alliance between France and England was weakening, wrote to Henry in a most friendly fashion. He guessed how that young bantam, Henry, would be feeling and was determined to exploit the situation to the full.

Ferdinand did not like to see lack of good faith in families, he wrote. He thought fondly of his dear son and daughter. And to prove this he did an extraordinary thing; he sent Henry a collar studded with jewels, two horses caprisoned in the richest manner, and a jewelled sword.

Ferdinand, it was said, was either genuinely seeking Henry's friendship this time or in his dotage to send such gifts.

But it was very pleasant for Katharine, nursing the child in her womb, basking in the tenderness of her husband, enjoying the atmosphere of tolerance which had grown up about them—all this and reunion with her own country!

All will be well, thought Katharine. I am happy because I have learned to take life comfortably as it comes along; I no longer fight, I accept. Perhaps that is the lesson of life.

She did not greatly care. She busied herself with the preparations for her confinement.

She had never felt so calm and confident.

That September the Cardinal's hat arrived from Rome.

This, Wolsey assured himself, was the greatest moment of his life so far; but he was convinced that it was nothing compared with what was to come.

He determined that the country and the Court should be aware of his rising greatness; they should not be allowed to think that the arrival of a Cardinal's hat was an everyday affair.

He was a little angry with the Pope for sending an ordinary messenger, and he immediately sent word that he was to be detained as soon after disembarking as possible.

He announced to the City that a great procession was about to take place, and the people, who liked nothing so much as the pageantry provided by the Court and were only content with their colourless lives because of it, turned out in their thousands.

Wolsey knew that Mistress Wynter and his children would be watching; and the thought added to his pleasure.

The Pope's messenger was persuaded to discard his simple raiment in exchange for one of fine silk; this he was happy to do, for the clothes were his reward for taking part in the ceremony.

Then he rode towards London, and was met at Blackheath by a great and vividly coloured procession made up of the members of the Cardinal's household. There they were, his higher servants and his lower servants, all aping their master, all giving themselves airs and strutting in a manner which implied: "We are the servants of the great Cardinal and therefore far above the servants of every nobleman in the land. Only the King's servants are our equals, and we wish the world to know it."

So through the City the hat was borne so that all might see it and marvel at it.

"It is being taken to the great Cardinal," said the citizens, "who is not only beloved by the people but by the Pope."

In his apartments at the Palace of Westminster Wolsey waited to receive the hat.

Taking it reverently in his hands he placed it in state upon a table on which tapers glowed.

He then declared that this was in honour of England and he would have all Englishmen under the King pay homage to the hat. None should consider himself too important to come forward and pay his homage in deep obeisance.

There was a murmuring among the Dukes and Earls of the realm; but Wolsey was creeping higher and higher in the King's favour, for Henry believed that he could not do without him if he were to pursue his life of pleasure. It gave him great content, when he hunted through the day, to think of friend Thomas grappling with state affairs. He believed in this man, who had come to his present position from humble beginnings. He had proved his genius.

Therefore Wolsey insisted that all those disgruntled noblemen—chief among whom was the Duke of Buckingham—should pay homage to his hat; and one by one they succumbed; so it was that Wolsey acquired at that time not only a Cardinal's hat but the hatred and envy of almost every ambitious man in the land.

What did he care! If Katharine believed this was her year, Thomas Wolsey knew it was his.

Before the year was out he could count his gains. Cardinal Wolsey, papal legate, Archbishop of York and Lord Chancellor of England, Prime Minister of State. Under the King he was the richest man in England, and many believed that his wealth might even be greater than Henry's. In his hands was the disposal of all ecclesiastical benefices; he held priories and bishoprics, among which were the rich ones of York and Durham, Bath and Hereford; he also held the Abbeys of St. Albans and Lincoln.

He had come as far as he could in this country; but he did not believe that was the end. His eyes were firmly fixed on Rome.

CHAPTER XIV

The Death of Ferdinand

Ferdinand was often thinking of his daughter in England. Indeed lately he had begun to ponder on the past, a habit he had never indulged in before. This may have been due to the fact that his health was rapidly declining. His limbs were swollen with dropsy, and, although he longed to rest them, he found it difficult to breathe within closed walls because of the distressing condition of his heart.

There were times when he had to battle for his breath, and then would come these sessions of reminiscence. His conscience did not trouble him. He had been a fighter all his life and he knew that the only way he could have preserved what he had, was to have fought and schemed for it.

He had heard an alarming rumour that Henry of England believed his wife to be incapable of bearing healthy children because not one of them so far had lived. Ferdinand knew the significance behind such rumours.

But Catalina is strong, he told himself. She is her mother's daughter. She will know how to hold her place.

It was not for him to worry about his daughter; his great concern was to keep the breath in his body.

There was one place where he felt more comfortable, and that was out of doors. The closeness of cities was intolerable to him, for the air seemed to choke him. He would not admit that he was old; he dared not admit it. If he did he would have young Charles closing in on him, eager to snatch the crown.

He could feel angry about young Charles. The boy did not know Spain, and did not even speak Spanish; he was Fleming from the top of his flaxen head to the toes of those—if he could believe reports—ungainly feet. He lacked the dignity of the Spaniard.

"If I could only put his brother Ferdinand in his place, how willingly would I do so." Ferdinand thought lovingly of his grandson who bore the same name as himself, and who had been as the son he had longed for. He had had the boy educated in the manner of a Spanish grandee, he himself supervising that education; he loved young Ferdinand.

His eyes glinted. Why should he not give his possessions to Ferdinand?

He laughed to picture the disapproving face of Ximenes who would remind him of his duty and that Charles was the heir, the elder of mad Juana's sons. Ximenes would rigidly adhere to his duty. Or would he? He had a great affection for young Ferdinand also.

But I have many years left to me, he assured himself, refusing to think of death. It was true he was nearly sixty-four years old—a good age—but his father had been long-lived and, but for this dropsy and the accursed difficulty in breathing, he would not feel his age. He had a young wife, and he still endeavoured to persuade her that he was young, yet he was beginning to wonder if the continual use of aphrodisiacs did not aggravate his condition.

As he sat brooding thus he was joined by the Duke of Alva who looked at him keenly and said: "Your Highness yearns for the fresh air of the country. Come to my place near Placencia. There are stags in plenty and good hunting."

Ferdinand felt young at the thought of the hunt.

"Let us leave this very day," he said.

When they came into the country he took deep breaths of the December air. Ah, he thought, this suits me well. I am a young man again in the country. He looked at Germaine who rode beside him. She was so fresh and youthful that it did him good to see her; yet his thoughts strayed momentarily to his wife Isabella who had been a year older than he was, and he felt a sudden desire to be back in those old days when he and Isabella had fought for a kingdom, and at times for supremacy over each other.

As usual the fresh air was beneficial and he found that if the day's hunting was not too long, he could enjoy it. Alva, concerned for his health, made sure that the hunt finished when the King showed signs of fatigue, and Ferdinand began to feel better.

In January he decided that he should travel on to Andalusia, for he was never one to neglect state duties for pleasure.

Perhaps the hunt had been too strenuous, perhaps the journey was too arduous, but Ferdinand was finding it so difficult to breathe that by the time his party reached the little village of Madrigalejo not far from Truxillo, he could not go on.

There was great consternation among his followers as there was no place worthy to provide a lodging for the King. Yet stop they must, and certain friars in the village came forward and said they had a humble house which they would place at the King's disposal.

The house was small indeed; rarely in his adventurous life had Ferdinand rested in such a place; but he knew that he could not go on, so he gasped out his gratitude to the friars, and allowed himself to be helped to a rough bed.

He looked round the small room and grimaced. Was this the place where the most ambitious man in Europe was to spend his last days on Earth?

Almost immediately he laughed at himself. His last days! He had never been easily defeated and he would not be now. After a little rest he would be ready to go on with his journey; he had learned one lesson; he would take more rest; he would give up his rejuvenating potions and live more as a man of his years must expect to live. If he curtailed his physical exercise he could direct state affairs from a couch. He thanked God that he was in possession of his mental powers.

But as he lay in that humble dwelling news was brought from the village of Velilla in Aragon. In this village was a bell which was said to be miraculous; when any major disaster was about to befall Aragon the bell tolled. Certain bold men had sought to stop the bell's tolling only to be dashed to death. The bell, it was said, rang and stopped of its own volition, when the warning had been given.

Now, said rumour, the bell of Velilla was tolling for the imminent death of great Ferdinand of Aragon.

So stunned by this were those about him that Ferdinand asked what ailed them; and one, unable to withstand the insistent interrogation, told Ferdinand that the bell of Velilla had given a warning of imminent disaster.

Ferdinand was horrified because until this moment he had not believed death could possibly come to him. To other men, yes; but in his youth he had seen himself as an immortal; such self-made legends died slowly.

But the bell was tolling . . . tolling him out of life.

He said: "I must make my will."

He thanked God . . . and Isabella . . . in that moment for Ximenes, because thinking of the tolling of the Velilla bell, his great anxiety was not for himself but for the good of his country. Ximenes he could trust. There was a man who was above reproach, above ambition, who would never give honours to his friends and family unless he honestly believed they deserved them. He remembered even now all he owed to Isabella, and he would serve Isabella's family with all his powerful ability.

Then Cardinal Ximenes, Archbishop of Toledo, should be the Regent of Spain, until such time as his grandson was ready to rule it.

Ximenes would support Charles, he knew. Ferdinand grimaced. Oh, that I were not on my death-bed! Oh, that I might fight for a kingdom and bestow it on my grandson Ferdinand!

But this was a matter outside the control of a dying man. There was no question of the succession of Castile; as for the succession of Aragon and Naples they must fall to Juana— mad Juana, a prisoner in Tordesillas—and to her heirs. The Regency of Castile should go to Ximenes and that of Aragon to his dear son the Archbishop of Saragossa.

Ferdinand could smile wryly, and it seemed to him then that his first wife Isabella was at his bedside and that he snapped his fingers at her. "Yes, Isabella, my bastard son, my dear one on whom I bestowed the Archbishopric of Saragossa when he was six years old. How shocked you were, my prim Isabella, when you discovered his existence! But see, he is a good and noble boy, of sound good sense and beloved by the people. The Aragonese love my illegitimate son more than you did, Isabella."

He would not forget his grandson Ferdinand. He should have an annual income of fifty thousand ducats and a share in Naples. As for Germaine, she must be provided for. She should have thirty thousand gold florins, and five thousand should be added to that while she remained a widow. Would that be long? He pictured her—gay Germaine—with a husband who did not have to resort to potions. Jealous anger almost choked him and he had to restrain himself in order to get back his breath.

He saw a man standing at his bedside and demanded: "Who is there?"

Some of his servants came forward and said: "Highness, it is Adrian of Utrecht who has arrived here, having heard of the indisposition of Your Highness."

Ferdinand turned his face to the wall to hide his anger. Adrian of Utrecht, the chief adviser of his grandson Charles.

So, he thought, the carrion crows have arrived already. They sit and wait for the last flicker of life to subside. They are mistaken. I'm not going to die.

He turned and gasped: "Tell . . . that man to go. He has come too soon. Send him away."

So Adrian of Utrecht was forced to leave the house. But Ferdinand was wrong.

A few days later when his gentlemen came to his bed to wish him good morning, they found that he was dead.

CHAPTER XV

The Princess Mary

The Christmas festivities were over and Katharine was glad. She was expecting the child in February and was determined not to exhaust herself by over-exertion.

Henry continued tender. He was quite happy for her to be a mere spectator at those entertainments in which he played the central part. He could tell her solicitously that she was to retire to bed and rest; then he would be off to Elizabeth Blount or perhaps to some other young woman who had caught his passing fancy.

Katharine did not mind. She was patiently waiting.

That winter was a hard one—the coldest in living memory—and it was while the frost was at its worst, and the ice on the Thames so thick that carts could pass over it, that news was brought to Henry of the death of Ferdinand.

He received it with elation. Ferdinand, that old trickster, was dead. Henry would never have completely forgiven him for duping him as he had. It was the passing of an era; he knew that well. There would be a new ruler in Spain. Henry wanted to laugh aloud. It would be that boy whom he had met in Flanders—that slow-speaking young oaf, with the prominent eyes and the pasty skin. There would be one who was a complete contrast to Ferdinand.

He was far from displeased. Now he would turn his hatred and envy of the Spanish ruler to the King of France, that sly-eyed, fascinating creature who was bold and had begun his reign—as Henry had longed to do—by offering his people conquest.

But for the time being, Ferdinand was dead.

"This will be a shock to the Queen," he said to Wolsey when they discussed the news. "It would be better to keep it from her until after the child is born."

"Your Grace's thoughtfulness is equalled only by your wisdom."

"You agree, eh, she should not be told?"

"It would be unwise to tell her in her present state. There might be another disaster."

The King nodded. His eyes had become cunning. Wolsey followed his thoughts. Katharine had lost a powerful ally in her father. If the King should decide to repudiate her now, there would be no great power in Europe to be incensed by this treatment of her, for in place of a warlike and cunning father-protector she had only a young and inexperienced nephew.

Wolsey thought: Bear a healthy son, Katharine, or you will be in acute danger.

"I will let it be known," said Wolsey, "that on pain of Your Grace's displeasure, none is to tell the Queen of her father's death."

It was on the 18th day of February of the year 1516, in the Palace of Greenwich, when Katharine's child was born.

Katharine came out of her agony to hear the cry of a child.

Her first thought was: "Then the child is alive."

She saw faces about her bed, among them Henry's. She heard a voice say: "The child is healthy, Your Grace. The child lives."

She was aware of a great contentment. How she loved that child! All my life I shall love it, she thought, if only for the joy it has brought me in this moment.

But why did they say "the child?"

"A . . . boy?" she asked.

The brief silence told her the answer before it came: "A bonny girl, Your Grace."

There was a faint intake of breath. But it was too much to hope for a boy and a child that lived.

Henry was beside her bed.

"We have a healthy child, Kate," he said. "And the next . . . why, that will be a boy."

Days of acute anxiety followed; she was terrified that events would take the same tragic course as on so many other occasions. But this little girl was different from the beginning; she lived and flourished.

When it was time for her christening it was decided that she should be called Mary after Henry's sister who, having returned to England and been publicly married to the Duke of Suffolk at Greenwich, was now installed high in the King's favour.

It was the Queen's great delight to watch over the Princess Mary. She loved her with deep devotion which could scarcely have been so intense but for all the disappointments which had preceded the birth.

Even the grief she suffered when she heard of her father's death, and the faint fear which, knowing something of the exigencies of state, this event must arouse in her, was softened, because at last she had her child, her healthy little Mary, the delight of her life.

Katharine, playing with her daughter, knew that this was the happiest period of her life. The child was charming; she rarely cried but would lie solemnly in her cradle or in Katharine's arms.

Katharine would stand with the wet-nurse, Katharine Pole, and the governess, Margaret Bryan, wife of Sir Thomas Bryan, about the little Princess's cradle; and they made an admiring circle, while they watched the child playing with the gold pomander which had been a present from her Aunt Mary, now Duchess of Suffolk. The child seemed to love that ornament which later she might stuff with perfumes and wear about her waist, but which at the moment she liked to suck.

Henry would come in and join the circle. Then Katharine Pole and Margaret Bryan would draw back and leave the parents together.

Henry's eyes would be glazed with tenderness. This was his child and he told himself that more than anything on Earth he wanted children. He marvelled at those plump wrists, at the fingers, at the eyes which looked solemnly into his. He was delighted with the down of reddish hair on that little head, because it was his own colour.

Katharine watching him loved him afresh; they had something they could share now: this adorable little daughter.

"By God, Kate," murmured Henry, "we've produced a little beauty."

He wanted to hold her; and he was delighted when she did not cry as he picked her up. He would sit, looking a little incongruous, that big figure, glittering with jewels, holding the baby somewhat awkwardly yet so tenderly in his arms.

He insisted on having her brought to the banqueting hall or his presence chamber when his courtiers were present or when he was receiving foreign ambassadors.

"My daughter," he would say proudly, and take her in his arms, rocking her to and fro.

She never cried as most children would, but her large solemn eyes would stare at that big face at this time all suffused with tenderness and love.

The ambassadors would look on, admiring the baby, and the courtiers were continually discovering new likenesses to the King.

"She has the temper of an angel," said the Venetian ambassador.

"You are right there," cried Henry. "By God, Mr. Ambassador, this baby never cries."

Mary was almost perfect in the eyes of the King. If she had but been a boy she would have been quite so.

Before Ferdinand's death he had recalled Caroz and sent in his place Bernardino de Mesa, a very different type from Caroz. De Mesa was a Dominican friar, quiet, seemingly humble but in truth one of the shrewdest of Spaniards. It was a master stroke for Ferdinand to have sent him because his outward meekness was just what was needed to offset Wolsey's arrogance and ostentation.

Ferdinand had realized too late that the Cardinal was the real ruler of England. However, de Mesa immediately began an attempt to repair the damage Caroz had done; and it was on de Mesa's suggestion that Ferdinand had sent Henry the handsome present.

But Ferdinand was dead; de Mesa would have a new master; Katharine was no longer interested in politics as her attention was focused on her daughter; but Wolsey favoured the Spanish ambassador because he was knowledgeable in that field which was one of the utmost interest to the Cardinal—the Papal Court.

De Mesa waited apprehensively for new policies. While Ximenes was Regent he imagined that there would be little change; but what would happen when young Charles took the reins of government, guided no doubt by his Flemish favourites?

De Mesa sought to speak to the Queen of these matters but Katharine had become half-hearted, since her father's perfidy and death had shocked her deeply.

She no longer wanted to feel herself a Spaniard; she had her daughter to absorb her; and all the time de Mesa was seeking to draw her attention to European politics she was thinking: How she grows! To think that we can dispense with Katharine Pole's services now! She will be easily weaned. Was there ever such a good tempered child? They say sweet temper means good health. Soon she will have her own household, but not yet. For a while her place will be in her mother's apartments.

She smiled absently at the Spanish ambassador, but she did not see him; she saw only the bright eyes of her daughter, the round, chubby cheeks and that adorable fluff of reddish hair on the top of the exquisite little head which so delighted the child's father.

And when Henry's sister, Margaret, Queen of Scotland, came to London to seek her brother's help against her enemies, Katharine's great interest was in discussing Margaret's children with her and trying to win her sister-in-law's admiration for the beloved little Princess.

CHAPTER XVI

" 'Prentices and Clubs"

The following Spring there was disquiet in the streets of London.

During recent years many foreigners had settled there, and these people, being mostly exiles from their native lands—serious people who had fled perhaps for religious reasons—were by nature industrious. Day in, day out, they would be at their work, and so they prospered. There were Flemings who were expert weavers; Italians who were not only bankers but could make the finest armour and swords. The Hanseatic traders brought over leather, rope, wax, timber, nails and tar; and of course since the coming of Katharine to London to marry Prince Arthur there had always been Spaniards in London.

Life was hard for the citizens of London. During the cruel winter many had died of starvation in the streets and there had been rumblings of dissatisfaction all through the year.

With the coming of Spring the young apprentices gathered in the streets and talked of the injustice of foreigners coming to their city and making a good living, while they and their kind lived in such poor conditions.

They themselves could not understand the joy some of these cordwainers and weavers, these glaziers and lacemakers found in the work alone. They did not seem to ask for pleasure as the apprentices did. They cared for their work with the passion of craftsmen, and those who lacked this skill were angry with those who possessed it.

They met in Ficquets Fields and near the Fleet Bridge, and talked of these matters.

There was one among them, a youth named Lincoln, who demanded: "Why should we stand by and see foreigners take away our livings? Why should we allow the foreigners to live in our city at all?"

The ignorant apprentices shook their fists. They had a leader; they craved excitement in their dull lives. They were ready.

So on a May morning of the year 1517, instead of rising early to go and gather May flowers in the nearby countryside, the apprentices gathered together and, instead of the cry "Let's a-maying," there were shouts of " 'Prentices and Clubs!"

The revolt had begun.

The apprentices stormed into the city; there were hundreds of them and they made a formidable company. Through the streets of London they came, carrying flaming torches in their hands; they broke into the shops of the foreigners; they came out carrying bales of silk, the finest lace, jewels, hats, textiles.

When they had ransacked these shops and houses they set them on fire.

News was brought to the King at Richmond.

Henry was first angry; then alarmed. The people could always frighten him because he had a dread of unpopularity.

He decided to remain at Richmond until others had the revolt under control.

Chaos reigned in London.

The under-sheriff of the city, Sir Thomas More, pitying the plight of the apprentices and knowing that they would be quickly subdued, went among them, risking his life, for tempers were running high, imploring them to stop their violence.

Wolsey meanwhile had taken the position in hand and had sent for the Earl of Surrey who arrived with troops and very soon had hundreds of people under arrest and others hanging from gibbets which had been quickly erected throughout the city.

Meanwhile Henry waited at Richmond, determined not to go into his capital until order was restored.

It was eleven days after the uprising that he rode into the city and took his place on a dais in Westminster Hall. With him came three Queens—Katharine, Mary—who had been Queen of France and was far happier to be Duchess of Suffolk—and Margaret, Queen of Scotland.

"Bring the prisoners to me," cried Henry, his brows drawn together in a deep frown, "that I may see these people who would revolt against me."

There was a sound of wailing from the spectators as the prisoners were brought in. There were some four hundred men and eleven women, all grimy from their stay in prison, all desperate, for they knew what had happened to their leaders and they expected the same fate to befall themselves; they even came with ropes about their necks; and in the crowd which had pressed into the Hall and clustered round it were the families of these men and women.

The King raged in his anger. They had dared rise against his merchants; they had burned the houses of his citizens; they deserved the worst death which men could devise.

His troops were stationed about the city; his guards surrounded him, and he was eager to show these people the might of the Tudor.

Wolsey came close to him. He said: "Your Grace, I beg of you in your clemency spare these men."

Henry's little eyes glittered. He hated them, those wild-eyed men and women. They had dared show criticism of his rule. Yet . . . they were the people. A King must always please his people.

He caught Wolsey's eye; the Cardinal was warning him: "It would be as well, Your Grace, to pardon these men. A fine gesture . . . here in the heart of your capital. A powerful King but a merciful one."

Yes, he knew. But here was the spirit of the masque again. He must play his part as he always had done.

He scowled at Wolsey and said: "These prisoners should be taken from here and hanged by the neck on gibbets prepared for them within the city."

Katharine was watching the faces of some of the women who had pressed into the hall. They were mothers, and some of these boys who stood there on the threshold of death, the halters round their necks, had been their babies.

It was more than she could bear. Stripping off her headdress so that her hair fell about her shoulders—as became a supplicant—she threw herself at the King's feet.

"Your Grace, I implore you, spare these prisoners. They are young. Let them grow to serve Your Grace."

Henry, legs apart, his fingers playing with the great pearl which hung about his neck, regarded her with assumed tenderness and said: "You are a woman, Kate, and soft. You know nothing of these matters. . . ."

Katharine turned to Mary and Margaret and they, seeing the appeal in her eyes and being moved themselves by the sight of those miserable prisoners and their sorrowing families, loosened their hair and knelt with Katharine at the King's feet.

Henry regarded them, and his eyes were a brilliant blue.

Three Queens knelt at his feet! What a spectacle for his people!

He appeared to consider.

Wolsey—the great Cardinal who, when he went abroad, rode through the streets in a procession which rivalled that of a king's—also appealed to Henry.

His appeal was a warning, but there was no need for the warning. Henry was about to make the grand gesture.

"I am not proof against such pleading," he declared. "And I know full well that these foolish men and women now regret their folly. They shall live to be my very good subjects."

There was a sudden shout of joy. The prisoners took the halters from their necks and threw them high into the air.

Henry stood watching them—sons rushing into their mother's arms, wives embracing husbands—a smug smile of pleasure on his face.

As Katharine watched, the tears flowed down her cheeks.

CHAPTER XVII

The King Triumphant

Little Mary was growing up to be a model child. She was now two years old and had her separate establishment at Ditton Park in Buckinghamshire. Katharine could not bear to be separated from the child, and consequently she spent a great deal of time in her daughter's nursery; and she contrived to be often at Windsor Castle so that the child could be ferried over to her there.

Katharine was going to supervise her education as Isabella had her children's. She was going to take her mother as an example; Mary should learn to love and depend on her mother as she, Katharine, had on hers.

Already Mary was showing great promise. She had a lively intelligence, could speak clearly and knew how to receive important personages. It was a constant delight to present them to her that she might charm them as she charmed her parents.

Henry was almost as devoted as Katharine. He enjoyed taking the child in his arms or on his knees and playing with her. Only occasionally would the frown appear between his eyes, and Katharine would know then that he was thinking: Why is this child not a boy?

Mary quickly showed an aptitude for music, and, young as she was, Katharine taught her how to play on the virginals. The Queen would sit with the little girl on her lap, the four feet long box in which the keyboard was set, placed on the table; and there the childish fingers would pick out the notes.

Her progress was amazing, and Henry as well as Katharine liked to show off her talent as much as possible.

What happy days they were; and to crown her pleasure, Katharine discovered that she was once more pregnant.

"Now we have a healthy girl, we must get us a boy," said Henry.

His tone was playful but there was a faint threat beneath it. He was determined to have a boy . . . from someone.

Autumn had come and the King hunted all through the day and returned in the late afternoon to banquets and masques.

Katharine was spending the days in happy preoccupation with her domestic affairs. There was so much to occupy her days. She liked to sit sewing with her women; and it was her delight to embroider Henry's linen, and garments for little Mary. She had moved away from the sphere of politics and was happier for it.

Her hopes of bearing another healthy child were high. Mary was a joy in more ways than one. Not only was she her charming self but she was a promise of future children, a symbol which insisted that what could be done once could be done again.

This was the happiest of her pregnancies—apart from the first one. This time she could feel almost complacent.

"But let it be a boy," she prayed. "O Holy Mother, intercede for me and give me a boy."

She was seated at the table on the dais; the hunters had returned hungry from the forest, and Henry was in his place at the centre of the table where there was much jesting and laughter.

Elizabeth Blount was present. Katharine always looked for her among the guests, and she marvelled that Henry could have been faithful to a woman for so long. Elizabeth was, of course, a beauty; and she was entirely the King's. The marriage to Sir Gilbert Taillebois was one in name only. They could be certain of this. Sir Gilbert would not dare to be a husband to Elizabeth while she was the King's paramour.

Poor Gilbert! thought Katharine with some contempt. He stands by, like a cur, waiting for his master to throw the bone after he has finished gnawing it.

She felt no jealousy of Elizabeth; she felt nothing but this great desire to bear a son.

She did notice, however, that Elizabeth looked different tonight. She was even more attractive than usual. A diamond glittered at her throat. A gift from the King of course. She was dressed in blue velvet with cloth of silver, and those colours were very becoming to her fair beauty. She was subdued tonight. Had she perhaps noticed that the King was less attentive? Yet she seemed radiant. Had she another lover?

Katharine ceased to think of the woman. It was no concern of hers if Henry discarded a mistress, because there would be another if he dispensed with this one. She was not a giddy girl to look for faithfulness in a man such as Henry.

There was a burst of laughter at the table. The King had made a joke. It must be the King's, for only his jokes provoked such abandoned laughter.

Katharine set her face into a smile, but she was not thinking of the King nor of Elizabeth Blount.

The child stirred suddenly within her.

"Holy Mother, give me a healthy child . . . a healthy male child."

Henry's hand touched that of Elizabeth in the dance. She raised her eyes to his and smiled.

He pressed her hand warmly. He too had noticed the change in her tonight.

"But you are more fair than ever," he whispered.

"Your Grace . . ." Her voice faltered.

"Speak up, Bessie."

"There is something I must tell you."

"What is this?"

"I . . . wish to tell you as soon as we can be alone."

"You're frightened, Bessie. What's wrong?"

"I pray Your Grace. . . . When we are alone."

Henry narrowed his eyes, but she was whirled away from him in the dance.

*   *   *

She was waiting for him in the ante-chamber where he had bidden her go.

"Slip away," he had said when their hands had touched again in the dance. "I will join you. None will notice us."

At one time she would have smiled at his belief that, when he did not wish to be noticed, he never was. As if everyone in the hall was not aware of the movements of the King! But tonight she was too preoccupied with her thoughts and fears.

He shut the door and stood looking at her.

"Well, Bessie?"

"Your Grace . . . I . . . we . . . I am with child."

Henry stared at her.

Then he began to laugh. "By God, Bessie," he cried, "I had begun to think you were a barren woman. When I considered all the nights we have been together . . . and no sign of a child. I began to wonder what was wrong with you . . . or . . ."

He frowned, as though admonishing himself.

He came towards her then, and there was a tender smile on his lips.

"Your Grace is not displeased . . . ?"

Bessie was thinking: This will be the end. He will not want a pregnant woman. There will be someone else. Nothing will ever be the same again.

"Displeased!" He took her face in his hands and gently pinched her cheeks. "There's nothing could have pleased me more."

He seized her in his arms and held her so tightly that she would have cried out with the pain if she had dared. Then he swung her into his arms and held her up, looking at her.

Displeased! he was thinking. He had said that nothing could please him more; that was not true. If Bessie gave him a son he would be delighted, but a legitimate son was what he desired more than anything on Earth.

Now that Bessie carried their child he could look more closely at the fears which had been trying to intrude into his mind.

When there was failure to produce children it was natural to presume that something might be wrong with the would-be parents—both of them perhaps. Katharine was not barren. She could become pregnant; her failure lay in not giving birth to a healthy male child. Among her offspring there had been boys—but still-born, or, as in the case of the first, living only a few days.

If Bessie Blount bore a healthy child, it would prove, would it not, that the fault did not lie with him.

True there was Mary—but one living girl in all those pregnancies! It was almost as though God was against him in some way, as though He had said, you shall not have a male heir.

His high spirits began to overflow. He began dancing round the small chamber with Bessie in his arms.

Then he was sober suddenly. "We must take care of you, my Bessie," he said, lowering her gently to the ground. "We must cherish this little body of thine now that it shelters a royal child."

They returned to the ballroom and were covertly watched.

The King does not grow out of his love for Bessie Blount, it was whispered. See, he is as enamoured of her now as he was when he first saw her.

Katharine was in her daughter's apartments. Mary was seated at the table, propped up with cushions so that she was high enough to reach the virginals which had been placed on the table.

The plump little fingers were moving over the keys with a dexterity astonishing in one so young.

Katharine watched her. She was not yet three years old; surely there was not another child like her in the whole of the kingdom.

"My precious daughter," she murmured.

Glancing through the window she saw that the November mist was wreathed about the trees like grey ghosts; the ghosts of unborn children, she thought, and shivered.

She placed her hands on the child in her womb; and involuntarily the prayer rose to her lips. "A boy. Let it be a boy."

If I have a boy—as healthy, as bright as my little Mary, then Henry will be pleased with me. It is all he needs to make him happy. What need have I to concern myself with the Elizabeth Blounts of the Court if only I can have a healthy boy.

The child had finished her piece. Margaret Bryan clapped her hands, and the Duchess of Norfolk and her daughter, Lady Margaret Herbert, who were both in attendance on the little Princess, clapped with her.

Katharine rose to embrace her daughter and, as she did so, she felt the now familiar nagging pains begin.

She cried out in alarm. It was not the pains which frightened her. It was the grey mist out there. It looked like ghosts ... ghosts of children who had made a brief appearance on Earth and then had gone away. It reminded her that this was but November and her child was not due to be born until the Christmas festivities should begin.

So it was over.

She lay frustrated, sick, weary and a little frightened. She heard voices which seemed to come from a long way off but which she knew were in her bedchamber.

"A daughter ... a still-born daughter."

Oh my God, she thought, then You have forsaken me.

There were other voices, but these were in her mind.

"They say the King fears his marriage does not find favour in Heaven." "They say it is because he married his brother's wife." "They say it would not be difficult to end such a marriage ... now, for the Queen's father is dead and there is no need to fear her nephew ... he is but a boy. Why should the King fear him?"

She closed her eyes. She was too weak to care what became of her.

She thought: This was my last chance. I have tried so many times. We have one daughter. But where is the son he so desperately needs, where is the boy who could make him tender towards me?

He was standing by her bedside, and they were alone. When he had that look in his eyes, people slunk away from him. Even his dogs were aware of it. She had seen him often standing, legs apart, eyes blue fire, chin jutting forward—the sullen, angry boy. The dogs waited in corners and the clever men like Cardinal Wolsey were called away on urgent state matters.

Now they had left him with her; and she lay helplessly looking up at him.

She said: "I am sorry, Henry. We have failed once more."

"*We* have failed? I did my part. It is you who fail to do yours."

"I do not know where I failed, Henry."

Those were the wrong words. How easy it was to speak the wrong words.

"You would suggest that it is something in me!"

"I do not know what it is, Henry."

She thought he would strike her then.

O God, she thought, how much it means to him! How angry he is!

He had taken one step towards the bed and stopped; then he turned and began pacing the room. He was holding in his anger. He was hurt and bewildered. He had thought, after Mary, that they would get a son.

She knew that with each attempt she lost some charm for him. Each time she took to her bed in the hope of giving birth, she rose from it more wan, more listless; each time she left some of her youth behind.

She understood him well enough to know that these failures hurt him so much because they brought an insidious doubt into his mind. He would admit this to none, but she who had lived close to him for nine years knew him perhaps better than he knew himself, for he was a man who would never know himself well because he refused to look where it was not pleasant to do so.

Yet he could not drive the question from his mind. Is it in some measure due to me? Am I incapable of begetting a healthy son?

He could not bear that he should be anything but perfect. He loved himself so much.

Even in that moment she, who was so much wiser, was sorry

for him. If she could, she would have risen from her bed and comforted him.

He had paused before the device which hung on the wall. The device of the pomegranate—the Arabic sign of fertility.

Oh, if I could but go back to the happy days in Granada before I had seen England, when my beloved mother was alive, I would never have chosen this as my device.

Henry began to laugh, and his laughter was not pleasant to hear.

He lifted his hand, and she thought that he was about to tear the device from the wall and trample on it. As though with difficulty he restrained himself; then, without another look at her, he strode from the room.

Henry rode out to a certain Priory, and with him he took only his most intimate friends. Compton and Bryan were among them, and they chatted and laughed gaily as they went along.

But Henry had not his heart in the raillery. He listened half-heartedly and there was a strained expression on his face. And after a while they fell silent.

Henry believed what was waiting for him at the Priory was of the utmost importance. He was praying, as he went along, for a sign. He would discuss his thoughts with no one, for as yet he was afraid of them; but if what he hoped should happen, then he might begin to reshape his life.

When they reached the Priory, he rode ahead of his friends into the courtyard, and grooms who clearly were expecting the important visitor hurried out to do them service.

Henry leaped out of the saddle; he was striding into the building and as he did so he was met by two excited nuns; their faces under their black hoods were flushed and their eyes alight with excitement.

"What news?" demanded Henry.

"It is all over, Your Grace. Her ladyship is well and will be eager to see you."

"And . . . is there a child?"

"Yes, Your Grace, a bonny child."

Holy Mother of God, they torture me, thought Henry.

He shouted. "Boy or girl?"

"A bonny boy, Your Grace."

Henry gave a shout of triumph.

He called to Compton who was close behind him: "Did you hear that? A boy! Bessie has my boy!" Then he seized the nearest nun by the shoulder. "Take me to them," he cried. "Take me to Lady Taillebois and my son."

They led the way, running, for this was an impatient King.

He saw her on her pillows, her red gold hair spread about her as he had seen it so many times before. She was pale and triumphant. She was his beautiful Bessie who had given him what he wanted, now as she always had.

"Why, Bessie." He was on his knees by the bed. "So you've done it, eh, girl? You've come through it, eh?" He took her hand and kissed it loudly. "And the child? Where is he?" Suspicion shot up in his eyes. "Where is he, I say?"

A nun had appeared; she was holding a child.

Henry was on his feet, staring down at the burden in her arms.

So small. So wrinkled. Yet a child. His child. He wanted to shout with joy. There was the faint down on that small head—and it was Tudor red.

Tears were in his eyes. The smallness of the child moved him; this little one, his son!

Then he thought, Holy Mother, how could you do this to me. . . .? You give Bessie my son . . . when I want to give him my crown.

He took the child from the woman.

"Your Grace, have a care. He is young yet."

"Do you think to tell me to have a care for my own child? Let me tell you, woman, this child means as much to me as my crown. This is my son. By God, this boy shall know great honours. . . ." He was overcome with love for the child, with gratitude to Bessie, who had not only given him a son, but proved his capability to beget sons. He said rashly: "This child might have my crown."

Bryan and Compton exchanged glances.

The remarks of an exuberant father on beholding his son?

Mayhap. But both Bryan and Compton were wondering what effect the existence of this young child could have on the Queen.

Henry had summoned the whole Court to that Manor which he had some time since bought for Bessie Blount. This was the occasion of the christening of his son.

It was to be a grand ceremony, for he would have everyone know that since he welcomed his son into the world with such joy, so must they all.

There was one guest at the ceremony whom many thought it was cruel to have asked. She had come, pale and resigned, looking like a middle-aged woman since her last pregnancy.

Poor Katharine! How sad it was that it was she who, out of so many pregnancies, had been only able to produce one daughter while Bessie Blount should give the King a healthy son.

She brought presents for the child. She showed no resentment for she had already learned that it was wise to hide her true feelings.

The King seemed unaware of the indignity he was heaping upon her; he seemed at that time unaware of her.

And when the name of the newly-born child was asked, it was Henry himself who answered in a deep, resonant voice which could be heard by all: "This child's name is Henry Fitzroy."

And as he spoke he looked at Katharine. She was startled; she had always known that there was cruelty in his nature; but now she read his thoughts: You see, I can get me a son. But not through my wife. Here is my boy . . . my healthy boy. Is it not strange that you should have tried so many times and failed? Is it because our marriage is frowned on in Heaven? Is it, my wife? My *wife*!

Now her nightmares had taken shape. They were no vague phantoms.

She saw the speculation in those blue eyes.

She thought: I am the Queen. None can change that. And

she would not meet his gaze for fear she should be tempted to look into the future.

She was here in the Manor he had bought for his mistress; she was attending the christening of his only son—and a son by that mistress.

For the present she was the Queen of England. She would not look beyond that.

Bibliography

Lives of the Queens of England, Agnes Strickland.

England in Tudor Times, L. F. Salzman, M.A.

Catherine of Aragon, Garrett Mattingly.

Henry VIII, Francis Hackett.

Henry VIII: A Difficult Patient, Sir Arthur Salusbury Mac-
Nalty, K.C.B., M.A., M.D., F.R.C.P., F.R.C.S.

The Private Character of Henry the Eighth, Frederick
Chamberlin.

The History of England under Henry VIII, Edward Lord
Herbert.

British History, John Wade.

The National and Domestic History of England, William
Hickman Smith Aubrey.

Henry VIII, A. F. Pollard, M.A., LITT.D.

The Wives of Henry VIII, Martin A. S. Hume.

History of England: Henry VIII, James Anthony Froude.

Life of Wolsey, Cavendish.

Wolsey (Great Lives), Ashley Sampson.

History of the Reign of Ferdinand and Isabella the Catholic
(2 vols.), William H. Prescott, Edited by John Foster Kirk.

Cardinal Ximenes and the Making of Spain, Reginald Merton.

The History of Spain, Louis Bertrand and Sir Charles Petrie.

A History of Spain (2 vols.), Ulick Ralph Burke, M.A.

Spain: Its Greatness and Decay (1479–1788), Martin A. S.
Hume. Revised by Edward Armstrong.

The romance and intrigue you have come to expect from the pen of

VICTORIA HOLT

Published by Fawcett Books.